A Cowboy for Keeps

BOOKS BY JODY HEDLUND

The Preacher's Bride

The Doctor's Lady

Unending Devotion

A Noble Groom

Rebellious Heart

Captured by Love

BEACONS OF HOPE

Out of the Storm: A BEACONS OF HOPE *Novella*

Love Unexpected

Hearts Made Whole

Undaunted Hope

ORPHAN TRAIN

An Awakened Heart: An ORPHAN TRAIN *Novella*

With You Always

Together Forever

Searching for You

THE BRIDE SHIPS

A Reluctant Bride

The Runaway Bride

A Bride of Convenience

COLORADO COWBOYS

A Cowboy for Keeps

A Cowboy for Keeps

Jody Hedlund

a division of Baker Publishing Group
Minneapolis, Minnesota

© 2021 by Jody Hedlund

Published by Bethany House Publishers
11400 Hampshire Avenue South
Bloomington, Minnesota 55438
www.bethanyhouse.com

Bethany House Publishers is a division of
Baker Publishing Group, Grand Rapids, Michigan

Printed in the United States of America

All rights reserved. No part of this publication may be reproduced, stored in a retrieval system, or transmitted in any form or by any means—for example, electronic, photocopy, recording—without the prior written permission of the publisher. The only exception is brief quotations in printed reviews.

Library of Congress Control Number: 2020944642

ISBN 978-0-7642-3639-6 (trade paper)
ISBN 978-0-7642-3819-2 (casebound)

Scripture quotations are from the King James Version of the Bible.

This is a work of fiction. Names, characters, incidents, and dialogues are products of the authors' imagination and are not to be construed as real. Any resemblance to any person, living or dead, is purely coincidental.

Cover design by Kirk DouPonce, DogEared Design

Author is represented by Natasha Kern Literary Agency

21 22 23 24 25 26 27 7 6 5 4 3 2 1

Cast thy burden upon the LORD, and he shall sustain thee:
he shall never suffer the righteous to be moved.

—Psalm 55:22

CHAPTER 1

COLORADO TERRITORY
AUGUST 1862

"Stop or we'll shoot!" A dozen feet up Kenosha Pass, three robbers with flour sacks over their heads blocked the way, their revolvers outstretched.

Walking alongside the stagecoach, Greta Nilsson didn't have to be told twice. She froze—all except her pulse, which sped to a thundering gallop.

Next to her, the Concord jerked to a halt.

"Come out and put your hands up where we can see 'em," called the lanky robber at the center, peering through unevenly cut holes in his mask.

Greta raised her gloved hands and hoped they weren't trembling. Likewise, the two gentlemen hiking near her wasted no time in obeying.

Before she'd left Illinois, everyone had warned her of the trouble she might encounter on the route to the west, including the growing problem of stagecoach robberies. Over the past eight weeks of traveling, she'd braced herself for the possibility, had mentally rehearsed such an encounter and what she'd do.

But today, on the last day of the journey, she'd finally allowed herself to relax and believe that for once things might work out in her favor, that she hadn't made a big mistake in moving to Colorado.

Apparently, she'd assumed too much too soon.

At the rear of the stagecoach, several men had been pushing it the final distance to the top of the pass, and they now eased out into the open, their arms up. The driver sitting on his bench atop the stagecoach set the brake, then released the reins controlling the two teams of horses that had been straining to pull them up the mountain. He, too, cautiously lifted his hands.

She guessed, like her, the other passengers were well aware of the tales of murder and mayhem along the wilderness trails. And they weren't taking any chances either.

At least Astrid was inside the coach. After trekking uphill for the first hour, the little girl's poor lungs hadn't been able to handle the exertion. As much as Astrid had loathed returning to the bumpy conveyance, she'd been able to have a seat to herself since everyone else had gotten out to lighten the load.

Last time Greta had peeked through the open windows, her sister had been sprawled out asleep, and now Greta prayed the precocious child would stay that way.

The middle robber inched toward them, his revolver swinging in a wide arc. His leathery hands and dirt-encrusted fingernails contrasted with the ivory handle of his revolver. "Nobody move."

Morning sunlight filtered through the aspens, their white bark and green-gold leaves making the trail feel more open and airy than other parts of the mountainous road. A cool, dry breeze rattled the leaves, swishing like ladies' skirts brushing against grass.

Just minutes ago, Greta had been marveling at how different the dry and cooler climate was from northern Illinois, where oppressive humidity plagued the summers and made every chore feel like a burden. What she wouldn't give at this moment to be back there shucking corn or snapping beans, even if she was dripping with perspiration.

"Anyone left inside?" one of the other robbers asked.

"No," Greta said quickly. "Everyone's out."

Just then the stagecoach door inched open.

The lanky robber with the uneven eye slits swung his revolver toward the door and clicked the hammer.

"No!" Greta threw herself between the robber and the stagecoach, shoving against Astrid's strong push.

A short distance away beyond the trees, the mountainside overlooked the sprawling grasslands of South Park, nestled between the Front Range in the east and the Mosquito Range in the west. Their destination was within eyesight. If only it was also within shouting distance so they could call for help.

The bandit shifted the barrel's aim to Greta, his arm stiff, his fingers taut. "Woman, unless you want to find yourself eating a bullet, you'd best step aside and let that person out."

Inside, Astrid cried out in protest and once again attempted to open the door. But Greta flattened the full length of her body against it.

"Move on outta the way, woman," the robber said, louder and more irritably.

"It's her little sister." One of the other passengers moved to stand beside Greta, a middle-aged man who'd introduced himself as Landry Steele yesterday morning when they boarded the stagecoach in Denver. He'd spent the majority of the journey conversing with the other gentlemen. However, during the few brief interactions she'd had with him, he'd always been considerate.

"The girl is ill and is of no concern to you." Beneath the brim of Mr. Steele's bowler, he shot Greta an apologetic look, as though realizing she'd wanted to keep Astrid hidden away and out of the conflict.

"That so?" The gunman's revolver didn't waver. "If she's of no concern, then let her on out."

Greta pressed against the door harder. She hadn't brought Astrid all this distance to have her die at the hand of a robber. "She's only eight years old—"

"I'm nine," came Astrid's indignant voice.

"Allow her to come out," Mr. Steele said with a quiet urgency. "You don't want her to end up an orphan, do you?"

Astrid an orphan? Never in Greta's plans had she counted on dying before Astrid. The truth was, Astrid's days were numbered, and Greta hoped to lengthen and make them as pain-free as possible. But she couldn't do that if she let the robber kill her.

Swallowing hard, Greta stepped away from the stagecoach. The door flew open with a *bang*, and Astrid tumbled out. She landed with an *oomph* onto the grassy road but then bounded up as nimbly as a barn cat. Though the consumption had emaciated the girl so that she was thin and petite for her age, somehow she still retained a fresh and vibrant spirit that made up for her physical frailty.

Her big silver blue eyes, so much like Greta's, took in the

scene—the robbers, their guns, and all the passengers standing motionless with hands in the air. Astrid's hair was also the same color as Greta's, a golden brown now sun-streaked from so many days of neglecting her bonnet. Astrid had refused to allow Greta to plait her hair when they'd arisen at half past four in the morning for a hasty departure from the stagecoach station, and now it hung in tangled waves.

Even so, Astrid was the picture of perfection. She had dainty porcelain but beautiful features that drew attention everywhere she went. Greta had never considered herself to be a beauty, not like some of the other young women back home and certainly not like Astrid.

But too many people to recall during the journey west had exclaimed how much she and Astrid looked alike. The admiring glances and flattery had been strange but not unwelcome. At times, she wondered if maybe she was prettier than she'd realized, if maybe she'd been hasty in accepting the first mail-order bride proposal that came along.

Astrid took several steps in the direction of the closest robber. "Why are you wearing a sack over your head?"

"Astrid, come here this instant," Greta whispered in her sternest tone.

The thief's gaze darted over to the passengers, revealing a crooked, lazy eye that didn't focus. "It's what robbers do, kid."

"W-e-l-l." Astrid drew the word out and cocked her head. "It makes you look kinda silly, like a scarecrow."

Greta lunged for Astrid, but the girl dodged away and skipped toward the robber.

His gun wavered, as though he was considering turning the weapon on Astrid.

"Astrid!" Horror rose in Greta's throat, threatening to strangle her. "Don't you dare go a step closer."

Astrid halted and held out her hand. "Here's some money, Mister. It's mine, but you can have it since you need it more than me."

The man's lazy eye shifted to Astrid again. "Drop it on the ground."

Astrid released a crumpled wad and a few coins. They bounced in the grass near the robber's feet. "My sister has more—"

"No!" Greta couldn't let these bandits discover her secret stash since she'd taken pains to sew the cash into the lining of her coat after the passengers had been warned not to carry valuables.

It was her jam money. Her earnings from picking and preserving the wild berries that grew on the farm. The accumulation of two years of working every spare minute.

Astrid turned her pretty eyes upon Greta. "They have to wear flour sacks instead of hats. Guess that means they need the money more than we do. Right, Mister?"

"Right, kid." This time the robber's voice hinted at amusement.

The thieves made quick work of emptying the locked box next to the driver and then divested each of the passengers of anything of value. Within a few minutes they ran off into the woods with their loot.

Greta stood with the others, surveying their belongings strewn over the grass surrounding the stagecoach. Astrid had lost interest in the robbers and was intent on picking a bouquet of wildflowers.

"We got lucky." The driver broke the silence, his voice

shaky as he closed the now-empty box next to him. "Last time the Crooked-Eye Gang struck, they killed three men—"

Mr. Steele cut off the driver with a glare and a curt nod toward Astrid.

The driver clamped his mouth closed, and everyone set to work repacking their bags and trunks.

Greta fingered the frayed coat hem. Although Phineas Hallock, her intended, had informed her he had plenty of money since he was part owner of a gold mine, she couldn't keep dismay from weighing upon her.

She'd corresponded with Phineas by letter on several occasions last year, and she sensed in him genuine kindness, especially since he'd so readily agreed to take care of Astrid. He also made all the arrangements for the trip, including paying for their fare.

Though the small daguerreotype he'd sent in his last letter the previous autumn had shown him to be a plain-looking and somewhat older man, his face held a look of integrity as well as honesty. Maybe he wasn't handsome or young, but that didn't matter. What she needed was a husband who was reliable, dependable, and able to provide for her and Astrid.

Besides, after making up her mind, Greta had wanted to move as quickly as possible to get Astrid to the healing air of the Rockies. Why waste time corresponding with other men when Phineas had been so eager and ready to help her?

Maybe she'd acted rashly. But what was done, was done. She was on her way to marry Phineas. She would, in fact, wed him by the day's end.

Still, she blinked back tears. All of her savings was gone. If only Astrid knew how to obey better. If only the little girl had a real mother and father to raise her. Instead, she was stuck with a mere half sister who clearly didn't know how to keep her in line.

Greta sat back on her heels and watched the young girl with a mixture of frustration and helplessness.

"Don't be too hard on her." Mr. Steele bent next to Greta and retrieved a shiny leather shoe.

"She's a handful."

"She saved us from meeting our Maker today."

"She did?"

The gentleman removed his bowler and smoothed back his dark hair, which had hints of gray at his temples and streaking his long sideburns and mustache. "The gang leader liked her and showed mercy on us as a result."

Mercy? Each of the passengers had lost everything of value. But she supposed that was better than losing their lives.

"I have a son about Astrid's age." Mr. Steele replaced his hat, watching Astrid wistfully.

"You must be looking forward to seeing him when we arrive in Fairplay."

He focused on the child a moment longer, his expression filled with sadness. "Unfortunately, I won't be seeing him anytime soon. He lives in New York with his mother."

"I'm sorry." Greta didn't know what else to say.

Mr. Steele shook his head, as if by doing so he could shake away his morose thoughts. "Tell me again why you're moving to Fairplay."

Greta hadn't told him anything yet, since he hadn't asked. But she wouldn't be so impolite as to say so. Instead, she gave him the rehearsed line she'd spouted to everyone else who'd wanted to know. "My fiancé lives in Fairplay, and I'm traveling there to marry him."

"Your fiancé? Is that so?" Mr. Steele's eyes lit with interest. "May I ask who the lucky fellow is? I'm mayor and have gotten to know many men in the area."

All the misgivings she'd had since agreeing to marry Phineas soared. What if she'd made a mistake in coming west and agreeing to marry a stranger? What if he wasn't who he had claimed to be? What if he mistreated Astrid?

Just as quickly as the doubts assailed her, she tossed them aside. If Phineas wasn't the man he'd portrayed in his letters, then she'd have no obligation to stay with him. In fact, perhaps Mr. Steele would be able to advise her regarding the true nature of Phineas's character. Then if her fiancé had any glaring faults, she'd be well aware of them before arriving in Fairplay.

She cast a sideways glance at the other passengers, who were in the finishing stages of stowing their belongings and were thankfully heedless of the conversation. "I haven't actually met my intended."

Mr. Steele, in the process of picking up another shoe, paused.

"We've written to each other."

He straightened and gave her his full attention. "You wouldn't happen to be Phineas Hallock's mail-order bride, would you?"

Something in his tone made the skin at the back of her neck prickle with unease. "Yes, Mr. Hallock is my fiancé. Do you know him?"

The gentleman shook his head, his features creasing. "I knew him well. He was a good man."

Her heart began to patter fast and hard. "Knew?"

"I'm sorry, Miss Nilsson. Phineas Hallock is dead."

"The mine owner Phineas Hallock, originally from Connecticut?"

"Yes, he left for California last October. Said he was traveling there to purchase supplies for his new bride and that he planned to be back by late spring. When the thawing came and he didn't return, we all thought he was delayed. Until a body was discovered on Hoosier Pass."

"His body?"

"As far as we can tell, after so many months of being exposed to the elements . . ."

She stared at Mr. Steele, but somehow he faded from her vision. All she could see was the black-and-white photograph of Phineas.

In his last letter, he'd mentioned his trip to California and his excitement over picking out additional furniture and items for their home. He expressed his desire to have the newly built house well-stocked and ready for her arrival. She hadn't heard from him since and assumed he hadn't had the opportunity to send further correspondence. Even if he had, mail delivery via the Pony Express and stagecoach wasn't reliable. Letters were sometimes lost or stolen.

Besides, she'd been busy preparing for the trip, sewing clothes for Astrid and her, packing their belongings, and saying good-byes. She'd never in her wildest imagination believed Phineas Hallock hadn't written again because he was dead.

He was dead.

She swayed, her vision growing fuzzy.

Mr. Steele's grip on her elbow steadied her. "I'm truly sorry, Miss Nilsson."

With a deep breath, she tried to bring the world back into

focus. The sunlight streaming through the aspen branches above splashed across her face as though to wake her from a nightmare.

The man she'd come west to marry was dead. Every penny of her savings had just been stolen. What would she do now? How could she, a lone woman with a sick child, survive in the wilderness knowing no one and having nothing?

Chapter 2

The cold barrel of a revolver jammed into back of Wyatt McQuaid's neck and stopped him short in the middle of Fairplay's dusty Main Street.

"Quit stealing my business." The voice—and the sour body odor—behind Wyatt belonged to only one man: Roper Brawley.

"I ain't stealing your business—"

"Jansen's steers were mine." Brawley dug the steel into Wyatt's flesh, bumping and loosening his hat so it tumbled to the street.

Against the black felt, the chalky line from dried sweat was all too visible and encrusted along the brim with dust, grease, and mud spots. The center was dented where a heifer had recently trampled it. And the hatband of braided horsehair hung loose.

Even if his hat wasn't pretty, it was still his pride and joy. And he wouldn't stand for anyone knocking it from his head.

With a jab backward, Wyatt elbowed Brawley's stomach, forcing the man to double over. With the pressure gone, Wyatt spun, latched on to Brawley's gun arm, and slammed it down hard against his knee, giving Brawley little choice but to release the revolver.

The weapon flew several feet, landing in the gravel, far enough away that Brawley couldn't easily reach it.

"This here is a free country." Wyatt swiped up his hat and situated it on his head. Although the sun was on its evening hike down to Sheep and Horseshoe Mountains, the rays were still strong and hot. "The miners can sell their oxen to anyone in the blazes they want to."

Nursing his stomach, Brawley straightened. A black patch covered a missing eye but couldn't hide the thin, white scars scattered across his cheek—wounds he'd gotten fighting Indians. "Me and my men were here in South Park first."

That was debatable. Wyatt had arrived in the summer of 1860 and tried gold mining like thousands of other prospectors. After scraping by and managing to pan only enough nuggets and gold dust to fill his pockets, he'd tried his luck at something different—ranching.

With the passing of the Homestead Act earlier in the year, he'd been one of the first to file an application and pay the registration fee at the land office in Denver. He'd gotten himself the one hundred sixty acres allowed under President Lincoln's new legislation fair and square.

His pasturelands spread out to the southeast of Fairplay. Wyatt had spent the spring and summer laboring from sunup to sundown, building a house and a barn on his claim. He and Judd had buckled down and made the place livable for both man and beast. And over recent weeks, he'd started adding more steers to his small herd.

And now, Roper Brawley was determined to keep him from succeeding.

Brawley crossed his arms and nodded at several cowhands loitering outside Cabinet Billiard Hall. At their boss's signal, they sauntered toward Wyatt, their spurs jangling, their hands resting on the handles of their six-shooters tucked into their holsters.

Wyatt made eye contact with Judd, who stood next to the livery guarding the two bone-thin steers Wyatt had just purchased. The white-haired man limped forward too. He didn't reach for his Colts—didn't have to. Judd was the fastest gunslinger in the Rockies. He could shoot iron quicker than the twitch of a cow's tail.

Fortunately, Brawley and his men knew it. They stopped a dozen paces away, feet spread, hands at the ready.

Brawley spit a stream of tobacco into the street, then wiped his sleeve across his mouth. "This place ain't big enough for the two of us, McQuaid."

"If that's the way you feel, then I guess you oughta be moving on."

"You're the one needing to move on." Brawley's bottom lip rounded out from the chew stuffed inside, and his thin, scraggly beard and mustache were stained with the juice. Brawley probably wasn't much older than Wyatt's own twenty-three years, but his lean, leathery face and somber eyes spoke of hardships that had aged him too soon.

"Come on now, Brawley." Wyatt attempted to dredge up some empathy for the man. After all, he knew a bit about hardships himself. "This land here in South Park can handle more than one ranch. Let's aim to live in peace—"

"Peace?" Brawley scoffed. "You buying up all the cattle and leaving me with none ain't aiming for peace."

Wyatt almost snorted but held himself back. Brawley had

things backward. He was the one buying up the weak and worn-out oxen as rapidly as the miners and teamsters came over the passes.

The rumbling of wheels and the pounding of hooves from the northeast end of town cut off their discussion. *Discussion* was too kind a word for Brawley's attempt to intimidate Wyatt into leaving. It wasn't the first time the rancher had made threats, and it probably wouldn't be the last.

As the stagecoach rolled closer, the clatter and dust rose higher. Brawley bent and retrieved his revolver and then headed toward his men. Across the street, Judd watched with unswerving intensity, his bushy white eyebrows narrowed and his white mustache pursed until the men disappeared into the billiard hall. Once they were gone, Judd tipped the brim of his hat at Wyatt before he shuffled back toward the newly purchased steers.

Wyatt rolled his shoulders and tried to release the tension. At the rate he was going, he'd never make enough profit to send for his ma and siblings. Even if he could help his family with the costs of traveling to Colorado, how would he support them once they arrived?

What he needed to do was purchase a herd of purebred Shorthorns from the breeder he'd met in Missouri during his days transporting livestock for Russell, Majors, & Waddell. Beeves like that would thrive on the buffalo grass, wheat grass, and moss sage.

He peered beyond the buildings that lined the street to the grassy plains that spread out to the distant Tarryall mountain range in the east. Since the grass was endless and free, he'd have no trouble fattening up the cattle for butchering.

The miners always had a hankering for beef, tiring easily of the fish they caught in local streams or the canned goods they bought for exorbitant prices.

In fact, if Wyatt could purchase a big enough herd of Shorthorns and start his own breeding, he'd be able to send a stream of beef to the markets in the east. Eventually, he might make enough from sales to buy up more of the surrounding land and expand his ranch.

The trouble was, he didn't have a tail feather left, not after pouring every penny of his savings into the start-up costs of his place. He could hardly afford the worn-out oxen that newcomers were practically giving away. Besides, he couldn't rely on that supply forever, especially with Brawley's hackles rising every time Wyatt made a purchase.

As the stage rolled to a jerking halt in front of the Fairplay Hotel, Wyatt expelled a pent-up breath. What he needed was an investor, a partner who'd be willing to help him build up his herd.

The gold mines in the mountains surrounding South Park had made millionaires out of numerous men. Would any of them be willing to invest in his ranch?

Wyatt scanned the buildings lining Fairplay, most having the typical false storefronts that made the businesses appear bigger and more significant to draw men in. Set at the center of the flat grasslands along the intersection of Beaver Creek and the South Platte, Fairplay had earned its name from its first prospectors who'd vowed that their mining camp would be different from the others in the area, that they'd operate with integrity and fairness.

Although the town had its share of taverns and dance halls, it was a shade tamer than some of the other colorful mining towns that had sprung up in the area, towns like Buckskin Joe and Tarryall.

Of all the mining towns Wyatt had lived in and visited, he liked Fairplay best, mainly because he liked and respected the men who ran it.

Men like Landry Steele . . .

Steele stepped down from the stagecoach, wearing his usual dark suit coat, vest, and matching trousers. He turned around and offered his hand to a woman in the stagecoach door.

The woman accepted the help descending. The brim of her bonnet hid her face, but from the litheness of her movements and the womanliness of her form, she was awful young to be Steele's wife. In a blue dress, the woman was also too plainly attired to be Steele's fancy eastern wife. Besides, Steele had yammered on more than once about his wife refusing to live in the Wild West.

As the woman planted both feet on the ground, Steele reached up to the doorway again and, this time, offered his hand to a little girl.

Wyatt couldn't contain his surprise and released a low whistle. Maybe Steele's wife had decided to come west with their child after all, although hadn't Steele talked about a son, not a daughter?

The girl bounded down, her bonnet pushed back, revealing long, loose hair the color of a newborn fawn. Petite and pretty, the child smiled her thanks to Steele before skipping away.

"Astrid, stay close." The woman spun after the child and revealed her face. Her hair was the same light brown as the child's, and her features were just as pretty but fuller and slightly rounder.

Astrid didn't heed her mother and frisked away from the stagecoach in the direction of Simpkin's General Store.

"Astrid, please." The woman grabbed a fistful of her skirt and picked up her pace, then cast a glance over her shoulder at Steele.

Steele smiled and waved her on. "Go and explore. You know where to find me."

She nodded, her expression emanating gratefulness, before she hustled after her child.

Stroking his mustache, Steele watched the young woman until she disappeared into the store behind the little girl.

Wyatt needed to stop staring, but his curiosity got the better of him. If this woman wasn't Steele's wife, then who was she? Couldn't be his mistress. Steele had never struck Wyatt as the type of man who'd cheat on his wife, no matter how much he had a hankering for a woman.

As if sensing the scrutiny, Steele's gaze swung to Wyatt, where he still stood in the middle of the road. Steele touched the brim of his bowler in greeting.

Wyatt repeated the action.

"Don't look at me like that, McQuaid," Steele called.

"Like what?" Blast it all. Why hadn't he walked away before Steele had caught him staring?

"Like I'm doing something I shouldn't be."

"She ain't your wife, is she?"

"No, of course not." Steele huffed.

"I took you for a God-fearing man who took his marriage vows seriously."

"And I am."

"Then what are you doing with a pretty lady like that?" Wyatt glanced at the dusty window of the general store but couldn't see inside past the grime to the woman in question.

Steele pressed his lips together and crossed toward him. "Do you think she's pretty?"

Wyatt hadn't seen her long, but it had been enough to know she was a real beauty. "A man'd have to be blind not to think so."

Steele halted in front of him. The dust from the journey lightened the black of his suit coat to a charcoal gray. "Good. Then I want you to marry her."

CHAPTER 3

Marry her? In the process of drawing in a breath, Wyatt choked and began to cough. Steele must have knocked his head hard during the bumpy stagecoach ride. Or maybe Wyatt had heard him wrong. He cleared his throat. "Come again?"

"I want you to marry Miss Nilsson." This time Steele spoke more decisively, as if the matter was settled.

Wyatt opened his mouth but couldn't find the words to respond.

"She's a good woman in dire straits." Steele peered up and down the street, as though gauging who else might be listening in on their conversation. At the early evening hour, the town wasn't yet as busy as it would be once the miners finished their work and swarmed the taverns. "Miss Nilsson is Hallock's mail-order bride."

Wyatt shot another look at the general store and wished he could get a second glimpse of the woman Phineas Hallock had boasted about to no end.

From the moment Hallock had put the ad in the *Chicago Daily Tribune* for a bride, Wyatt teased his friend. It hadn't taken long for Hallock to start exchanging letters with a woman. Wyatt had been surprised along with everyone else when the woman had accepted Hallock's proposal. Even though Hallock was a decent fella, he was shy and eccentric, with a balding head, a paunch, and too much nose hair. And to top it off, he was ancient enough to be Wyatt's father.

"The stage got robbed up at Kenosha Pass by the Crooked-Eye Gang," Steele continued, "and Miss Nilsson lost the entirety of her savings."

Wyatt shook his head. It wasn't fair some men thought they could get rich off honest, hardworking fellas. But they didn't have a regular lawman in these parts, which only made crime worse. When things got too rough, about the best they could do was organize a vigilance committee to serve up justice.

"Now Miss Nilsson has no husband and no money. And she has her sick little sister to care for."

"The girl is her sister?"

"She brought her west to see if the mountain air would cure her consumption."

"So that's why she agreed to marry Hallock?" Wyatt could feel his ire rising.

"Now, hold on, McQuaid. Lots of marriages begin as partnerships."

Yep. Like Ma's with Rusty. And look how that had ended. "What was in it for Hallock?"

Steele's brows shot high. "You saw her. I think the answer's clear enough."

Hallock hadn't been so shallow that he'd marry a woman for her beautiful face and body. More likely he'd been lonely and eager for companionship.

"You knew Hallock better than anyone," Steele said. "He was a good man with a big heart. And he would have wanted to help Miss Nilsson's sister if he could."

Wyatt removed his hat and brushed his fingers through his overlong hair, letting the dry evening breeze cool his forehead. Steele was right. Hallock had been generous and kind.

"After getting to know Miss Nilsson during the journey, I can see that Hallock picked a very sweet woman."

"That may be." Wyatt settled his hat on his head. "But she ain't my problem."

"Hallock was your friend. What would he want you to do?"

"He sure as cow patty wouldn't want me to marry her."

"I wouldn't be so sure if I was you."

Wyatt's chest tightened as he remembered the excitement on Hallock's face when he'd said good-bye last autumn. He'd been so happy to have a woman who wanted to marry him that he'd decided to travel to California and spend his gold on all the fancy things a woman could ever want.

When Hallock still hadn't returned by late May, everyone concluded that the decomposed body several miners found in the pass leading north to the Overland Trail had been Hallock's. From what they'd been able to tell, Hallock had died a gruesome death, having been mauled and mutilated—maybe by a wild animal. Knowing such a gentle and peace-loving man had died so violently hit Wyatt hard. Still did.

As difficult as Hallock's death had been, he couldn't marry his friend's mail-order bride.

"She'll need to find another taker, Steele." He'd wasted enough time on a conversation that was going nowhere. He tipped his hat to Steele and started to move away, but the man spread his feet and crossed his arms, clearly not done.

Wyatt paused and bit back a sigh as his ma's training on respecting his elders held him in place.

Steele scrutinized him long and hard. "I'm sure plenty of other fellows in the area would pluck Miss Nilsson up and marry her today. But I can't think of any other man I like half as much as you."

"Thank you kindly, Steele, but I ain't lookin' for a wife." Wyatt worked at keeping the irritation out of his voice. "Not when I'm too busy lookin' for an investor."

"Investor?"

Wyatt kneaded the back of his neck. "All I'm saying is I don't have the means to support a wife and child right now. Not when I'm pouring everything I've got into building my ranch."

Steele's eyes took on a glimmer. "What kind of investor you looking for?"

Wyatt's ready retort faded. Just minutes ago he'd been contemplating which of the rich men in town might be willing to invest in his ranch. But he hadn't really expected anyone would want to take such a risk. After all, no one had ever done full-scale ranching in the high country before, and there were no guarantees he'd be able to succeed. The honest truth was that the odds weighed against him.

Yet, without an investor, his chances at making a go of it were even slimmer. He'd be left fighting Brawley for every scrawny ox that made it west. And it'd take years to form a large enough herd to start turning a profit.

A picture of Ma flashed into his mind from the last time he'd visited home three years ago. She'd had a swollen bruise under her eye. She'd claimed one of the colts had kicked her, but he knew their stepfather had hit her again.

Wyatt was trying as best as he could to make a new way for Ma and his four siblings. He'd been trying since the day he'd left home at the age of fifteen.

And now he was so close. He had plenty of land and plenty of know-how. He just had to get the cattle.

Was Steele the answer to his problem?

Wyatt narrowed his gaze upon Landry Steele. A shrewd entrepreneur, Steele had arrived in South Park shortly after gold had been discovered. After visiting mines in the area, he'd invested in several. Two had been profitable, including the one in Fairplay. Steele had taken his profits and invested in other mines farther up near Leadville as well as businesses that catered to the miners' needs.

Would he see the benefit in investing in cattle? It wouldn't hurt to ask, would it?

Wyatt swallowed his trepidation and forced out the words he needed to say. "Next spring, I'm aiming to buy a herd of Shorthorns and drive them up here."

"And you need someone to loan you the cash for the purchase?"

"Yep. In addition to the loan payback, I'd offer a percentage of the market sales."

"Of course." Steele's attention drifted to the end of Main Street to the treeless, grassy plains that surrounded Fairplay for miles and miles. Wyatt hoped Steele was seeing the same thing as him—hundreds of cattle roaming the fertile land, fat and content and ready to sell for a huge profit.

"I might be new to ranching." Wyatt tried to tamp down his growing excitement. "But I've got a whole heap of experience with livestock. My pa raised cattle on our farm, and I worked alongside him since the day I was born. After he died, I got a job driving cattle from Ohio to New York. And you know about my work freighting livestock for Russell, Majors, & Waddell."

Steele continued to stare at the boundless land. "I don't doubt your experience, son. And I don't doubt your determination."

"But . . . ?"

"But if I'm going to invest, I want to make sure you're planning to stick around and follow through for the long haul."

The excitement bubbling inside Wyatt pushed higher. "I wouldn't have built a cabin and a barn on my homestead if I wasn't fixin' to make a go of this place."

Steele turned his focus back onto Wyatt, and the sadness in his eyes set Wyatt off-kilter. "I telegraphed my wife again when I was in Denver. She's still refusing to come out here to Fairplay. Says she won't move until I make it into a bigger town with more to offer."

Wyatt wasn't sure what Steele's personal business had to do with agreeing to invest in his cattle ranch. Even so, he had to offer a word of consolation. "I'm sorry. I reckon you miss her an awful lot."

Steele's jaw worked up and down.

"You've already built a church and a theater," Wyatt continued. "There ain't much more you can do."

"If we get more families here, the town will become more civilized."

Wyatt nodded, still unsure of the direction Steele was taking the conversation. "Yep. I agree."

"Then you'll agree to marry Miss Nilsson, settle down permanently, and start a family?"

As the conversation came full circle and slammed into Wyatt like a steer from behind, he had to catch himself. Protest rose swiftly, but he captured and stuffed it since Steele was watching his reaction.

"I am settling down here, Steele, but that doesn't mean I wanna get married."

"She has no place to go. I'd let her stay in Hallock's house, but I can't kick out the renters."

"Give her some of Hallock's gold."

"You know I can't do that. They weren't married, so she has no legal claim to his assets."

Across the street, the front door of the general store opened, and Miss Nilsson stepped out onto the plank sidewalk.

Her bonnet hung down her back, revealing a worried crease between her eyebrows. She searched the street, taking in each of the wooden signs that hung above the businesses, before she lifted a hand and twisted a loose strand of her hair.

Wyatt held his breath and waited for her to glance toward him and Steele. No doubt if she did, she'd catch on real fast that she was the topic of their conversation. Thankfully, however, after only a moment more of hesitation, she started toward the hotel. Once she disappeared inside, Wyatt allowed himself to breathe again.

"She needs a husband," Steele said firmly. "You need an investor. And I need a civilized town for my wife."

"Don't know how one woman's gonna make much difference in civilizing the town."

"Good Christian women in the community attract other women, which eventually leads to schools, community events, charities, and all the other things women like to participate in."

"Reckon so, but that doesn't mean I need to rush in to getting hitched."

Steele situated his hat, readying to leave. "If you marry Miss Nilsson today and take her home as your wife, then I'll give you what you need for buying cattle."

Wyatt felt as though he'd been kicked in the gut by a wild horse and that his prize was galloping away even as he chased it. He wanted to plead with Steele to reconsider the ultimatum, but the hard set to the man's mouth told him he wouldn't be swayed, that for some crazy reason, he'd already made up his mind.

Why him? What did Steele think Wyatt had to offer a wife?

"Mull it over."

"I might." He'd already thought all he was going to on it, but Wyatt bit back his response.

Steele tipped the brim of his hat, then started back to the stagecoach and the luggage the driver was in the process of unloading.

"When you're ready for the wedding," Steele said over his shoulder, "I'll be at the Hotel Windsor taking a meal."

Wyatt nodded, then spun on his boots and headed toward Judd, who was still waiting near the livery. Frustration thrummed through Wyatt's body and echoed in each thud of his footsteps against the hard earth.

How could he walk away from the opportunity to buy a herd of cattle and finally make something worthwhile of his life? And yet, how could he possibly marry a complete stranger?

CHAPTER 4

No luck. Again.

Greta stepped out of the dry goods store and closed the door behind her. The evening sky had turned a shade bluer over the past hour of job hunting. Nighttime would soon be upon her, and she still had no work, no place to live, and no money.

She reached up and twisted a loose strand of hair. She'd come to the edge of town. There were no more businesses to visit—at least none for a woman like her.

The lively music pouring out of the closest tavern taunted her every bit as much as some of the men had. *"There's plenty of work to be had for a woman as purty as you."* The leering grin and ugly words from the owner of the dry goods store had followed her outside and still rang in her mind.

She hadn't stayed to ask the man what kind of work he was referring to. She hadn't needed to.

Down the street near the livery, the stagecoach sat empty, the teams of horses unhitched, the luggage gone, and the driver nowhere to be seen. Or any of the other passengers, including Mr. Steele.

She had hoped to prove the kind gentleman wrong. He'd warned her that in a mining town like Fairplay, a single woman wouldn't have other options besides becoming a dance girl. She supposed that's why he'd offered to give her shelter in his home.

She'd wanted to remain optimistic that one of the hotels would hire her to do their cooking or that one of the stores might need help, but he'd been right. No one was willing to pay others to do the work he could do for himself.

"God," she whispered as she lifted her face heavenward. "What am I to do now?"

She breathed in the clean air laden with the scent of campfire smoke and roasting game. Her stomach gurgled, reminding her that she and Astrid hadn't eaten anything all day except for the biscuits, dried venison, and milk she'd purchased before leaving the stagecoach station hours ago. And now, without any money, she had no way to buy them an evening meal.

Of course, along with giving her a room in his house, Mr. Steele had been kind enough to suggest taking Astrid and her to supper tonight. He'd emphasized that he was happily married and didn't have any ulterior motives for his kindness.

Nevertheless, she was hesitant to accept his assistance. Maybe he was as noble as he appeared. Maybe he was simply a Good Samaritan. Maybe she was worrying for nothing. But the fact was, Mr. Steele lived alone. And staying with him would only cause problems.

Lowering her head, she blinked back swift tears. She was always a burden and had been for as far back as she could remember. She'd been a burden on Pappa as he labored to take care of Mamma when she'd been bedbound. Of course, he'd loved Greta the best he could, but with managing his farm all by himself, he'd been stretched too thin, even though many within their Swedish immigrant community had reached out to help him.

After Mamma had died, Pappa quickly remarried so he wouldn't have to watch over a six-year-old in addition to everything else he had to worry about. Her stepmother, a newly arrived Swedish immigrant widow, had two boys, and Greta had felt as though she was adding to the woman's heavy workload, especially after Astrid and Liam were born.

Over the past few years, as her older stepbrothers had gotten married and the number of people living in the farmhouse grew, Greta sensed she was wanted even less. If not for her role in taking care of Astrid after her stepmother and Liam died, Greta guessed her stepbrothers would have married her off long ago. But no one else had the energy or desire to oversee the sick little girl.

After her pappa and stepbrothers left to join the War of Secession, her sisters-in-law had made it quite clear they saw her and Astrid as a burden on their limited resources. They encouraged her to get married and take Astrid with her. They even brought her mail-order bride ads in the newspaper and suggested she accept an offer.

She'd come west so she wouldn't need to encumber anyone. And she didn't want to burden a new friend on her first day in town. But it seemed no matter where Greta went or what she tried to do, she ended up being an unwanted responsibility to those around her.

With heavy steps, she started back toward Simpkin's General

Store, where Astrid had been playing checkers. The moment Astrid had walked into the establishment and noticed the board set up on top of a barrel, she'd challenged the store owner to a game.

When Greta had checked on Astrid a short while ago in between job hunting, the two had been on their fourth game, with Astrid having won each round. The store owner's placating smile had long since vanished, replaced by a brow furrowed with determination. Greta should have warned the man, but she hadn't wanted to ruin Astrid's fun, especially because the game was keeping the girl occupied.

The traffic on the street had steadily increased, and as Greta retraced her steps to the store, she could feel the stares of the men coming and going from the hotels and taverns. She garnered a whistle or two along with a few calls. But she chose to ignore such vulgar behavior, hoping the men would eventually choose to ignore her too.

She supposed the only thing to be done for the night was to take up Mr. Steele's offer and stay with him. She had no other option, unless she and Astrid camped out under the stars. Of course, Astrid would love every minute of camping.

But Greta had heard too many stories during their journey—and some even before leaving—that had opened her eyes to the perils of the West. She'd clung to the hope that the danger, risks, and hardships they encountered would be worth it if the Colorado climate helped to heal Astrid's consumption.

She'd first heard about the clean mountain air being medicine for the lungs from a physician who'd passed through her small Illinois farming town. After that, she'd done more investigating and learned the West was considered an Eden, that the open air was life-giving, and that it could cure those with the white death.

In recent days, Astrid seemed to have gained more energy along with color to her face, but her delicate body was still too thin and the cough still too frequent. Maybe the Colorado air wouldn't be able to cure Astrid after all. Or maybe they just needed to give this mountain wilderness more time to work its miracle.

Whatever the case, they couldn't think of leaving yet, not when they'd just arrived. Besides, even if she wanted to go home to Illinois, she had no money to pay for the return stagecoach trip. She'd have to stay in Fairplay and earn the fare. By the time she saved up enough, she and Astrid would likely be snowed in the high country until spring—at least she'd heard some mountain trails became impassable from November's first snowfall until the spring thaw.

With a shake of her head, she tried to forget her worries. But as her footsteps slapped against the plank sidewalk, they only echoed the steady dreadful thud of her heartbeat.

"Miss Nilsson?" came a voice from the side of the blacksmith shop.

Startled that anyone other than Mr. Steele would know her name, Greta halted and searched the shadows. A man leaned against the building, his arms folded and his legs crossed at his ankles. She couldn't see him clearly, but it was enough to tell he was broad shouldered, well built, and muscular.

Seeing he had her attention, he pushed away from the wall and straightened, adding several inches to his height, making him too imposing for a woman unchaperoned on the street.

Gathering her skirt and the starched petticoat underneath,

she hurried on her way, ducking her head and pretending not to notice him.

"Miss Nilsson, hold on."

She picked up her pace.

"I need to talk to you." He sounded almost desperate.

Still, she kept her head down and continued toward the general store, now only a dozen paces away.

"Heard you're in a bad way, and I've got a proposal for you."

Proposal? Her footsteps faltered. What kind of proposal?

"Phineas Hallock was a good friend of mine."

She slowed and then stopped. If this man had been friends with Phineas, then surely he was someone she could trust. Hesitantly, she turned.

The stranger had halted and now held himself motionless, as though he was facing a doe about to bolt. "Name's Wyatt McQuaid."

Underneath the brim of a battered felt hat, eyes the color of richly brewed coffee peered at her intently. The eyes were framed by dark, thick lashes and brows. The scruffy layer of hair covering his chiseled jaw and chin was the same inky shade as the hair that curled up around the edge of his collar and neckerchief.

His loose-fitting shirt and vest were dusty, as were his woolen trousers. But he wasn't as sloppy or ill-kempt as some of the men she'd met. In fact, under other circumstances, she might have been impressed by the rugged handsomeness of his features.

But not tonight. Not now. Her situation had become too woeful for her to care that such a good-looking man was stopping her in the middle of the street. "You knew Phineas?"

"Yep. And as his friend, I know he'd want me to do the right thing. . . ."

Something in the way the man assessed her—as though measuring her worth—made her stand up a little straighter. Was it possible this Mr. McQuaid was approaching to offer her a job? Maybe for Phineas's sake?

When she'd dressed that morning, she wanted to look her best for Mr. Hallock and donned one of her Sunday outfits. After the day of traveling, she should have known she looked wilted.

She brushed a hand over her calico skirt of blue with sprigs of red flowers and wished it wasn't so dusty. The matching bodice with velvet-covered buttons was equally dusty, and she guessed the once-white collar pinned neatly in place was now a dull gray. She wasn't making a good impression.

"I've got a ranch—a homestead—southeast of Fairplay—"

"If you're in need of a cook, I won't disappoint you or your ranch hands. I promise."

"Right now, it's just me and my friend Judd."

The hope that had begun to rise stumbled back a step. He wouldn't need a cook for just the two of them. But maybe he was searching for another ranch hand. "I can help with the cattle. I've lived my whole life on a farm, and my pappa raised a few cows, mostly for dairy. But I'm a quick learner, and I'm sure it won't take me long to learn everything I need to know about ranching."

Mr. McQuaid tugged at his neckerchief as if the thing was strangling him. He cleared his throat and then seemed to force himself to speak again. "Thank you kindly for the offer, but I had a different proposal in mind."

Her hope fell away, and wariness rushed in to replace it.

After spending the past hour fending off advances and offensive suggestions, she had the feeling she knew exactly what kind of proposal he was about to offer. And she didn't want to hear it.

She spun on her heels and strode toward the store. "I'm not interested in a *different* kind of proposal, Mr. McQuaid."

"Hold on. Hear me out."

She reached the door and tossed a final comment over her shoulder. "I'm looking for honest work or none at all." She flung open the door, eager to get Astrid and escape.

"I'm not aiming to make you an employee." He trailed after her. "I'm aiming to make you my wife."

Wife? She stopped so abruptly Mr. McQuaid bumped into her from behind. He caught himself and pulled up short. As she spun, he took a rapid step back, almost as if he expected her to haul off and slap his face.

His dark brows furrowed above his expressive eyes—eyes that now radiated worry.

She couldn't keep from studying his face again, this time more carefully, noting the perfect nose, the shadowed hollow lines that defined his cheeks, and the well-rounded chin. His eyes were deep and serious and altogether too beautiful for a man.

She dropped her gaze to his chest, noting again how powerfully built he was all the way down to his solid waist, where he wore a holster and a gun, along with what looked like a small whip of braided rawhide. His legs were long and sturdy with his trousers tucked into a pair of Texas-style leather boots with a pointed toe.

Reaching the end of her inspection, she met his gaze. One of his brows had cocked just slightly, as if questioning whether he had her approval. If she went by appearance alone, this man would have won first prize.

Why, then, was he proposing marriage to her? Obviously, there weren't many women in these parts to choose from, which was why Phineas had placed an ad for a bride. But Phineas had been—well, he'd more than made up in kindness what he lacked in appearance.

This man, on the other hand, could have his pick of women.

"If you're looking for that little girl of yours," the store owner said, "she took off."

"What?" All thoughts of Mr. McQuaid fled as Greta scanned the store's interior. Everything was the same as when she'd entered after she arrived on the stagecoach. The shelves were overflowing with all manner of food items: flour, sugar, oats, lard, baking soda, and canned goods. The scent of onion hung heavy in the air along with the mustiness of potatoes.

The checkerboard on a barrel near the counter was deserted, the pieces in place on their respective ends. The two stools on either side were empty. Several other men loitered near the counter reading week-old editions of the *Rocky Mountain News* that had been brought up on the stage from Denver, full of reports of the war back East. They eyed her with interest. But there was no sign of Astrid anywhere.

"Where did she go?"

The store owner shrugged. "Said she was gonna find her sister. Told her she oughta wait for her ma—for you. But she said she don't have a mamma no more."

Greta was used to people thinking she was Astrid's mother and having to explain her real relationship to the little girl.

But at this moment, in a strange new town with the evening beginning to fade, she didn't have time to set this man aright.

"How long ago did she leave?"

"Don't quite remember." The store owner busied himself with folding the newspaper pages his patrons weren't reading.

"Did you see which direction she went?"

"Can't rightly say."

Greta's body tensed with frustration. She'd simply have to go door-to-door down Main Street until she found Astrid. Hopefully, the little girl hadn't gone far.

"Come on now, Captain Jim." Mr. McQuaid stepped into the store next to her. "You know the business of every fly living on a horse's hind end this side of the Continental Divide."

The other men guffawed, and the store owner cracked a smile.

Apparently Mr. McQuaid had his fair share of charm as well as good looks.

"If you didn't see where that little girl was headed," Mr. McQuaid continued, "then I reckon this town better invest in a telegraph to take your place."

Once more the men laughed, and Mr. McQuaid's grin came out briefly. He was definitely a charmer.

Captain Jim leaned back against the wall plastered with old newspapers. "Well, I suppose I did hear one of the fellas walking past say he saw a little child heading out by way of the river path off Front Street."

"The river path?" Greta shivered at the prospect of Astrid getting anywhere near a river. "Where's that?"

"I'll take you there." Mr. McQuaid nodded his thanks to the store owner.

As Greta followed Mr. McQuaid outside and down the street, she rushed to keep up with his long stride. She didn't want to be dependent on this stranger to find Astrid, but since the child had a knack for getting into trouble, Greta needed to locate her before anything happened.

He led her onto a side road, past a number of log cabins that most likely belonged to the miners. The structures were tiny, at best one room, and flimsy enough to blow over with the first fierce storm. The canvas tents near the cabins were also small and crowded together.

Men milled about, some hunched over campfires in front of pots and pans. Others washed their faces from basins or hung clothing on lines suspended between cabins and tents. At the sight of her, the men stopped what they were doing to stare.

At a few whistles and calls, she hastened her steps so she was directly behind Mr. McQuaid. The road narrowed into a path, winding through tall grass, and turning into a path that descended and grew rockier. As they reached the edge of a ledge, Mr. McQuaid halted, pushed up the brim of his hat, and scanned the area below.

Greta stopped next to him, her breathing shallow from the exertion of the hike. In the distance, thick clouds were moving in and obscuring the setting sun, and the sky had turned a mixture of deep purple and orange.

Darkness was settling fast, and she was running out of time.

She followed Mr. McQuaid's gaze downward to a river winding through a rocky embankment littered with all manner of mining equipment.

During the stagecoach ride up into the mountains, she'd

come across other mining camps and had begun to learn the names of the tools, like sluice and rocker boxes. But at the moment, she wasn't interested in the mining process.

The only thing she cared about was finding Astrid.

She squinted downriver. "Do you think she came out this far?"

"It's possible."

A familiar weight of failure settled over Greta. Somehow she was always doing things wrong with Astrid. "She runs off now and then but has never gone this far before."

"Maybe she heard the men in the store talking about finding gold."

After the robbery that morning and Greta's scolding, Astrid had finally realized they had no money. And after learning Phineas had died and that they had no place to go, her sister had been unusually quiet.

If she'd heard the fellas in the store telling tales about gold, had she thought she could walk down to the river and find nuggets so they would have money again?

Greta sighed. "She's probably hoping to get rich quick in order to make up for losing our money during the stagecoach robbery."

"Steele mentioned you all were robbed."

She swallowed a rising lump in her throat. "I'm told I should be grateful our lives were spared, and I am. But I may have no other option but to take up gold digging right alongside Astrid."

Mr. McQuaid pursed his lips even as he continued to scrutinize the riverbank below.

"Do you know Mr. Steele?" She tried to turn the conversation away from the pain of her loss.

"Yep. He's the one who told me I should help you."

"By help, you mean marry?"

"Yep." Mr. McQuaid's expression was as hard as granite. He hadn't seemed too thrilled about the possibility of getting married before. And he still didn't. So why had he asked?

She wanted to question him more, but what was the point? She wasn't planning to seriously consider his offer, was she? He was a stranger. Then again, Phineas had been a stranger too. Though they'd corresponded, no one could ever truly get to know a person without meeting face-to-face.

If Phineas had lived and she'd met him tonight, she might have decided she couldn't marry him after all. Of course, she couldn't afford to be too picky about a spouse. He had to be God-fearing, clean, and kind. And as long as he agreed to accept Astrid along with her, what more could she want?

"There." Mr. McQuaid pointed to a section of the river farther down. "I think she's across from the sandbar."

Greta strained to see the spot Mr. McQuaid had identified. "I don't see anyone."

With another hard look in the direction of the sandbar, he started down the path that cut through gravel and rock, giving Greta no choice but to follow him and pray he was right. As she descended, she slipped and slid on the loose stones. How did the miners make it down to the river every day without falling?

By the time she reached the riverbank, the rushing water and the cold breeze made her wish she'd brought their shawls. Hurrying after Mr. McQuaid, she picked her way through abandoned metal pans, broken boards, and piles of pebbles and rocks pulled from the river in the quest to find the gold buried in its depths.

He cast frequent glances toward the west and the dark clouds that seemed to be rolling toward them with the speed of a galloping team of horses. During the stagecoach ride up from Denver, they'd gotten caught in a thunderstorm. One moment the sky had been sunny and blue. The next, it had been black and flashing with lightning. Another passenger had informed her that in the mountains, storms came from out of nowhere.

With a new sense of urgency, Greta shouted Astrid's name, hoping the little girl would hear her and come running. But the rushing of the river drowned out her voice.

As they rounded a particularly large boulder, Mr. McQuaid halted and motioned her to stop with one hand while with his other, he removed his revolver and aimed it at something along the bank.

"What—?"

He pressed a finger against his lips, urging her to silence.

Finally, she saw what he did, and the air squeezed from her lungs. Crouched on a rock overlooking the river was a mountain lion—its yellow eyes fixed with unswerving intensity upon a little girl panning for gold in the river.

Chapter 5

Greta tried to pray, but she couldn't push the words past the fear clogging her throat.

With ears flat against its head, the lion swished its tail back and forth. It was on the opposite side of Astrid, a dozen paces away. If only the girl would turn around, see the danger, and run toward them. Instead, she'd waded into the river up to her knees and was bent over pouring a handful of muck into a rusted mining pan.

Mr. McQuaid cocked the hammer on his gun.

Greta braced herself for the shot and tried not to think about what would happen if he missed.

Before he could release a bullet, the mountain lion leapt to the ground.

"No!" The cry slipped out instinctively.

At the sound, Astrid straightened and turned in their direction. "Hi there, Greta." The girl held up the pan, water pouring out the bottom holes. Her discarded boots and socks sat in a dry heap near the shore, but her skirt was soaked past her knees. "I'm searching for gold."

"I can see that." Greta worked at keeping her voice calm even though her pulse was about to pound out of her body.

"I think I found some." Wading out of the river, she dug into her pocket and pulled out a handful of stones.

Greta pushed past Mr. McQuaid, heedless of his arm blocking her way. She had to direct the mountain lion's attention away from Astrid to herself. That was the only thing left to do.

He fumbled after her, but she dodged away from his grasp.

The cat's attention shifted from Astrid and onto Greta. She had to keep it that way until she positioned herself between Astrid and the creature.

"Who's that?" Astrid stared past Greta, noticing Mr. McQuaid. "And why does he have a gun? Are we getting robbed again?"

Greta picked up her pace as the large cat crouched closer to the ground, preparing to leap. "No. He's not robbing us. He's a new friend, Mr. McQuaid, and he brought me out here so I could find you." She was surprised at how natural her voice sounded when her insides were twisting with the ferocity of a funnel cloud.

She reached Astrid just as the mountain lion released a long, low growl. After grabbing Astrid's arm, she jerked the girl behind her, putting her sister out of harm's way.

Only then did Astrid see the danger. "What's that, Greta? I've never seen a kitty so big."

Before Greta could answer, the mountain lion bared its teeth and released a cry that sounded more like a scream, making the hair on Greta's arms stand on end.

"Drop to the ground," Mr. McQuaid ordered from behind her. "Now."

All Greta wanted to do was pick up Astrid and run. But she dropped down and threw herself over Astrid, figuring Mr. McQuaid knew how to outsmart a mountain lion better than she did.

As the creature released another scream, a shot rang out. Greta hugged Astrid closer and watched the bullet ping against a boulder near the cat's head, startling it and causing it to bolt. With silent, graceful strides, it bounded up the riverbank and disappeared.

Greta pushed up and ran her hands over Astrid's frail body. "Are you alright?"

The little girl was shaking. Her eyes fixed upon Mr. McQuaid, who had his revolver still aimed at the riverbank.

"What was it?" Astrid's voice was small and trembling.

"A mountain lion." Greta pulled her sister into a tight hug. "It could have hurt you."

Astrid sank into Greta's embrace, burying her face and letting Greta hold her, which she didn't allow as often now that she was getting older. Greta kissed the girl's silky, soft hair and offered silent prayers of thankfulness for God's protection. She'd brought the child west with the hope of bringing her healing. But so far, all she'd done was put Astrid into one dangerous situation after another. Had this trip been a big mistake? The question rose to taunt her again.

A sizzle and flash of light was followed by a crack of thunder.

Mr. McQuaid glanced up at the sky in time to get hit in the face by several drops of rain.

As large plops landed on Greta, she hovered over Astrid

more protectively. At another dangerous bolt and resounding boom, she shuddered and peered back the way they'd come. She had to get Astrid out of the storm.

She stood and pulled the girl to her feet. Just then, the sky opened, the wind roared against them, and rain fell in a deluge.

"This way!" Mr. McQuaid shouted above the stormy clamor. "We'll take shelter in that rocky cleft until the storm blows over."

He was pointing toward the embankment farther down. But the rain and increasing darkness obscured her vision. "I'll follow you!"

He nodded and started forward.

Greta took a step but then remembered Astrid wasn't wearing shoes or socks. Greta tried hefting the girl, but the rain made everything too slick.

"Here." Mr. McQuaid returned to her side and lifted Astrid into his arms as though she weighed nothing more than a doll. Before Greta could say anything, he strode off, and she practically had to run to keep up with him. He disappeared up a rocky embankment but several moments later was back, grasping her arm and hefting her up.

Within seconds, she found herself scrambling into a low cavern out of the rain. Another flash of lightning revealed Astrid huddled underneath the overhang and shaking.

"I'm sorry, Greta," she sobbed. "I didn't mean to cause trouble."

Greta crawled toward her sister. "It's okay." She drew the girl into her arms. "We'll be okay."

"I was just trying to make things better. That's all."

"I know you were." She swallowed her need to scold Astrid. Sometimes it seemed scolding was all she ever did.

Mr. McQuaid had crept under the cleft with them. The space was tight, and as he sat next to her, his shoulder brushed hers. With water dripping from the brim of his hat, he smelled distinctly of wet leather and hay. He settled his back against the wall and stretched his legs out, crossing them at his boots.

The rain poured off the ledge above and ran in rivulets underneath them, and the wind gusted every few seconds, blowing a mist of rain inside. But at least they were out of the worst of the storm and away from the danger of lightning.

The steady pounding of the rain drowned out all other sounds except for the occasional boom of thunder. The temperature had dropped significantly, and now that they were nearly drenched, a chill permeated Greta's wet layers to her skin.

She rubbed Astrid's arms to warm her. After a couple of minutes, the girl stopped shaking and scooted forward, attempting to take stock of their shelter. Though it was dark, the evening sky along with the lightning kept them from utter blackness. Greta could see the rain descending like a waterfall over the opening of the cavern. And she could see Astrid's outline as she inched closer to the edge.

"Stay back, or you'll fall out."

The girl stuck her hand into the stinging drops. "It's really pouring."

"It's good drinking water," Mr. McQuaid said. "If you can manage to catch it."

"Catch it?" Astrid squinted through the darkness as though trying to get a better look at the man.

"Yep." He leaned forward, cupped his hands together to form a bowl, and then let the water fill it. When the rainwater reached the top, he lifted his makeshift bowl to his mouth and downed the water.

Astrid watched him, fascination radiating from her little body.

"You try it." He nodded toward the falling water.

She eagerly held her hands out into the rain but managed to capture only a scant amount. Mr. McQuaid showed her again, then helped her to cup her hands so she caught a little more before it leaked out.

"Keep practicing." He leaned back, his shoulder brushing Greta's again.

Astrid chattered away as if there was nothing strange about sitting in a cave during a thunderstorm with a man they didn't know. Although from everything Greta had witnessed of him so far, he seemed like a decent fellow. He'd gone out of his way to help her find Astrid. He'd saved them from certain mauling, possibly even death, from the mountain lion. And he'd aided them into this shelter where they were safe from the storm.

As if that wasn't enough, he'd been kind and gentle with Astrid, giving her something to do to occupy her time. She could see now why both Phineas and Mr. Steele counted Mr. McQuaid as their friend.

"Thank you, Mr. McQuaid." Her words seemed somehow inadequate.

"Ain't nothing," he replied so quietly, she almost didn't hear him over the rain slapping against the rocks.

"I owe you our lives."

"No, ma'am. You don't owe me. I don't expect nothing for helping someone in need."

Her estimation of him rose another notch. If Mr. Steele

had suggested that Mr. McQuaid approach her about marriage, did she need to give the idea more consideration? Certainly a man of such high caliber wouldn't suggest a match unless it was a good one.

Would Mr. McQuaid ask her again? She waited, letting Astrid's prattle fill the silence. This was the perfect opportunity for him to leverage the situation to his advantage. With all he'd just done for her, she'd have a hard time turning him down.

When Mr. McQuaid didn't say anything more, she tugged on one of her loose strands of wet hair and let her self-doubts come calling. What if he'd changed his mind? Especially after seeing how difficult her life was with Astrid? And what if he'd taken a closer look at her and decided she wasn't pretty enough?

Had she thrown away her chance with him? Did she even want a chance?

"Mr. McQuaid," Astrid said when she'd had her fill of drinking rainwater, "have you found any gold out of the river?"

"Nothing that amounts to much." He shifted his legs and made room for the little girl to sprawl out next to him. "I learned that getting rich fast only happens to a lucky few. Most of the rest of us have to set store by hard work, the way the good Lord intended."

"I don't like working hard," Astrid said with her usual honesty.

"Astrid," Greta reprimanded.

"It's the truth."

Mr. McQuaid took off his hat, combed through his damp hair, and then leaned his head back as though he was taking time to think before he gave an answer. Greta preferred that much better than someone who liked to hear himself talk.

"My pa always told me and my brothers that even if we don't like doing hard things, it's those hard things that make us strongest."

"You're sure strong," Astrid replied. "That must mean you've done a lot of hard things."

"Yep. Reckon I have." His answer was decidedly sadder. What kind of hardships had he experienced to make him so sad?

"Do your pa and brothers live here in Fairplay too?"

"No, Pa—well, he died a while back. And my brothers are living in Pennsylvania."

"Are they younger than you?"

"That's enough now, Astrid," Greta cut in. "You know it's not proper manners to pry into someone's private life."

"It's alright. Yep, my brothers are younger."

"What are their names?"

Greta sighed with exasperation, but Mr. McQuaid was already answering before she could rebuke Astrid again. "Flynn is closest to me at twenty-one. Then there's Brody. He's nigh to eighteen. And Dylan—I think he's about fifteen."

"So you had four boys in your family?"

"Yep, and I've got a little sister. It's been a few years since I've seen her, but last time I did, she was full of questions too."

"How old is she?"

"Last time I checked, she was only knee-high to a grasshopper."

Astrid giggled. "No, really. What's her name?"

"I reckon she's about eleven, and her name's Ivy."

"Since I'm nine, maybe she can be my new friend."

"She'd probably like that." Mr. McQuaid was quiet for a heartbeat, and the steady patter of the rain echoed in the cavern. "I'm hoping to move my family out here next summer."

Greta sensed a wistfulness in his tone, a missing of his family. Why had he moved away from them? Was that one of the hard things he'd had to do?

It hadn't been hard to move away from family. In fact, leaving had been more of a relief for her—and for them too. The trouble was thinking she might have to go back. She dreaded what her sisters-in-law would say if she and Astrid showed up on the farm needing a place to stay.

It would be humiliating to burden them again.

She straightened her spine. She had to find a way to make it on her own.

"I don't think me and Greta will still be here next summer," Astrid said, as if reading Greta's mind. "Unless I find more gold to see us through."

Greta smiled wryly. "I highly doubt what you found today was gold."

"It was shiny."

"I'm sure most of the gold lying on the surface has already been scooped up by the miners living in town. Isn't that right, Mr. McQuaid?"

He shifted his body, clearly uncomfortable in the tight, damp space. "All the valuable land around here is claimed. Some of the mines, like Mr. Steele's, are producing more gold than others."

"Greta's fiancé had a gold mine."

"Yep. He was part owner and doing well for himself."

"Too bad he had to die." Astrid piled her new rock collection on Greta's lap. "I liked him, even if he was old."

"Astrid."

"It's true. He was a lot older than Thomas."

At the mention of her best friend, Greta's throat closed up with emotion. More than a year after his death, she couldn't think of him without missing him.

"Who's Thomas?" Mr. McQuaid asked.

"Greta was set to marry him, but then he went off to war and got killed." Astrid spoke the words matter-of-factly, but to Greta, Thomas's death from pneumonia while at training camp had been anything but matter-of-fact. It had been devastating, even worse than learning of her pappa's fatality at the Battle of Shiloh in April.

In the months leading up to the conflict, the conversation around the dinner table invariably ended with talk of the Mason-Dixon line and the need to keep the shame of slavery from spreading into every new territory. Her pappa and stepbrothers spoke proudly of President Lincoln, who hailed from their fair state, and they denounced the Southern states for seceding.

Once the president had called for troops, the men had rushed off to put the South in her place. Like everyone else, Greta had expected a quick victory for the North, had never believed it would drag on for a year and a half.

Again, silence fell over the cavern. The lightning and thunder had ceased, and the rain had softened to a low patter. The chill in the air, however, hadn't diminished. It had only seemed to increase, and Greta couldn't hold back a shudder. She crossed her arms, hugging herself for warmth.

"The rain won't last much longer," Mr. McQuaid said.

"I don't mind." Astrid yawned, leaning her head against Greta's leg. "Maybe me and Greta can live here in this little cave. It's real nice."

Greta's thoughts tumbled together as she fought against another shudder. Though plenty of time had passed since she'd lost Thomas, thoughts of him always made her melancholy. She'd first met him when his father, Reverend Lawson, had performed her mamma's funeral.

After the memorial service, Thomas offered her a peppermint, winning her affection. After that, he'd become a fast friend. He'd been a safe place, the only one who'd made her feel needed and important, at least until her half-siblings had come along, and she'd proven her worth by helping to take care of them.

Thomas had been there for her when she'd been devastated by her little brother Liam's death from consumption, and when her stepmother had died not many months later. He held her and comforted her and promised her that God was there still with her.

And when she'd felt the pressure from her family to get married and take Astrid with her, Thomas had been the one to offer his hand, to tell her he loved her and always would.

When Thomas died, her future had crumbled, and she'd been floundering ever since. Then when she'd learned Pappa was gone, she realized she didn't have a single soul left who cared what became of her. While Pappa had always been working and never affectionate, at least he'd been solid and secure and looked after her.

With the engagement to Phineas, she'd thought she'd reestablished her footing. But today, the solid ground had given way to raging rapids that seemed to be carrying her away.

Greta closed her eyes, wanting to give in to the temptation to let the drowning waters take her wherever they would. But as Astrid started to cough, Greta pushed aside her own woes. She had too much responsibility to wallow in self-pity.

She needed to keep fighting for Astrid's sake.

Patting her sister's back and encouraging her to breathe through the coughing, Greta watched as the rain tapered away and the sky lightened, cringing at what Mr. McQuaid must think of Astrid's coughing. The constant hacking sound could get annoying after a while—at least that's what her sisters-in-law had said.

Thankfully, Mr. McQuaid didn't seem to mind and even asked if there was any way he might be of aid to Astrid. When the rain completely stopped, he ventured out. He came back a minute later to let them know the storm was over and they could walk back to town.

He assisted both Astrid and her down to level ground. Though wet with puddles, the path along the river was manageable. Astrid, still coughing slightly, skipped ahead. She stopped now and then to pick up a rock, examine it, and ask Mr. McQuaid if it was gold.

By the time they climbed the ravine and were nearing the miners' tents and cabins at the edge of town, Greta knew what she had to do.

She slowed her footsteps. "Mr. McQuaid, does your proposal from earlier still stand?"

He halted and looked at her intently.

Her feet were soaked through her boots and the wet leather rubbed against one of her big toes, forming a blister. Her skirt was damp and tangling in her legs. And her hair was loose and matted from the rain. "You're seeing me at my worst. And you've experienced Astrid with her coughing. At least you know honestly what you're getting."

He hesitated. Behind him, the sky above the mountain range was laced with hues of lavender, rose, and lily of the valley, with a few remaining dark clouds to frame the work of art. The storm had moved to the southeast, the dark clouds still flashing lightning in the distance.

"It's okay if you changed your mind." She started forward, picking up her pace through the grassy path. "I understand that I might not be what you were looking for."

"No, that ain't it." He easily caught up and matched his stride to hers. "There's nothing wrong with you. Mr. Steele was right when he said you're a very sweet woman."

This time she stopped abruptly. "Mr. Steele thought I was sweet?"

Mr. McQuaid nodded, his expression earnest. "And he figured you and Astrid would be safe with me."

Mr. McQuaid had proven himself to be a hero. If she had to marry a stranger, she'd likely find no better man than this handsome rancher.

"The thing is . . ." His forehead furrowed. "I know why you want—need—the marriage partnership—so you and Astrid can stay here in Colorado so Astrid can get well. But you might be wondering why I'm needing it . . ."

For a few seconds, she waited for him to continue. When the silence lengthened, her face flamed. What was he insinuating? That he wanted a wife because he had manly needs?

"What I'm trying to say," he continued awkwardly, "is that Steele is wanting to make Fairplay a stable town with more families and children."

So Mr. McQuaid wanted a family of his own? Again,

Greta's face grew hot. While she hadn't thought much about the marriage bed, she'd assumed it would be one of her wifely duties with Phineas. And if she went through with marrying Mr. McQuaid, she assumed it would be with him too. So why was he bringing it up? Did they really need to talk about it?

He rubbed a hand over his jaw and chin. "I'm making a mess of this, ain't I?"

She couldn't look him in the eyes. Instead, she focused on Astrid, who'd stopped and was now staring and waving at the miners in their camps.

Mr. McQuaid took a deep breath. "Steele's offering me a deal 'cause he thinks he can convince his wife and son to come west if Fairplay has more families—"

"I understand, Mr. McQuaid." She had to assure him before he said something even more embarrassing. "All I need to know is that you're willing to help me for Phineas's sake. That's a good enough reason for me."

He lifted his hat, smoothed his hair, then situated it again. "Alright, then."

She let out a breath, and the tension eased from her shoulders. As with Phineas, she was taking a big risk in agreeing to marry a stranger. But she had to keep doing whatever she could for Astrid, no matter the personal sacrifice.

They started walking again.

After a moment, he cleared his throat. "I'm guessing you'll want to change into something dry before the wedding?"

"You want to get married tonight?" She didn't know why his question surprised her. After all, she'd expected to marry Phineas right away. Why not Mr. McQuaid instead?

"I guess we can wait if you want to—"

"No, tonight is just fine." There was no reason to put it off. She might as well get it over with so she could move on with her life and provide a home for Astrid.

"You sure?" His voice wavered. Who was he asking: himself or her?

"Mr. McQuaid, I haven't been sure about anything for a long time. But that hasn't stopped me yet."

He was quiet for several steps, so that their squeaking boots sounded too loud against the wet grass and gravel. "I'll go get the preacher."

Chapter 6

Steele's front parlor was hotter than the scorching sun on a Kansas prairie. Wyatt tugged at his neckerchief and collar. Even with every window wide open in the sparsely furnished room, allowing in the cool night air, he was perspiring worse than a pack mule at midday.

"You're doing the right thing," Steele said again, as he had a dozen times since Wyatt had found him at Hotel Windsor reclining in a chair, smoking a cigar, and waiting for him.

The Methodist minister, Reverend Zieber, stood with Judd across the room and had been carrying on a mostly one-sided conversation since he'd arrived. Although Wyatt considered both of the older and wiser men to be friends, their personalities were about as different as a columbine and a cactus.

Reverend Zieber was ruggedly built, sturdy, and had only a smattering of gray in his hair. He'd moved to Colorado from Wisconsin the previous year and had been traveling from one mining camp to another preaching, tending the sick, and burying the dead. He always had news to share as well as plenty of godly advice. While he had a cabin in Buckskin Joe, he spent a heap of time in Fairplay now that Steele had built a church.

Judd, on the other hand, was short and wiry with hair as white as a fresh winter snowfall. Judd had come up from Texas to mine for gold and had saved Wyatt from getting killed in a gunfight over a claim the first week he'd been in the Rockies. Ever since then, they'd been friends. Judd had given up on finding gold about the same time as Wyatt and had taken his offer to stay and help him build the ranch. Judd rarely spoke unless he had something important to say, but Wyatt had come to rely upon his friend for just about everything.

When Wyatt had returned to town after the storm and told Judd about his decision to marry Miss Nilsson in exchange for Steele's investment in a herd of Shorthorns, Judd had shaken his head. Wyatt hadn't been able to interpret whether Judd thought his decision was good or bad, and he hadn't had the time to ask.

And now it was too late. Sure as a gun, he was getting hitched to Miss Nilsson.

If only she'd hurry it up and get on down to the parlor.

He tugged his neckerchief again. He'd taken Steele up on the offer to borrow a clean, dry shirt. Even if his trousers were still damp and dirty, at least he was halfway decent for his wedding day.

Wedding day. The very thought made his head itch. Marrying had been the last thing on his mind when he'd ridden into town today. In fact, marrying had been the last thing on his mind since the day his ma had married Rusty. Their neighbor had always been mean and hardfisted, but Wyatt had been barkin' at a knot trying to convince his ma of that. After she'd married the lowlife, Wyatt hadn't been surprised when the marriage had gone sour.

That didn't mean he'd never planned on getting married. A part of him wanted a family and a place to belong. But he'd moved around too much to make any real connections with the women who'd paid him attention. The handful who lived in the high country were already married and worked alongside their husbands. The rest lived in the dance halls and taverns catering to the lusts of the miners. They were the kind of women Wyatt had decided long ago to steer away from, no matter how tempting they might be.

Instead, he'd stayed busy and focused.

Until today . . . Until he'd met Miss Nilsson.

How in the name of all that was holy had he gotten roped into marrying a woman he hardly knew?

He glanced through the parlor door into the hallway. Did he have time to make an escape?

At just that moment, Miss Nilsson stepped into the entrance, and he froze at her image of perfection. Somehow over the past hour, she'd transformed herself from pretty to stunningly beautiful, and he could only stare stupidly at her like the other men were doing.

She'd changed out of her wet blue gown into a dark green one that contrasted with her light skin and made her eyes more blue than gray. The bell-shaped skirt hugged her hips and emphasized her tiny waist, and a matching bodice was formfitting over her curves. A simple but elegant pendant on a chain graced her neck. And she'd transformed her rain-soaked tangles of hair into a stylish knot.

She searched the room until she found him. As her gaze

connected with his, he couldn't look away. She was so wide eyed and innocent. And yet her gaze was also intense, fanning a strange new heat to life low in his gut.

Something in her expression asked him whether he really wanted to go through with this wedding. A moment ago, he'd been about to bolt from the house. But now he wasn't sure he could move his feet even if the place began to burn down around him.

Wyatt sucked in a lungful of air, and his breathing felt shallow and quick, like it had when he'd first moved to the area and had to get used to the high altitude.

"The flowers I picked earlier today all wilted," came Astrid's childish voice as she sidled past her sister into the parlor. "But I managed to find these for the wedding. Aren't they pretty?"

The girl was attired in fresh garments, too, and her hair neatly brushed and plaited. Miss Nilsson had spent as much time cleaning up Astrid as she had herself. And if the girl's shenanigans were any indication of how things usually went, then Miss Nilsson was nigh on to becoming a saint for her patience.

"What do you think, Mr. McQuaid?" Astrid crossed toward him, holding out the handful of weeds with a few flowering cow parsnip in the bunch.

He gave her plait a gentle tug. "I think it's mighty sweet of you to be giving your sister flowers, that's what."

The compliment earned him one of her impish smiles, one he suspected she'd used to get herself out of trouble plenty of times.

As Miss Nilsson drew farther into the room, Wyatt was suddenly in tune to her every movement in a way he hadn't been with a woman in a mighty long time, if ever. Each soft step, the quick intake of her breath, a tilt of her head, the way she fingered the pendant against her neck.

He fumbled through introducing her to Reverend Zieber and Judd. For a short while, Reverend Zieber yammered on with both Steele and Miss Nilsson about the stagecoach ride as well as the robbery, before finally getting to the ceremony.

Reverend Zieber led them through Scripture readings and prayers. When he instructed Wyatt to face Miss Nilsson and hold her right hand, Wyatt hesitated to touch her. Thankfully, she offered up her hand, and he situated her fingers within his and then spoke his vows.

A moment later, as Miss Nilsson began to recite her vows, she abruptly stopped. "I take thee—"

Wyatt waited.

"I don't remember your given name," she whispered, her cheeks flushing.

"Wyatt," he whispered back, embarrassment stealing through him, tightening his muscles, and reminding him of the foolishness of so hasty a marriage. They hardly knew anything about each other for crying-in-the-rain. She didn't even know his first name and was standing here vowing to marry him. Were they making a mistake?

"I take thee, Wyatt, to be my wedded husband, to have and to hold, from this day forward, for better, for worse, for richer, for poorer, in sickness and in health, to love, cherish, and obey, till death do us part, according to God's holy ordinance: and thereto I give thee my faith."

The instant she finished, she loosened her hand from his and wrapped it back around the weeds Astrid had given her. Wyatt self-consciously stuffed his hand into his pocket.

"What about a ring?" Reverend Zieber asked under his breath as he leaned in toward Wyatt.

Wyatt shook his head, again chagrined, but Steele stepped forward and handed the minister a simple silver band with a nod to Wyatt. "You can use this until you have the chance to purchase something more permanent."

Wyatt nodded back.

"Excellent." Reverend Zieber closed his eyes. "Bless this ring, O Lord, to be a sign of the vows by which this man and this woman have bound themselves to each other, through Jesus Christ our Lord. Amen."

After placing the band upon his open prayer book, Reverend Zieber held the book out to Wyatt. "Go ahead and place the ring on her finger and repeat after me: Greta, I give you this ring as a symbol of my vow, and with all that I am and all that I have, I honor you, in the name of the Father, and of the Son, and of the Holy Ghost."

Wyatt fumbled with the ring but somehow managed to slip it down Miss Nilsson's finger, noting the slender shape as well as the strength. Once the ring was in place, she stared at it for a moment, as though she wanted to bury it in the boneyard.

He had to stop thinking of her as Miss Nilsson and call her Greta. As improper as such casualness felt, she was no longer Miss Nilsson. She was Mrs. McQuaid. Mrs. Wyatt McQuaid. His wife.

He swallowed past a swelling lump of fear. What in the name of the Almighty had he done?

Reverend Zieber closed his prayer book with a snap that brought their attention back to him. "Now that you've given yourselves to each other by solemn vows, with the joining of hands and the giving and receiving of a ring, I pronounce that you are husband and wife, in the name of the Father, and of the Son, and of the Holy Ghost. Those whom God has joined together let no one put asunder."

Astrid clapped and fairly danced in place. "Now they have to kiss! Right, Reverend Zieber?"

Wyatt started to protest at the same time as Miss Nilsson—Greta. But before either of them could speak, Steele was clapping Wyatt on his shoulder—hard. "Of course they need to kiss. May as well begin right now getting to know each other."

Something in Steele's tone and in his squeeze warned Wyatt that he had to fulfill his part of the bargain and make this a real marriage. He couldn't playact or pretend. He had to take his vows seriously. And he had to produce a family in order to help this community grow.

Guilt prodded him as it had earlier when he tried to explain the cattle bargain to Greta. He'd sounded like a bull in heat and botched the entire conversation, telling her just about everything . . . except the part that really mattered—that he was marrying her so he could get a loan from Steele.

He'd have to find a way to be aboveboard with her eventually, although he didn't expect it would make much difference. She'd said all the explanation she needed was that he wanted to help out Phineas. That had been good enough for her.

"Go on now." Steele's fingers dug into his shoulder. "Give your wife a kiss, a nice one."

"And a long one," Astrid chimed in, much too eagerly.

"Astrid." Greta cast the girl a mortified look.

Wyatt took a step closer to Greta. What was the best way

to go about the business of giving her a kiss? Should he put his hands on her tiny waist? Or maybe on her shoulders? Or would she prefer he not touch her at all and just lean in?

When she glanced up at him, he was surprised that her eyes were filled with curiosity more than reticence. A woman as pretty as her had likely been kissed before. Maybe by Thomas. The man she'd planned to marry before he'd gotten killed in the war. It had been clear his death had been painful and that she hadn't wanted to talk about it. How close had they been?

His attention fell to her lips. Slender like the rest of her, they were slightly open as though she was readying herself. Part of him resisted the notion of kissing this woman. But another part prodded him closer, urging him to do it, to prove to Steele and himself that he was up to the task of having a wife.

"Kiss her!" Astrid said again.

Greta dropped her attention to the girl, as though to issue another rebuke. In that instant, Wyatt swooped in and pressed his lips to hers, gently cupping her cheek to guide their kiss. At the softness of her mouth and the intake of her breath, every other coherent thought fled, and he couldn't think of anything else except their connection.

He deepened the pressure, urging her to respond. For a second, she didn't seem to know what to do, and then tentatively she let herself press back softly, curiously.

The movement awakened him, almost as if he'd been asleep, making him conscious of need pulsing through his body—need he'd kept as cold as a wagon tire.

He didn't want that need awakened. Didn't want to need a wife. Didn't want to need anyone.

Though the kiss was thrilling, even pleasurable, he forced himself to break the contact and pull back.

She dropped her gaze as more pink infused her cheeks.

His thoughts returned to the way she'd looked standing in front of the mountain lion, her shoulders braced for an attack, chin jutted with determination. She'd been desperate to save Astrid, so much so she'd placed herself between the girl and the wild animal without a second of hesitation. And now here she was, so desperate to save Astrid she'd sacrificed herself again. By marrying a stranger.

Although he'd only known Greta a short time, she'd already proven herself to be a good and kind woman. The least he could do in return was demonstrate he was worthy of the sacrifice she'd made.

No matter Steele's pressure for them to have a real marriage, no doubt she'd appreciate having the chance to get to know and trust him before he kissed her a second time.

Chapter 7

The oh-so-handsome Wyatt McQuaid was her husband. Greta wanted to pinch herself and wake up to reality, but she was clinging to the seat with both hands as the wagon bumped over the uneven earth. She didn't dare let go for fear of falling off.

Mr. Steele had insisted they use his wagon and team to transport them, along with her trunk and bags, back to Wyatt's ranch. At first, Wyatt had wavered in accepting the offer, only doing so after Mr. Steele insisted.

Now she knew why he'd been reluctant. The ride had been jarring and uncomfortable—more so than the weeks of stagecoach traveling.

The wagon dipped into another rut, tossing her up from the bench and then slamming her back down. She winced. She'd have new bruises in the morning.

She checked over her shoulder to the wagon bed. Cushioned by mounds of hay, Astrid had stopped talking, and her eyes were closed. The little girl had tried valiantly to stay awake to see her new home. But the day had taken its toll on her frail body and now sleep was claiming her.

"Not long now," Wyatt said above the rattle of the wagon and wheels.

A half-moon overhead drizzled enough light that they'd been able to see their way well enough. The treeless prairie was covered with sage and shrubs, along with pale grass Wyatt said the cattle loved.

He'd spent the majority of the five-mile ride from town answering Astrid's questions about his ranch. Though Greta had tried to quell her sister's unyielding stream of curiosity, it had been a useful way to glean more information about the man she'd married.

She learned he had three horses, close to eighteen head of cattle, along with four hens and a rooster. She also discovered that Judd had planted and taken charge of a large vegetable garden, while Wyatt fished trout from the river running through his property and hunted wild game.

Apparently the two men had hauled in and hewn logs from the nearby foothills to build the house and barn since the lumber from the new mill in Fairplay was costly. From the tone of Wyatt's voice, she could tell he was pleased with his accomplishments.

He mentioned that he'd purchased two more cattle earlier in the day and was slowly building up and fattening his herd. With Wyatt occupied transporting her and Astrid in the wagon, Judd had offered to drive the two steers back to the ranch. According to Wyatt's explanation to Astrid, *"The cattle take their sweet old time, chewing up every lick of grass they come across."*

"There's the house." Wyatt nodded ahead.

She didn't mean to look at him again. But her attention shifted as if it had a mind of its own. His chiseled profile, even in only the moonlight, was strong and masculine. His defined jaw and the dark covering of stubble on his cheeks drew attention to his mouth.

That mouth. Those lips . . . against hers.

Strange heat bloomed in her cheeks. He'd really and truly kissed her. The kiss, restrained and yet containing a hint of passion, had been unexpectedly pleasant and unlike anything she'd experienced before. If she didn't know better, she could almost believe he'd enjoyed it and found her attractive.

She was tempted to lift her fingers to her lips and capture the memory all over again. But she'd done so a dozen times already, and eventually he'd catch her in the act and realize she was thinking about their kiss.

It surely hadn't meant as much to him as it had to her. He'd likely kissed plenty of women in his life. What was one more?

For her, the kiss was her first. Thomas had wanted to kiss her on the day he'd left for the war. But she'd been too upset and told him he had to wait until he came home for a kiss, hoping to give him an incentive to return.

It hadn't worked. And she'd regretted not kissing him good-bye ever since.

"It ain't much," Wyatt said. "But hopefully it'll get us through the winter."

She squinted through the dark to the outline of a stout, low-lying structure that looked more like a hovel than a house. It was built out of logs with thick chinking and had a gabled roof of simple boards. A single stovepipe protruded from the roof, and a small lone window had been cut out of the wall next to the door.

Dismay settled into her sore bones, bringing a fresh wave of weariness. She wasn't sure what she'd expected, but not a cabin that looked as though it could fit into the spacious kitchen of her childhood home. Although modest, the two-story farmhouse had been airy and open with plenty of windows that afforded natural light along with several stoves for warmth in the winter. With four upstairs bedrooms, she'd always considered it too small for everyone living there. But it was a mansion compared to this place.

As Wyatt blessedly brought the wagon to a halt, she attempted to mask her disappointment, especially in light of how proud he was when talking about it. She'd seen other log structures over the past weeks, and Wyatt's was well constructed compared with some. He and Judd had obviously put many hours of labor into it, and she couldn't complain.

"The barn is there." Wyatt cocked his head to the east.

She followed his gaze to another building, this one slightly bigger, with a zigzag log fence forming a corral off to one side. It was all very basic, almost rudimentary. But from what she could tell, he kept his place tidy and in good repair.

He hopped down and started rounding the wagon bed. "The river's not far, maybe a hundred paces behind the house and Judd's garden."

She had to find her voice and say something. This might not be the kind of life she'd envisioned for herself, not after Phineas's letters detailing the big house he was building for her and the furniture he was buying to fill it. But this was better than being homeless.

"Looks like you're off to a good start," she offered as he came to her side of the wagon.

"Yep." He reached up to assist her. "We've got a lot of hard work ahead of us to make something of the ranch. But it's a start."

We. Not I. But *we*.

She gave him her hand and allowed him to aid her down. Was that the real reason he'd married her? Because he needed the help to get his ranch working? Maybe he couldn't afford to hire more workers and had decided on a wife instead.

It made sense. Maybe that's what he'd meant when he mentioned having a partnership.

His hand in hers was firm but polite. And as he steadied her on the ground, she breathed a silent prayer and tried to be grateful. Maybe her new home and situation weren't ideal. But she'd work hard alongside him and do her best to help him succeed. It was the least she could do after all he'd done for her.

He released her without lingering and started toward the door. "I'll light a lantern and show you inside before unloading."

Greta peeked over the side of the wagon. Astrid was curled up in the hay asleep.

"Will she be alright for a minute?" Wyatt paused in the door. "I can come back for her and carry her in."

"She'll be fine." Though the consumption tired Astrid easily, she'd had more energy than usual all evening. Greta could only pray that meant the drier air of the West was helping. If only Astrid could finally sleep through the night without waking up coughing.

Greta followed Wyatt into the cabin and waited by the

door as he fumbled to light a coal-oil lamp. At the touch of the flame to the wick, the room sprang to life. Wyatt lifted the lantern and hung it from a nail protruding from one of the rafters.

A medium-sized stove in one corner was rusted and dented in places and seemed as though it had seen better days. Several blackened pots and pans sat on the range, congealed grease lining them. A simple table with benches took up most of the rest of the living space. An open door off the back revealed a second smaller room with a bed built into the wall.

Wyatt had made it clear enough earlier he wanted a family of his own. And she knew very well what that meant: She'd have to share the marriage bed with him from now on.

She hugged her arms around her middle to ward off a sudden chill. Although he'd given her a sweet kiss after their wedding and she knew she had nothing to fear from him, the thought of being together during the coming night wasn't something she was looking forward to.

Feeling Wyatt's gaze upon her, gauging her reaction to the home, she tried for a smile. "It's a cozy place."

He peered around the room as though seeing it through her eyes. "I know it ain't much—"

"No, it's very nice."

He hesitated, took his hat off, and raked his fingers through his black hair.

"Really. I mean it." And she did. He'd done a fine job. "You have every right to be proud of what you've accomplished so far."

He replaced his hat and nodded. "If you need anything, just let me know. And I'll do my best to make it or get it for you."

"I'm sure I'll get along fine." Her attention strayed to the bedroom again. The bed was small for the two of them. When she realized Wyatt was watching her, she ducked her head.

A lengthy silence filled the space between them, broken by the steady trill of crickets coming in from the open door.

"Judd and me," he finally said, "we'll bed down in the barn loft."

Her head jerked up. His brows were furrowed above his rich brown eyes made even richer by his long lashes. What was he saying? That he didn't plan to spend the whole night with her?

As if sensing her confusion, he focused on the match stub he'd left on the table and began to twist it. "I figured you and Astrid might want to use the bed."

"That's nice of you." She hoped her voice didn't squeak through her tight throat. "But I can make a bed for Astrid. Maybe a trundle I can pull out for her at night."

He flipped the match around and between his fingers. "Listen, Miss Nil—" He stopped himself.

She squirmed. It would be so much easier if they could simply do their marriage duty without having to talk about it.

"Greta," he said slowly and softly, as though trying out her name. "I ain't a brute. And I wouldn't feel right about—well, sharing a bed with you. Not until we've gotten to know each other better."

His declaration took her by surprise, so much so that for a moment she was speechless. What was he saying? Didn't he want to consummate their marriage yet?

"This is all mighty sudden." He wound the match through

his fingers faster. "Shouldn't we make sure this is gonna work—well, before we make it official?"

Did he want to test her out first? See if she was hardworking enough before he decided if he wanted to keep her? Was there the chance he might not like her and kick her and Astrid out?

Her nerves tightened. "I promise I'll do my best. I've been told I'm easy to get along with."

"That ain't it," he said in a rush. "I can tell you're a real nice woman and all."

"Then you're afraid you might get tired of Astrid?" That was understandable. Not even her family had been able to cope with the demands of Astrid's illness.

"Nope. She can talk a donkey's hind leg off. But she's a sweet girl, and I'm sure we'll get along just fine."

"But . . ."

His fingers pressed hard against the match, snapping it in two. "I don't want you to be stuck here if this ain't what you wanted."

Or maybe he didn't want to be stuck with her, if *she* ended up not being what *he* wanted.

He released a breath that was full of frustration. "Always figured I'd marry a woman I knew and liked. But since that didn't happen, I'm fixin' to wait—you know—until we get to liking each other."

Get to liking each other. "What if that doesn't happen?" The question popped out before she could stop it.

He fiddled with the two pieces of the broken match.

"It doesn't matter—"

"Let's give it three months. Come November, if you don't like me or like living here, I'll buy your passage out to wherever you wanna go."

She tried to ease the tension that had built in her shoulders. It was a fair deal. She had the rest of August and the autumn to prove herself and make him like her. If she couldn't do it by then, she'd figure out something else.

"Alright," she said softly.

He straightened and moved from the table. "I'll go get Astrid and carry her inside."

She nodded but couldn't make herself move from her spot after he went out to the wagon. Instead, she stared through the doorway to the bedroom, to the bed. She ought to feel relieved, even happy. Wyatt wasn't pressuring her into intimacies yet. In fact, she should be grateful he was giving her time to get used to her new home and to him. Not many men would be so noble.

Why, then, did she feel afraid?

She shook away the fear and doubled her resolve. She would work hard and prove he hadn't made a mistake in marrying her. She'd show him she was worthwhile. And she'd make sure she and Astrid weren't a burden. That was the last thing she wanted to be to anyone ever again.

Chapter 8

Wyatt splashed cold river water against his face, trying to wake himself after a restless night. He let the icy drops course down before he sat back on his heels and dried his skin with the sleeve of his union suit.

The eastern sky above the Kenosha Mountains was tinted with the first pink of sunrise, more beautiful at dawn than any other time of day. It was the time when he could pray the best. The solitude, peace, and magnificence brought him in tune with his Maker so that for a few minutes, he could forget about his worries and the pressing work of the day ahead.

But not so this morning. From the second he'd pushed himself up from his bed of hay in the barn loft, he'd done nothing but chew on the conversation he'd had with Greta the previous evening after they'd arrived home. And he got all riled up when he thought about Judd's reaction later.

"Steele ain't gonna be happy," Judd had remarked in his quiet but deep voice. "If he learns you're beddin' down in the barn instead of with your wife, he'll be airin' his lungs."

"It ain't his business." Wyatt closed the barn door for the night, shutting the two of them in with the livestock, along with the new steers.

"When you made the confounded deal with him, you made it his business."

All night, Wyatt had tossed and turned, wondering if he'd done the right thing in accepting Steele's bargain, marrying Greta but then keeping things friend-like between them.

He'd thought Greta would be relieved he wasn't pressuring her into a real marriage—at least not right away. But she seemed confused and perhaps worried.

Maybe he'd been wrong to offer her freedom in three months if she decided she didn't like living on his homestead. It's just that he'd seen the wariness in her expression when she looked at the place, as if she expected something better.

Although he had big plans for his ranch, he couldn't shake the nagging voice reminding him of the ways he'd already failed. The voice sounded a lot like Rusty's and the words pretty near the same as what Rusty had told him.

It had been after the first time Wyatt had come in from the fields to find the bruise on Ma's face. She hadn't wanted to talk about it. But Ivy hadn't held back anything, telling him how Rusty had slapped Ma for not having his noon meal ready when he'd walked in the house.

Wyatt had stormed out to the barn, found Rusty mucking a horse stall, and plowed into him with both fists swinging. Of course at the time, Wyatt had been half the size and weight of Rusty, and his new stepfather easily subdued him by pinning him to the ground and punching him in the gut.

Even with Rusty sitting on top of him, Wyatt bucked and

twisted like a wild bronco, trying to free himself so he could take another punch. Rusty just laughed.

"Go on and leave!" Wyatt shouted, breathless and sore. "We don't need you and can get by fine without the likes of you around."

"Get by fine?" Rusty's eyes narrowed. "Is that what you call the failed crop last year and almost losing this here farm?"

"We didn't lose it!"

"That's because your ma realized you were running the farm into the ground, so she married me to bail her out of the trouble you got her in."

"I didn't run the farm into the ground." As Wyatt wrestled against Rusty, his voice lacked the same bluster as earlier.

After Pa's death, he'd taken over and tried to do everything the way his pa taught him. But the summer had been exceptionally hot and dry, almost to the point that many farmers had called it a drought. Their farm hadn't been the only one in a bad way.

"The problem with you young'uns"—Rusty jammed his finger into Wyatt's chest—"is that you're proud and think you know better than the rest of us."

Maybe Wyatt had been too cocky when he'd taken over after Pa died. Maybe he figured he could be like his pa, but better. And maybe because of that, he'd brought a whole passel of problems on the farm, giving Ma no choice but to marry Rusty when he'd come proposing and promising to turn things around.

"The truth is," Rusty continued with a harder jab, "you were a failure, and you'll always be a failure."

Wyatt tried to push the bitter memories from his mind by leaning down and splashing more icy water against his face.

But no matter how hard he tried to shut out the accusation, it reverberated louder than a shooting iron in a narrow canyon. He was a failure and would always be a failure.

After his few years of driving cattle, he'd failed at his brief cow-raising venture in Iowa. Then once he'd had enough experience in the freighting business, he tried setting up his own transportation company. And that bit the dust too. When gold had been found in the Rockies, he'd decided to give mining a go, and he hadn't had any luck with that either.

At twenty-three, he'd tried and failed more times than many men did in a lifetime. Was he bound to fail again with his ranching plans?

At the crunch of footsteps behind him, he pushed aside his melancholy, his senses on high alert and his fingers already fumbling for the handle of his revolver in his discarded holster. Last week, Judd had seen several Utes in the area. He hadn't been sure whether they were hunting or just passing through. With the increasing tension as more and more miners came in and took over Ute land, it was just a matter of time before the conflict escalated.

At Greta's appearance on the path that sloped gently to the river, he let himself relax and released his gun. She was carrying buckets in each hand, swinging them in rhythm to her quick stride.

He hadn't expected her to be up at dawn the same way he was, especially on her first morning. But she was apparently an early riser. He didn't want to frighten the living daylights out of her, so he stood and straightened, mighty thankful he hadn't unshucked all the way as he often did before washing up.

She made it halfway down the path before she stopped

short at the sight of him. For several seconds, she stared with wide eyes, then dropped her attention to the tuft of tall yellowing grass in front of her.

He glanced down at himself. Barefoot and wearing only his one-piece under-rigging, he was decent. With the cotton leggings and long sleeves, his union suit covered just about as much of him as his outerwear. As far as he could tell, they didn't have anything to be embarrassed about, did they?

"Morning. How'd you and Astrid sleep?"

"Very well." She kept her focus on the ground. "Astrid's still asleep."

"Good." He shifted and waited for her to continue to the river. But she seemed completely frozen in place. After another heartbeat, he decided to try to break the awkward moment.

"Hope the mountain sickness ain't too bad for either of you."

"I'm feeling well enough."

Wyatt had been woozy and tired his first few days in the higher elevation. The sickness had lasted a day or two before he felt like new. "Want some help fetching the water?"

He'd already informed her last night after he carried the last of her bags inside the cabin that the river water was as clean and fresh as any well.

"I didn't realize you were here." She finally moved but only to spin around. "I'll come back after you've finished your grooming and dressing."

"No, don't go."

She paused.

"I don't mind none." He waved at the river. "The river's big enough for the both of us."

"If you're sure."

"I'm sure."

Her golden brown hair wasn't tied up in a knot as it had been yesterday. Instead, she wore it loose, and it shimmered around her shoulders and down her arms, almost all the way to her waist. It looked fine and soft and silkier than a chestnut's mane.

Averting her gaze, she hiked the final distance but veered downstream from him. He reached for the trousers he'd tossed over a rock and began to put them on. He'd wait to bathe till another morning.

When she peeked at him sideways, he had one leg in and was tugging up the second. Her gaze darted back to the bucket she was dipping in the river. Although the faint light of dawn left her in the shadows, he guessed pink was infusing her cheeks as it had last night when he'd mentioned staying in the barn with Judd.

Was she embarrassed to see him in his underclothes?

He jerked his trousers up the rest of the way and then grabbed his shirt. He supposed he'd gotten so used to living among men, he'd forgotten the niceties a proper woman expected.

He was buttoning his shirt by the time she finished filling the second bucket. As she stood, he could almost feel her relief that he was dressed. "I'm sorry for disturbing you."

"It's alright." He grabbed a boot and stuffed his foot inside without putting on his sock. Losing his balance, he hopped awkwardly.

She diverted her attention, giving him a view of her profile and the shy smile playing at her lips.

He reckoned he seemed like a madman in his race to put

his clothes back on. He'd have to use good manners by the time he moved his family to the homestead, especially because Ma would expect him to behave in front of Ivy. Might as well start now.

Greta was halfway up the hill by the time he shoved his foot all the way into his second boot, stuffed his socks in his pockets, and rushed after her.

"Hold on." He gripped the handle of one of the buckets. "Let me help."

She didn't break her stride. "I can get it just fine. I wouldn't want to keep you from your work."

"You ain't keeping me from nothin'."

She held the bucket a second longer before she relinquished it. "I suppose you and Judd will be wanting breakfast once you finish with your morning chores."

"Judd's been taking care of the grub. I just leave it up to him."

"Now you can leave it up to me. Tell me when you want to eat, and I'll have it ready."

Before he could respond, she halted and touched one of the shrubs that grew along the river. "What kind of berry is this?"

He took a closer look at the dark red clumps amid tangled leaves. "Judd calls them chokecherries."

"Are they good to eat or poisonous?"

"They ain't poisonous. But Judd said they earned their name 'cause they're so tart they can choke a man."

She set her bucket on the ground and reached into the foliage. She plucked off a cluster, the berries so heavy and dark they appeared almost purple. "They look like blueberries."

"Definitely not as sweet. The birds like them. So do the bears."

"Bears?" She took a rapid step back, as if a bear were about to hop out of the bush and tear her to pieces.

He couldn't hold back a chuckle. "You don't have to worry about too many bears down here where it's dry and open. They like to stay farther up in the mountains."

Her shoulders relaxed. "Then I don't suppose they'd mind if I took some of the chokecherries, would they?"

"Nope, I don't reckon they would."

She began to pick more clusters, making a basket out of her apron. "I don't know how hard it is to get sugar up here. Or honey? It would be most beneficial if I could start my own bee colony eventually."

Honey? Bee colony?

"I sold jam back home from the berries—mostly blackberries and raspberries that grew in the wild around the farm." She was rapidly filling her apron with the chokecherries. "A few years ago, I planted several apple and peach trees. Last summer, my harvest was big enough to make apple and peach jam too."

Many women on farms put up jam every autumn. Even so, she seemed to have made a hobby of it. What other hobbies did she have? He knew so little about her.

"I could get right to work making jam," she said more tentatively. "And sell it, if you think people might buy it."

"Reckon so." He picked a grouping of the berries and added them to her apron. "Men around here are always looking for something sweet to add to their usual fare of pork and beans. I know for a fact just how old the same grub gets day after day."

"We can see if the hotels in town want to buy the jam too. I'd just need to find jars along with wax for sealing them."

He paused, his hand deep into the chokecherry bush. Not only would she need sugar, but jars and wax? The cost would add up real fast. How would he afford it when he barely had enough to dicker for the basic necessities?

Her fingers stilled, as if she'd sensed his questions. "Don't worry. I'll figure out a way to pay for everything without burdening you."

"Won't be a burden. It's just that I ain't got a penny to spare right now with trying to build my herd and all."

A mere foot away, she tilted her head and peered off into the distance. With her lips pursed in thought and her expression etched with determination, a sense of kinship swelled in his chest. She was the sort of person who wasn't afraid to take risks. And he could respect that, even if he didn't have much more than a wish and a prayer to lend her.

"I saw that you have some flour and sugar and lard," she said, as though thinking out loud. "If you'll let me borrow what you have, I'll make hand pies with the first chokecherries, sell them in town, and use the profits to pay you back as well as purchase more supplies."

"Don't care a lick about you paying me back—"

"I will. I promise I'll do this without costing you a cent except for a few initial ingredients I borrow."

"You ain't borrowing—"

Her brows furrowed.

"What I mean is that you ain't borrowing 'cause it's already yours."

"No, it's yours—"

"It's ours." He motioned back and forth between them. "You're my wife, and whatever we have is ours."

His wife. The realization was still strange. To think that yesterday when he'd woken up, he had no notion of getting married anytime in the near future. And today, he was hitched and had himself a wife.

A very pretty wife. The growing daylight reflected off her loose hair, turning the light brown to gold. And it made the silver blue of her eyes brighter and clearer, like a mountain lake.

"Thank you, Wyatt. I promise you won't regret it. Astrid and I'll come out later this morning and pick all the chokecherries we can find."

He didn't rightly know if many men would have a hankering for the sour berry any more than he did. Maybe she'd work some kind of magic and make them tasty. Regardless, he didn't want her to be disappointed if she went to all the hard work and people turned up their noses at her goods. "Could you use huckleberries instead?"

"Huckleberries?"

"They're like blueberries. But smaller. And they grow on the forest floors."

"They're sweeter?"

"Yep. When they're ripe, which is about right now."

"Okay. I'll try huckleberries too, but you'll have to tell me where to find them."

"I'll take you." The words were out before he thought about what he was saying. He didn't have time to gallivant through the foothills searching for huckleberries. He had his new cattle to brand, more fences to mend, the irrigation ditch to repair, and game to catch and smoke for the coming winter. One of the horses was barefoot, and the barn roof had a leak.

To top it all, his few acres of alfalfa would be ready for haying soon. He hadn't plowed much last spring since the ground had been harder than a stale biscuit. But he figured it wouldn't hurt to have the winter feed just in case the snow cover made grazing difficult for his livestock.

As if sensing his hesitation, Greta shook her head. "I'll be fine. You don't need to come along—"

"I'll aim to take you later in the week." While she and Astrid picked huckleberries, he'd do a little hunting. "And when you have your goods ready to sell, you let me know, and I'll help you take them to town."

Her lips curved into a smile, one that moved into her eyes. "I like you, Wyatt."

Somehow her words were a balm he hadn't known he needed. They settled deep inside and soothed him, giving him a strange sense of hope that maybe he hadn't made a mistake in marrying her after all, that maybe, for once, things might work out.

Greta dumped the chokecherries out of her apron into a chipped white basin she'd pulled down from the lone shelf above the stove. Then she collapsed onto a bench and laid her head onto the table.

Other travelers had warned her about mountain sickness, but she hadn't expected it and hadn't wanted to admit to Wyatt that she was dizzy and fatigued. But she'd started feeling poorly last night after she climbed into bed with Astrid, and she'd felt worse upon awakening.

Of course, it hadn't helped that she'd tossed and turned more than usual. She wanted to blame the unfamiliar night noises—the scratching, rummaging, and squeaking of critters—but the truth was, her thoughts hadn't been able to settle themselves. Her mind had been too full of all that had happened during the few short hours of the evening.

She'd lifted up a prayer of thankfulness that at least she had a roof over her head. But one thought clamored above all the others—whether she'd done the right thing by marrying Wyatt McQuaid.

Now, even at the early morning hour, the cabin was hot and stuffy and the flies were incessant. She'd discovered earlier that the greasy pan on the stove was blackened, not from burned food remains, but from flies that had gotten stuck in the lard.

At a clearing throat in the doorway, she shot up. Her skirt and petticoat tangled in the bench, but somehow she managed to find her footing.

"My apologies," came a deep voice. "Didn't mean to startle you."

She spun to find Wyatt's wizened cowhand standing on the threshold. Thin but muscular, he was shorter than her five-feet-five inches. He wore dark woolen trousers like Wyatt's tucked into his plain black leather boots with small spurs at the back. His neckerchief was a dull red that hung low to his loose-fitting vest he'd left unbuttoned to reveal a worn flannel shirt. He held a battered hat in his hands.

"Good morning, Judd." Although he'd been at the wedding at Mr. Steele's house, he'd left almost immediately after the ceremony, giving her no opportunity to speak with him.

He nodded. "Morning, ma'am."

"Call me Greta."

He opened his mouth as if he might protest, but before he could, Astrid stumbled into the room, wearing her long nightdress and yawning noisily. Her hair was mussed and her eyes still heavy with sleep, but her cheeks had a little color.

"Hi there, Mister." Astrid crossed toward Judd. "You look a lot like Saint Nicholas, what with your long white beard and white hair and all."

"Astrid," Greta said firmly. "Be polite."

"W-e-l-l, he sure does." Astrid stared up at the man, her head cocked to one side. "Except for the mustache. It looks like cow horns."

Exasperated, Greta pressed a hand against her head. "Astrid, please. Why don't you go back in the bedroom and get dressed?"

Judd's mustache curled up with the beginning of a smile.

Astrid swatted at a fly hovering in the air. "Sure are a lot of flies here, aren't there?"

"Yep." Judd flicked a finger at the same fly. It fell to the floor lifeless.

"How'd you do that?" Astrid bent to take a closer look at the unmoving insect. "Think you can teach me?"

"Sure."

"It would come in handy. Maybe I could go around clearing them all out of the cabin."

"You bother to kill one fly, several dozen more gonna come to its funeral."

Astrid paused and stared at Judd as though trying to make sense of what he was saying. Greta couldn't contain a smile.

"Came to get some grub started." He nodded at the stove.

"You needn't worry about doing the cooking anymore.

I was just about to make the coffee." Greta moved toward the stove but swayed and had to grab the table to steady herself.

Judd took a quick step but stopped and twisted his hat. "Wyatt said you're aimin' to do the cooking. But I figured you'd be unpacking."

She pressed a hand to her forehead again.

Judd's fluffy white brows furrowed. "Seeing as how you're so busy, I reckoned I could lend a hand."

She wasn't busy. And she suspected they both knew it. But with the way she was feeling, she didn't know how she could turn down his gracious offer.

"I reckon I could lend a hand too." Astrid's sweet voice imitated Judd's southern drawl, and when she moved beside him, Judd's mustache curled up again.

Greta forced herself not to smile at the child's antics. Instead, she pressed a hand on her hip and nodded to the bedroom. "I *reckon* you can go get dressed just like I asked you to and leave Judd alone."

"I don't mind none." Judd limped farther into the cabin, making his way to the stove. "Can always use a pardner."

"W-e-l-l then." Astrid's smile widened. "I guess I'll be your pardner."

"That'd be real nice." Judd's gaze met Greta's and was filled with a kindness that brought a lump to her throat.

Astrid had been shunned too often since getting sick. Though Greta had tried her best to shield the little girl from the comments and the glares slanted her way, no doubt Astrid had felt the rejection, which made her long for attention and love all the more.

But since coming to Colorado, where the sunshine seemed

to perpetually shine, perhaps it was shining down on Astrid in more ways than one. Greta could only pray her sister would finally get her share of happiness.

But a place deep inside her warned that sunshine never lasted forever.

CHAPTER 9

A deep, hacking cough shook Astrid's thin frame.

Greta watched helplessly until Astrid caught her breath, and then she finished rubbing salve onto the child's chest, the strong scent of elderberry and beeswax filling the bedroom.

Astrid sucked in several deep breaths.

"Time for some tea." Greta placed a hand gently underneath the girl and tried to lift her.

"I don't like it." Astrid resisted, her pale face blending into the bedcovers.

"You have to drink something."

"I'll have some of Judd's black water."

"Only tea. No coffee today." If Judd's weak brew could be considered coffee. Although the rest of his cooking was passable, Greta had to agree with Wyatt's nickname for Judd's watery coffee.

Greta wiped the sweat off her sister's forehead with the cool rag before she dipped the cloth back into the basin.

Astrid had woken halfway through the night with a fever,

accompanied by intermittent sweating and chills. Though Greta had done her best to control the fever, by morning Astrid's cough had worsened. It was no longer the dry hacking that came and went. This was the dreaded coughing accompanied by the spewing of phlegm. So far the discharge was white without any taint of blood, but nevertheless, Greta was more disappointed than she wanted to admit.

Just last night when kissing Astrid good night, Greta had marveled at the changes just a few days at the ranch had brought about. And she realized how long Astrid had gone without the fever. Weeks. At least since the stagecoach ride across Nebraska.

Astrid hadn't caught the mountain sickness, not even a little bit. Thankfully, Greta's dizziness had passed quickly, and she'd been back to herself in no time.

"I'll add a little more sugar." Greta rose from the edge of the bed. She wrung the cloth out again, positioned it on Astrid's forehead, and then crossed to the door. As she stepped into the main room, she stopped short at the sight of Wyatt standing near the table.

He held his hat in his hands and twisted the brim. "Astrid sick this morning?"

Greta gave a weary nod. "She's having a flare-up. I guess we won't be able to pick huckleberries today after all." Last night after dinner, he'd offered again to take her, said he had a few hours free in the morning if she still wanted to go. But she couldn't leave Astrid today.

"It's alright. We'll go some other time." He shifted his hat first to one hand and then the other. "Should I go after the doc?"

"I wish a doctor could help. But unfortunately, there's nothing he could do that hasn't already been tried."

Wyatt's brown eyes were almost ebony and overflowed with a compassion that made her chest ache. "Anything I can do?"

"No, there's nothing to be done except make sure she rests."

He shifted his hat again.

"I've got breakfast ready for you and Judd." She hurried to the stove, where she'd fried potatoes with several slabs of bacon. The potatoes had come from Judd's garden, which she'd discovered was enormous and well-tended. He'd told her to help herself to whatever she needed.

She hadn't asked him what he planned to do with all the vegetables once they were harvested, but she'd started a mental list of all the things she needed to do, including digging a cellar near the house for storing the produce.

Greta had spent the majority of the past two days exploring and getting familiar with the ranch, along with cleaning and airing out the cabin. Doing laundry had been the first priority. Though the cabin had but a few scant household linens, her and Astrid's garments had been in sore need of scrubbing after going weeks without a proper washing. She'd also gathered up Wyatt's and Judd's clothing and laundered it too.

When it came time for drying everything, she'd set to work shoveling two holes deep enough for the couple of posts she dragged over from behind the barn. Once she had both posts buried and sturdy, she rigged up a rope between the two and hung the bedsheets to dry and laid the clothing out in the grass and on brush.

All while she'd worked, she kept Astrid busy snapping beans and shelling peas and other small jobs. Astrid tired easily and had taken several naps during the day. Greta had supposed the girl was worn out from all the excitement of their traveling. But now she realized Astrid had been battling consumption again.

Greta lifted the lid off the pan, the waft of potatoes and bacon making her stomach rumble.

"Listen, Greta." Wyatt reached alongside her and took the lid out of her hold. "You go on and take care of Astrid. Me and Judd, we can fend for ourselves."

She shook her head and picked up the spatula she'd left inside the pan. Wyatt was directly behind her—much too close. He'd protested yesterday, telling her she didn't have to do so much, especially after seeing the laundry line she'd made. He told her next time she ought to ask him for help. But from what she'd seen, he was busy enough without having to stop and do things for her.

"No, I'm not letting you fend for yourself." She scooped a serving of the potato-bacon mixture onto a tin plate. "You married me to help you take care of the ranch, and that's what I intend to do."

He was still too close, so when he released a long sigh, she could feel the breath against the back of her neck. "Greta," he said softly, "look at me."

She let the spatula fall idle in the pan.

"Please?"

At the sweetness of his tone, she couldn't resist. She pivoted, plate in hand.

Without his hat, she had full view of his eyes, his beautiful, expressive eyes. "You're my wife. Not my slave."

"But as your wife, I have responsibilities—"

"You'll be running yourself ragged if you're not careful."

"I'm a strong woman. And it takes a lot to wear me out."

He studied her face, making her suddenly self-conscious. She hadn't taken care with her appearance this morning, hadn't had the time between tending to Astrid and trying to get breakfast for the men.

"I'm sorry." She smoothed back a flyaway strand. "I still need to plait it."

He lifted her hand away. "You don't need to. Your hair is pretty enough any way you wear it."

Pretty? Her heart pattered an extra beat.

At Judd clearing his throat behind them, embarrassment washed across Wyatt's face. He took several rapid steps away from her, bumping into the table and tipping one of the benches.

Judd reached out to catch the bench, righting it. He nodded at Greta, then leveled a look at Wyatt, one laced with humor.

Judd wasn't much for talking, but he, like Wyatt, had a kindness about him that put her at ease. He worked hard alongside Wyatt but seemed fond of taking breaks, especially those that involved puttering around in his garden.

"Heard Astrid coughing." Judd lowered himself to the bench and leaned his elbows on the table.

"It's the consumption." Greta handed a plate to Wyatt and then dished up Judd's breakfast. "A little extra rest today, and she'll be fine." At least Greta hoped so.

After giving Judd his food, she poured the men each a cup of coffee and then returned to Astrid's bedside with a spoonful of sugar. She sweetened the tea and made the little girl drink several sips. A few minutes later, when Astrid was dozing, Greta scurried back into the other room to the stove. Before the men could ask, she'd retrieved the pan and was dishing them up more breakfast.

"Reckon I can take you huckleberry picking next week." Wyatt nodded his thanks and dug his spoon into the steaming mound.

"I'm sure Astrid will feel better then."

"Go on today." Judd swallowed a bite of potatoes. "And I'll stay."

"You'll stay?" Wyatt's brows rose.

"That's right. I'll stay with the child so you can go get the berries."

"I don't want to inconvenience anyone." Greta returned to the stove and retrieved the coffeepot. "We can go another time."

"They're ripe now." Judd dangled his spoon above his plate. "Gotta get 'em now, or the critters'll chaw up every last one."

"It's kind of you to offer, but I couldn't impose."

"Best thing for her is the sun and the air," Judd said quietly but firmly. "Soon as she wakes, I'll carry her on outside."

Greta hesitated.

"Planning to dry the peas today," Judd added. "Wouldn't hurt her none to lend me a hand."

Wyatt took a sip of coffee and seemed to be gauging Greta's reaction. She didn't want to worry him needlessly. Surely Astrid would be fine with Judd there this morning and would sleep most of the time anyway.

"Very well. If you're sure you don't mind?"

"Not a bit." Judd scraped up a large spoonful of potatoes

and shoveled it in his mouth as if the subject was closed with nothing more left to say. She turned back to the stove and squelched the need to give the older man a list of instructions. Astrid was plenty vocal and would tell Judd if she needed anything.

A short while later, Greta was astride one of Wyatt's horses, riding after him as he led the way across the grassland toward the foothills in the east. The early morning sunshine was directly in her face, making her wish that instead of her bonnet, she had a hat like Wyatt's with a wide brim to shield her eyes.

Along with the thud of horse hooves, the quiet of the morning was broken by an unfamiliar, distant bird call. As far as she could see, she and Wyatt were the only two out in this wilderness for miles around, and the realization was daunting. If something happened to them, or if they encountered another wild creature like that mountain lion, or if they got lost . . .

She focused on Wyatt's back and the power emanating from him as he rode. With his revolver in his belt and a rifle secured to his saddle, she surely had nothing to fear. Even so, the high rugged Colorado country was nothing like she'd imagined. Truly, if she was honest with herself, nothing about her journey to the West had turned out the way she'd expected. Maybe by the end of autumn, she'd be more than ready to take up Wyatt's offer to return to Illinois. Maybe he'd been wise to suggest not rushing into the marriage bed.

Although she'd felt strange taking over his house and bedroom, he hadn't seemed to mind, had almost seemed relieved she'd cooperated so easily. In fact, he'd stayed well out of her way the past couple of days, only coming into the cabin for mealtimes. And they hadn't run into each other at the river either, though she'd waited until later to go down so she wouldn't chance seeing him half unclothed again.

Ahead, amid clumps of long grass and mounds of dirt, a prairie dog popped its head out of a burrow, stood high with its face pointed in their direction, and barked a scolding for disturbing it. As she and Wyatt passed, several more of the creatures took up sentinel posts, yelped warnings, shook their tails, and dove back into their holes.

Wyatt didn't seem to notice the prairie dogs but made sure to steer well away from the mounds and burrows and the honeycomb of holes that could cause injury to the horses. He pointed at something in the distance. "Look over yonder."

She lifted her hand to shield her eyes and saw what appeared to be a herd of some sort of deer. Several dozen were grazing in the open grassland. Against the rise of the foothills, the grandeur of the scenery washed over her, drowning the doubts and anxiety of earlier.

"It's awe-inspiring. Are they deer?"

"Pronghorns." He slowed, allowing his mount to fall into step with hers. "Like antelope but faster."

The slender, graceful creatures were brown, with portions of their bellies, legs, and rumps a snowy white. Most had horns, some longer and bulkier than others. "They're beautiful."

"And they're pesky, sneaking in and mowing my hay to stubs."

As they rode, Wyatt talked more about the pronghorns and the benefit of a bountiful supply of pronghorn meat, which he described as having a tender texture and mild flavor compared to other game.

He answered her questions about how much land he'd plowed and planted, along with the irrigation ditch he'd built from the river to the field. Since the rainfall in Illinois was usually sufficient during the growing season, Pappa had never needed to irrigate his crops. But Wyatt explained how the climate in the central mountain valleys was too arid to grow much of anything without the ditches.

"Might be wasting a whole lot of time growing my own hay," he said as they urged their horses onto higher terrain up a hillside dotted in aspens, ponderosa pine, and Douglas fir. "Some say there's enough natural grass here that we ain't got nothing to worry about. But Judd said we should have extra in case we get a bad winter."

"Sounds like a wise decision. Are the winters severe?"

"You'd think so since we're out here in the middle of the Rockies. But the past couple have been pretty mild. Lots of snow, but it don't stick around long enough here in South Park to keep the cattle from being able to graze."

"Better to be prepared than watch your herd starve to death."

"That's what Judd said." Wyatt reined in his horse and shifted to peer back over the direction they'd come.

She did the same. At the sight that met her, she sucked in a breath of amazement. The view was just as spectacular to the west as it had been a short while ago in the east when they'd watched the herd of pronghorns. A panorama of high-peaked giants lifted their bald heads to the sky. The expanse was vast against a cloudless hazy blue.

"I ain't been here long," he whispered reverently, "but already this land is winning me over something fierce."

"I can see why."

They sat in silence, taking in the landscape, letting the gentle morning breeze cool them as the sun warmed their heads. As with other times when she'd surveyed the wilderness, her thoughts turned heavenward with silent thanksgiving to the Creator who'd made such wonders.

But even as her heart swelled with praise to a God who was big enough to make the mountains and valleys and everything in between, her own insignificance taunted her. Why would the Lord of the universe care about someone so unimportant, small, and inadequate? Although she'd been taught to say her prayers, and did so regularly, she'd always wondered why God would listen to her. Not when He was busy with other more important matters elsewhere.

Of course, her stepmother and Thomas's father, the pastor at her Illinois church, had assured her the Lord heard everyone, from the least of them to the greatest, and that He didn't answer every prayer the way they wanted since He knew what they needed better than they did.

Greta understood that, and she believed it. But she still couldn't shake the feeling that her concerns were too trivial for so great a God, especially her concerns over Astrid's health. If only she had a stronger faith . . .

When Wyatt nudged his horse on, she released a sigh and put the thoughts from her mind. They rode a short distance farther into the wooded hillside before he stopped and slid down.

She was off her horse before he could come around to assist her. Already she spotted the pale purple huckleberries near the forest floor. The small plants bearing the berries were loaded, bent with the weight of the fruit.

They picked together until the area was cleared and one

of their bags was full. Then they rode to another shaded grove covered with the berries. This time, she picked alone while he hiked off with his rifle to hunt, telling her he'd be no more than a hoot and holler away. Although she worked quickly and efficiently, her progress was slower by herself. And too quiet.

During his absence, she realized she'd enjoyed spending time with him. They hadn't spoken of anything deep or revealing, but he was easy to talk to, knowledgeable, and interesting.

He reminded her of Thomas with his willingness to engage in conversation and treat her like a friend. But a current of something more told her Wyatt was no mere friend. Thomas had been ordinary, never standing out in a crowd. But Wyatt was so ruggedly handsome she couldn't keep from noticing him. And while Thomas had always brought her a sense of peace and comfort, Wyatt made her pulse patter faster with strange anticipation.

By late morning when she'd filled all the sacks they'd brought along, she rested on a large stone near where the horses were grazing along a small brook. She'd heard several shots and guessed Wyatt had some success with hunting. She hoped that meant he'd be back soon. After the time away from the ranch, she was anxious to see how Astrid was faring. It wasn't that she didn't trust Judd. Rather, she didn't trust Astrid. Even when the child was sick, she wasn't easy to handle.

At the crackle of branches in the woods behind her, she breathed out her relief and slid off the rock. "Hope you got what you came for . . ."

As she spun, her words died. Instead of Wyatt, three men

stood a short distance away, their horses behind them. The tall one in the middle wore an eye patch and aimed his pistol at her.

With a thin face and gangly limbs, he had the appearance of many of the men she'd encountered since starting her journey up into the mountains—ragged and undernourished. A look that testified to the scarcity of necessities and the difficulty of life in such a wild place.

He raked his gaze from the top of her head to her boots, making her feel like a prized heifer. "Got what I came for?" He arched a brow. "Reckon maybe I just did."

Chapter 10

At the echo of men's voices, Wyatt halted. With his rifle slung over one shoulder and two grouse he'd shot over the other, he bumped up the brim of his hat with his elbow to get a better look around.

The voices came again, this time followed by laughter and the angry shout of a woman.

His muscles tensed. Was that Greta? And was someone bothering her?

The Tarryall diggings were over the ridge along Tarryall Creek. Had some of the miners been out hunting this morning and happened upon her?

Urgency propelled him forward until he reached an outcropping above the huckleberry patch where he'd left her. She was still there, and sure enough, several men surrounded her.

As one of them grabbed her arm, anger flooded Wyatt. He dropped the grouse from his shoulder, grabbed his Colt, and fired a shot.

The bullet flew through the accoster's hat, knocking it from his head. Cursing, the man stumbled and fell, more from surprise than anything.

Wyatt trained his revolver on the second fella and let another shot rip, this one landing in the dirt and leaves, forcing the culprit to jump back. He, too, cussed a blue streak that would have made the vilest tavern dweller sound angelic.

Wyatt was tempted to put a bullet in the man's backside for using such foul language around Greta, but he'd already aimed his gun at the third fella and sent a shot flying, hitting his pistol and forcing him to release it.

Thankfully, Greta was a smart girl and hadn't needed him to instruct her on what to do. She'd scurried away, unwound the lead ropes of their horses already laden with the berry sacks, and was climbing on top of her steed by the time he'd fired his third shot.

Only then did he take a closer look at the scallywags, zeroing in on the tallest and scraggliest one with the eye patch who was picking himself and his hat up off the ground. "Roper Brawley, you oughta know better than to touch a woman without her permission."

Brawley's curses faded, and he squinted up the hill in Wyatt's direction. "McQuaid? That you?"

"Yep. And that there is my wife."

Brawley's homestead was north of Wyatt's and was near the foothills too. At first, Brawley had tried to file a claim for the same one hundred sixty acres as Wyatt. It was a prime piece of grassland because of the river winding through it, which would not only make watering a herd easy, but provide irrigation for crops.

Wyatt had gotten to the land office, finished the paperwork, and paid his fee, all in the same afternoon. Brawley had ridden in the next day, complaining that the homestead was his and that Wyatt had stolen it from him.

The surveyor hadn't budged on his decision, and Brawley had been forced to place a claim on the acreage north of Wyatt. It wasn't a bad parcel, even had a little creek flowing into Wyatt's bigger river. But they both knew Wyatt had gotten the far better place, and Brawley hadn't been able to forget it.

Brawley held up his hat and cursed again. "Look what you done to my hat, McQuaid." He poked a finger through the hole that went through one side of his crown and out the other. "You're gonna have to buy me a new hat now."

"I ain't buying you a new hat." Wyatt aimed his revolver on the second fella, who was reaching for his gun. "I'm thinking it'll serve as a reminder that next time you so much as blow a breath on my wife, I'll be blowing off your head instead of your hat."

From his periphery, he glimpsed Greta circling wide with the horses and heading up the hill toward him. Most women would have frozen up and acted all helpless, but she was doing everything just right.

"Didn't hear nothin' about you getting married." Brawley situated his hat on his head.

"Now you've heard." He fired another shot at Brawley's partner who was inching his gun too high. This time Wyatt took aim at the sack he'd dropped at his feet. The bullet pinged hard, and Wyatt hoped it showed off his gun skills enough that the men wouldn't try anything else. He might not be as fast as Judd, but his friend had taught him a fair share about shooting iron.

"She just arrived on the stagecoach the other day." Brawley's gaze narrowed upon Greta now, and Wyatt didn't like it. "How'd you end up getting married so quick?"

He couldn't very well explain to Brawley she was part of a cattle deal with Steele. The truth wasn't exactly something he was proud of. Besides, he didn't want Brawley knowing about the Shorthorns till the new herd was safe on his land. If his surly neighbor got wind of the bargain, no doubt he'd do everything he could to make sure the plans failed.

"She was Phineas Hallock's mail-order bride." Wyatt fumbled with the answer. He had to figure out what to say because every man this side of the Continental Divide would be pestering him once word spread. "Offered to help her out for my friend's sake."

"For your friend's sake?" Brawley's question ended in a laugh.

Wyatt ventured a glance in Greta's direction. She was drawing closer. He picked up his rifle and grouse with one hand and kept his revolver trained on the men with the other. Then he sidled toward her.

"We all know why you scooped up a pretty little thing like that." Brawley snorted. "But the real question is why she agreed to marry a clodhopper like you."

Wyatt hastened his pace, praying he could get Greta out of range before Brawley and his men decided to use them for target practice.

"When your ranch ends up failing and you have no choice but to give me what's mine, maybe I'll end up with her too."

"No how, no way!" Wyatt ran the last few steps to Greta.

She reached for his rifle and the grouse, freeing him to mount his horse. She waited to make sure he made it up before she nudged her horse forward. He did the same, trailing her. Once they were out of gunshot range, he kicked his horse into the lead.

The descent was rocky and challenging, especially since he was in a hurry to put as much distance between them and Brawley as possible. When they finally reached more level ground, he picked up the pace, working into a gallop. Greta stayed close behind, low to her mount, clearly understanding the danger they were still in.

They rode hard even after they were back on his claim. When the alfalfa field was in sight and the cabin and barn beyond, he tugged on the reins and halted. Greta pulled her mount alongside his and glanced over her shoulder.

"They won't follow us here," he said.

"Are you sure?"

"Yep." Brawley wouldn't dare. They might not have the same law and order in Colorado Territory that folks were used to in the civilized East, but a person couldn't get away with committing crimes—at least not forever.

As she shifted forward, only then did he notice that her face was pale and her pretty lips set tight.

His gut cinched. Blast it all. Had he gotten to her too late? If so, he'd go back after Brawley and pump him chock-full of lead. "Did he hurt you?"

"No, thank the Lord." Her voice wobbled.

Even with her reassurance, his stomach soured worse than bad whiskey. He slid down and was at her side in the next moment. "You sure?"

She nodded but bit her lip.

"Come on down," he said gently. "We'll walk a spell."

He took the grouse and rifle from her, then slung them

across his saddle. She was already on the ground by the time he turned to assist her. "You alright?"

"I'll be fine." She swayed just a little.

He reached for her upper arms to steady her. But then for a reason he couldn't explain, he drew her into an embrace. Maybe to comfort her, or express his relief, or assure himself that she really was fine. Whatever the case, she let her body sag into him and rested her head on his chest as though she didn't have the energy to hold herself up any longer.

"You did real good back there in getting away." He hardly dared to breathe for fear of frightening her.

"Did I?"

"Yep, real good." Her bonnet had fallen down her back and now loose strands of her hair ruffled in the breeze and tickled his chin and cheek. "Couldn't have done it much better myself."

Tension seemed to ease from her.

"I shouldn't have left you to fend for yourself."

"It's not your fault."

"Didn't expect to run into Brawley out there today. But don't matter. I should've been more vigilant."

She nestled in, not seeming in any hurry to end their embrace.

He tried to let himself relax, but she felt mighty good pressed up against him. She was warm and soft and womanly in all the right places. He bent and let her hair brush his face, and he breathed in the scent of her, a mixture of pine and fruit.

It had been longer than a coon's age since he held a woman. In fact, he couldn't remember the last time. And now that Greta was in his arms, he liked it a lot. A whole lot. He thought he'd been fine being single, reckoned it was better to be alone than land in a bad marriage. But what if he didn't have to end up in a bad marriage? What if he could do things right?

His pa had once loved his ma and had modeled for him and his brothers what it meant to be a devoted and kind husband. He could follow in his pa's steps instead of letting Rusty's bad example scare him off of trying, couldn't he?

All the same, he'd told Greta he wouldn't pester her to share the marriage bed, gave his word she could leave at the end of autumn if that's what she wanted. He wasn't about to go back on his promise.

She released a soft breath, one that only made his blood pump faster. Had he been too hasty in making the promise?

Just as quickly as the thought came, he spit it a shooting distance. He was merely being a friend. And there wasn't nothing wrong with holding and comforting a friend.

Judd was a good companion. But with Greta . . . well, the morning with her had been pleasant and the conversations a welcome change. He'd enjoyed her company and hoped maybe she'd learn to like his too.

She didn't make a move to break free, so he held her several heartbeats longer, until his thoughts once again jumped to how beautiful she was and how good she felt. At the fresh spurt of heat in his gut, he gently leaned back.

As she straightened, she offered him a smile. "Thank you, Wyatt."

He started to shake his head and tell her he didn't need any thanks, but she continued before he could. "The more I get to know you, the more I'm beginning to see how blessed I am that God brought you my way just when He did."

Wyatt wanted to take comfort from her compliment, but

all he could think about was the fact that God hadn't brought him her way. Steele and his cattle deal had.

He needed to tell her the truth, but the moment didn't seem right. Instead, he reached for his horse's lead line and prayed one day he'd be worthy of such praise.

Chapter 11

Greta stepped outside the general store and attempted to quell her growing despair. She'd assumed she'd have no trouble selling her sweets in Fairplay. But it seemed she'd been wrong and could hardly give the hand pies away.

At midmorning, the mountain community was teeming with men, horses, and teams pulling wagons. Everyone appeared too busy to be bothered, except for a few men who loitered outside one of the shops.

As with the last time she was in town, she didn't see women coming and going. Except for an old native woman who helped service the laundry, the only other women in town were those of ill repute. She'd been told the next closest neighbor was a grandmotherly woman who lived in Buckskin Joe and helped her husband run a hotel. If only the grandmotherly woman were closer. She'd surely appreciate and purchase some of the hand pies.

Greta glanced up and down the street. Wyatt had suggested selling her baked goods at the Fairplay Hotel, a place where many of the town's patrons ate. When the hotel owner scoffed at her, she picked up her basket and left without a word, heading to Simpkin's General Store. But Captain Jim wasn't willing to consider tasting a hand pie either.

Maybe she should have tried harder to find containers to make jam. But without jars or tins, she'd had little choice. Instead, she'd cooked up the chokecherries and huckleberries into a pie filling. In the process of creating the flaky treats, she used up every bit of flour, sugar, and lard in the cabin.

And now she had to sell her baked goods. After all, she'd told Wyatt her business venture wouldn't cost him a cent and that he wouldn't regret letting her do this.

At the sight of Wyatt exiting McLaughlin's Livery, where he'd gone to return Mr. Steele's wagon, she pretended she hadn't noticed him and started down the sidewalk the opposite way.

"Greta," he called, clearly having no intention of letting her pass by.

She slowed her steps and rearranged the towel over the hand pies so if he peeked into her basket, he wouldn't notice she hadn't yet sold a single one.

"Any luck?" He strode across the street, his long legs quickly eating up the space between them.

She tugged at the towel again, not wanting to meet Wyatt's curious gaze as he halted next to her. "I guess the men aren't as interested as I thought they'd be."

He was silent while a wagon rattled past. "Where have you been?"

"Only two places so far."

"Hotel Windsor?"

She shook her head.

Wyatt grabbed her basket and started down the street. Mortified she raced after him. "Don't worry about me, Wyatt. I promise I'll sell them all and repay you for the supplies I used up."

"I told you I ain't worried about the supplies." His boots thudded against the planks. As he reached Hotel Windsor, she tried to retrieve the basket and stop him before he entered, but he was too fast. He lifted it out of her reach and opened the front door.

With one of his disarming smiles, he stood back and waved her ahead of him. "After you."

At the cease of conversation within the dining area, Greta forced a smile and made herself walk inside with grace and poise, even though she wanted to run out and hide.

"There they are," Mr. Steele said, sitting at one of the center tables, a cigar in one hand and a newspaper in the other. "The newlyweds."

Greta was tempted to glance around and discover who the newlyweds were but then realized Mr. Steele was referring to her and Wyatt. They'd been married all of five days. She supposed he was right. They were still newlyweds.

Several of the men standing around offered Wyatt rowdy congratulations and backslaps. She took a measure of satisfaction at the sight of Wyatt flustered and tugging at his neckerchief. She wasn't alone in her discomfort.

"How are you holding up, Mrs. McQuaid?" Mr. Steele rose from his chair and politely bowed at her. "I hope your husband is treating you well."

"He's been as sweet as can be."

"McQuaid? Sweet?" One of the other men elbowed Wyatt. "Sure would like to see that."

"He has a soft spot for Astrid," she said in a rush, not wanting to cause Wyatt any further embarrassment. "He's kind to her."

Astrid was still weak and tired and coughing but soaking in the attention of both Judd and Wyatt. Upon arriving home from the berry-picking expedition, she'd found Astrid resting outside, stitching combed-out horsehair through the strands of a burlap bag and making her very own saddle blanket. Judd had promised to teach Astrid to ride a horse just as soon as she finished the blanket. And while Greta wasn't sure that riding was suitable for a sick child like Astrid, she'd been relieved to see some life back in Astrid's face.

Mr. Steele took a puff on his cigar and then released a cloud laden with a tangy tobacco scent. "I was just telling these fellows they ought to write back East for their own mail-order brides."

"If I could have me one as pretty as this gal, I'd give it a try," said a middle-aged man wearing an apron over his bulging midsection. He eyed Greta with too much interest, and she scooted closer to Wyatt.

The men teased the middle-aged man for a minute before they turned their attention back on Wyatt and Greta. Should she bring up the hand pies now? Maybe Mr. Steele would be willing to try one.

"Go on and show everyone what they're missing, McQuaid." Mr. Steele stepped back to his chair and narrowed his eyes at Wyatt.

"Come again?"

"Give them a taste of what they have to look forward to if they send away for wives."

Taste? Taste of what? One of her hand pies? Maybe selling them here in Hotel Windsor would be easier than she'd thought.

As the other men called out assent, Wyatt shook his head. "For crying-in-the-rain, Steele."

Mr. Steele's gaze didn't budge from Wyatt's. And somehow, Greta got the impression he was testing Wyatt, though for what, she didn't know.

"Go on!" someone shouted.

"You ought to be getting pretty good at this by now." Mr. Steele still held Wyatt's gaze.

Wyatt released an exasperated breath, then turned toward her, his beautiful brown eyes apologizing. She didn't have time to ask him what was wrong, because in the next second he bent down and touched his lips to hers, silencing her and taking her breath away in a single instant.

His kiss was as warm and gentle as it had been after their wedding. And although she'd relived that kiss more times than she wanted to admit, somehow this one was even better. Maybe because she'd gotten to know Wyatt a little bit. Maybe because in her secret thoughts she'd been wondering what it would be like to kiss him again. Maybe because he was so heart-stoppingly handsome that she couldn't keep from being attracted to him.

Whatever the case, she rose into the kiss, letting her mouth fuse with his in an exquisite moment of pure pleasure.

At the raucous chortles and laughter around them, she pulled away at the same moment he did, fighting down a wave of mortification.

She didn't realize she was twisting a loose strand of hair until Wyatt slipped his arm around her waist and drew her to his side. The pressure was reassuring, even as she fought the confusion that was making her forget rhyme or reason.

"Speaking of sweetness." Wyatt's grin was much too charming. "Greta's been baking up some sweet pastries that can tide you fellas over."

"I'd like to give one to Mr. Steele." She reached into the basket. "A small thank-you for all his help the other day."

At Wyatt's nod, she took out a hand pie and offered it to Mr. Steele. He made quick work of disposing his cigar, rubbing the butt against an empty plate, before taking an eager bite out of the square-shaped pastry.

Everyone in the room grew silent as they watched Mr. Steele chew. Greta's limbs stiffened in anticipation. Had she made a mistake letting him try it? What if he didn't like it? Then she'd have even more trouble selling the goodies.

He swallowed the first bite and took a second that was larger and full of the sugary mixture of huckleberries and chokecherries. This time as he chewed, his gaze met Greta's across the distance, glowing with the same fatherly warmth she'd seen the day they'd traveled together in the stagecoach. "Very tasty, Mrs. McQuaid. I don't think I've had anything as delicious in a long time."

Wyatt gently squeezed her arm, as though to tell her everything would be alright.

She released a pent-up breath. "Thank you."

Before she could say anything more, Wyatt was laying on more charm and convincing the men they were getting a good deal by paying a whole silver dollar. She tried to whisper to Wyatt that back in Illinois at the state fair, she'd bought a hand pie for ten cents. But he only shook his head and continued to gather the silver dollar pieces from the men, who seemed all too eager to hand over their hard-earned money.

By the time they exited the hotel a short while later, Wyatt had managed to sell a pie to every man present and then sold the rest to Mr. Fehling, the owner of the hotel, who planned to add them to his menu for the day, charging at least a dollar and twenty-five cents.

She wasn't sure whether to feel guilty or excited. "It's too much, Wyatt." She walked alongside him, swinging her now-empty basket. "I just don't feel right charging such a high price for them when they're not worth it."

"Everything costs more up here, especially something as special as the pies."

"Even so, I'd feel better asking for a fair price."

"A dollar's a real fair price seeing how it's all about the supply and demand. When there ain't much of something to go around, folks'll put out more cash for it." He told her that's what he had done already with his cattle when he sold off a couple last month. Since the miners were eager for fresh beef, they were willing to pay a high price for the luxuries they missed from back East.

When they halted in front of the general store, he dug into his pocket and pulled out a neckerchief full of coins. He reached for her hand and placed the bulging bundle in her palm. "Get all the supplies you need for making jam or more hand pies. And if you have any money left, buy yourself something special."

The weight of the silver pieces was strange but exhilarating. She'd never had so much money all at once, and she couldn't imagine using a cent on something *special* for herself.

Wyatt left her standing speechless, watching after him as he continued down the street. She hadn't been lying when she told Mr. Steele that Wyatt was a sweet man. And not just to Astrid. He was the kindest, most considerate man she'd ever met, even more so than Thomas.

Not only that, but she liked his lanky walk with his scuffling boots and muscular backside. With the jaunty tilt of his hat and the dark shadow of scruff on his jaw, her mind wandered back to his kiss and the tender pressure of his lips. Just the memory sent strange flutters around her belly, making her crave him and more of his touch.

As though sensing her admiration, he glanced over his shoulder at her, and his brow shot up.

With the heat moving up from her midsection and splashing into her face, she spun and fumbled for the door to the general store. She couldn't get into the store fast enough, and when she closed the door, she leaned against it and pressed her hands against her hot cheeks.

What was happening to her? Why was she reacting so oddly to Wyatt?

Breathing in deeply, she tried to calm her erratic pulse. Was it possible Wyatt wanted to have a real marriage after all? That maybe he'd changed his mind? Why else would he have kissed her again?

As she tried to make sense of what was happening between them, she made herself stay level-headed so she wouldn't get carried away with fancy notions. Wyatt had just been showing off for the men in the store, clearly trying to prove something to Mr. Steele.

She set to work gathering more baking supplies. At the sight of her silver dollars, Captain Jim was much more accommodating than he'd been previously. And within no time, she had most of what she needed, not only to make more hand pies but also for her jam. While the jars and other containers for the jam were sparse, Captain Jim helped her find enough to get started and promised to order more. With the freighters coming through the passes from Denver, each wagon drawn by teams of six horses, she'd have everything she could want in no time.

As Captain Jim helped her carry the supplies out and set them on the sidewalk, she caught sight of Wyatt at the far end of town, squatting beside a pair of skinny oxen, running his hand over the hind legs of one of the creatures and questioning the two men who appeared to be the owners.

She started toward him, curiosity lengthening her steps. Was he planning to purchase more cattle to add to his herd? The two Judd had brought back to the ranch earlier in the week had been nothing but skin and bones, much the same as these.

During the stagecoach ride along the Oregon Trail, they'd passed many dead oxen on the side of the road. Some travelers claimed the cattle became too worn out pulling wagons up hills and through sand to go any farther. Others said they'd died from alkali poisoning. The livestock that made it were clearly not much better off.

As she approached, Wyatt stood and wiped his hands on his trousers. "Sure do want to take these Herefords off your hands, but it'll take me a week or so to round up the cash."

"We're hoping to be moving on before that," said the older of what appeared to be a father-son pair.

Wyatt kneaded the back of his neck, watching the oxen.

Greta stopped next to him and examined the bulls, trying

to see in them what he did with his keen eyes and experience with cattle. He was obviously trying hard to build up his herd. But from what she'd been able to tell in the short time she'd been with him, the process was slow and hard and costly. At the rate he was going, it would be a long time before he'd have a self-sustaining ranch.

"How much are they asking?" she asked quietly.

"Only twelve dollars for the pair since they're so sickly." His reply was just as quiet.

She reached into her pocket and wrapped her fingers around the neckerchief and the leftover silver dollars. Though he'd instructed her to buy something special, she was too practical for that. She'd already decided she'd work on saving any extra earnings, just as she'd done with her jam money from back home, the money the stagecoach robbers had taken.

For an instant she let her fingers caress the solid pieces. Then she pulled out the neckerchief and held it out to Wyatt. "There's ten dollars left."

He took a rapid step back and held up his hands as if she'd pointed a gun at him. "I ain't gonna take your money—"

"*Our* money. Whatever we have is *ours*."

He paused, clearly recognizing her handing his words back to him.

"I've purchased all that I need." She nodded at the sacks and crates in front of the store. "And I'll make more next time we come to town."

He hesitated.

She shoved the bundle into his hand, giving him no choice but to take it. He stared down at the outline of the coins a moment, then looked up at her. His eyes were warm and full of gratefulness. "If you're sure."

"I'm sure."

"Thank you kindly."

"You don't have to thank me, Wyatt. We're just doing what we need to."

His lips lifted into another smile, this one throwing her off-kilter and making her slightly dizzy with happiness. As he ambled around the oxen and approached the father and son, she couldn't contain a smile of her own.

CHAPTER 12

"When will they be back?" Astrid asked for the hundredth time as she sat in the open doorway and peered outside.

The August day was stifling without the slightest breeze. In front of the stove stirring the bubbling pot of fruit, Greta plucked at a strand of hair sticking to her face. "They'll be back just as soon as they find the lost steer."

During the few days since the trip to town, Wyatt had branded the new oxen and set them out to pasture with the other cattle. But one of them had strayed. And today, Wyatt and Judd had decided to track it down.

Of course, today Astrid had managed to have enough energy to finish the horsehair saddle blanket that Judd had set her working on. And now, she was determined to take him up on his promise to teach her to ride in spite of her persistent cough.

Greta had already made one batch of jam with the supplies she'd purchased. And she had enough jars and wax to make one more set.

She lifted the wooden spoon and blew on the mixture of

huckleberries and chokecherries, hoping she'd gotten the consistency right. For yesterday's batch she'd added underripe chokecherries to help thicken and set the jam. And while she'd done the same today, she'd run short of huckleberries and added more sugar to the bubbling mixture to keep it from being too tart.

"Please thicken," she whispered to the liquid on the spoon. If she could keep contributing to the ranch in this small way, then perhaps Wyatt wouldn't regret marrying her.

Not that he appeared to have any regrets . . . In fact, he seemed to like talking with her. He was plenty busy, which didn't give them much time together, but whenever he and Judd came in for the morning and evening meals, he shared about all the things they were up to, everything from the poisonous plant one of the steers had nibbled to the porcupine quills in the nose of another. She and Astrid had laughed over his retelling of the attempts to hold down the steer and extract the quills while it kicked and bawled.

On Sunday, Wyatt had offered to take her to church. Judd insisted on staying home with Astrid while they went. In addition to getting to spend time with Wyatt, Greta had been excited to meet a young German woman a little older than herself who'd ridden down from her cabin up in one of the remote mines with her children so she could attend Reverend Zieber's services. Mrs. Mueller spoke limited English, but Greta learned her husband ran a sawmill that catered to the miners.

Only after they'd parted ways had Greta realized how much she missed female companionship, and the treeless grassland appeared all the more desolate and lonely as she and Wyatt had ridden back to the homestead.

Greta paused in stirring the jam and listened to the silence broken by the low buzz of insects—mostly locusts that flew up with a whirring every time anyone walked near.

"Judd said he'd show me how to ride on Dolly." Astrid reclined against the doorpost, her legs stretched out in front of her with the horsehair blanket at her side. She'd spent the greater part of the afternoon working on it, and now she was weary and ready for another nap. But she'd insisted on sitting up and waiting for Judd to return.

After the past week and a half, Greta was learning the rhythms of the ranch, and from the lengthening of the shadows, she guessed the men would be back soon. She'd already set grouse to roasting with vegetables from the garden. It had a similar taste and texture to chicken, and the scent of it wafted in the air, mingling with the sweetness of the fruit mixture.

"Maybe you ought to lie down and rest. Then by the time you wake up, he'll be back."

Astrid shrugged. "Do you really think he'll teach me?"

"Judd strikes me as the kind of man who keeps his word. If he said he'll teach you, then he will."

Even with the sunlight streaming in through the open window and door, the cabin was dark and shadowed, much gloomier than the wide-open kitchen of her family farmhouse in Illinois. With the close confines and the heat of the stove, the small room was also much hotter, causing her bodice to stick to her back and her skirt to tangle in her legs.

It wasn't an ideal setup, with little work space and few utensils and pans, but slowly she was getting used to it. Since most days were pleasant and sunny, she tried to be outside as much as possible, praying the sunshine and fresh air would heal Astrid.

Of course, Astrid hadn't had any trouble adjusting to their new home. For as sick as she'd always been, Astrid's ability to adapt always amazed Greta. During the many miles of journeying to the West, first by steamboat and then by stagecoach, Astrid had never once complained and had enjoyed each moment to the fullest, even on the bleakest of days.

Greta prayed Astrid would remain flexible and wouldn't get so attached to the ranch and to Wyatt and Judd that she'd have trouble letting go.

"I love this place," Astrid said, almost as if she'd read Greta's thoughts.

"Then you don't miss home?" Greta blew on the spoon again, then slurped a tiny amount.

"Not a bit. And I hope I never have to go back."

Greta paused in savoring the berries, a stab of regret piercing her. She'd tried to make Astrid's life bearable, tried to give her the love the rest of the family had withheld, but had she somehow failed?

"I hope we can stay here forever," Astrid continued.

"It wasn't all bad back home, was it?"

When Astrid didn't answer right away, Greta placed the spoon into the pot, wiped her hands on her apron, and crossed to her sister. "I'm sorry it was so hard."

Astrid looked up and smiled. "It's not your fault."

Greta took in every detail of the girl's delicate face, her dainty lips and nose and chin, and the new sprinkling of freckles from sitting in the sun more often.

"It's just that here, no one is getting mad at me and telling me to stop coughing or to go to my room and stay there. I can go wherever I want and cough as much as I need to."

Her sisters-in-law had been very vocal in their concern over Astrid's lingering illness. They'd only been trying to protect their own families, but over time, Astrid was bound to feel unwanted and unloved.

"My coughing doesn't bother Judd or Wyatt, does it, Greta?" The little girl's voice contained a note of worry, and a furrow formed between her brows.

"No, not at all." The two handled Astrid with patience and kindness, much better than anyone else ever had.

"You're sure?"

"They want to help you get well just like I do."

Astrid was quiet for a moment. "What if I don't get better, Greta?"

"You will. Already you're improving." At least, Astrid had been improving until the fever last week. And now she was pale and tired and listless again.

Greta stroked her sister's cheek. They had to be patient, had to give the high-altitude air time to work its healing.

At the approach of horse hooves, Astrid pushed herself to her feet. "It's Wyatt and Judd!"

Greta shielded her eyes and glimpsed the men riding in from the east pasture. Her sights locked upon Wyatt, his strong, proud bearing holding him well above Judd.

And at the perfect height above her. For that kiss. In the hotel dining room. *Oh my.*

Her skin tingled just thinking about being so close to him, feeling his lips and his breath. Even if he'd been pressured into kissing her, he hadn't seemed to mind. The trouble was, he hadn't made any effort to try it again.

As the men rode into the yard and dismounted by the barn, Astrid was already racing toward them, her excitement giving her new energy. Wyatt was the first one down, and Astrid was standing before him, chattering away and showing him the horsehair blanket.

Wyatt hoisted her up into a hug. "It's mighty fine," he said as she wrapped her arms around his neck and squeezed. "Better than anything I've ever seen Judd make."

Astrid laughed and the sound wafted around Greta, sweeter than the jam bubbling in the pot. She couldn't keep from smiling, a sense of completeness settling inside, that this place, these men, this life was where she and Astrid finally might belong.

And she couldn't keep from liking Wyatt better every day, especially when she witnessed him interacting this way with Astrid. His tenderness and attentiveness melted Greta's heart. Not many men could be as strong and rugged as Wyatt and yet display such gentleness with a little girl.

Wyatt claimed that Astrid reminded him of his sister and that's why he was able to interact with her like he did. But as Greta got to know him, the more she realized he was a man of deep character and principle, and the more she was amazed that he'd chosen to marry her.

As Wyatt returned Astrid to the ground, his gaze snagged on Greta above the girl's head. He straightened and seemed to give himself permission to look at her boldly, taking her in with an appreciation that did strange things to her insides.

She quickly turned her attention to Astrid, who was now throwing herself upon Judd. The older man lowered himself and hugged her back, then pulled away to examine the blanket. "It's real good."

"Then you'll teach me to ride?" Astrid hopped on first one leg, then the other.

"If Greta says you're fit."

All eyes turned in her direction. Greta smoothed back her flyaway hair and then twirled one of the loose strands around her finger.

"Please, Greta?" Astrid pleaded. "Please say yes."

"If you promise to lie down for a little bit first." Greta couldn't say no to Astrid getting on a horse even if the thought worried her.

"I promise."

"Then come on inside and let the men see to their mounts while you rest."

"Yay!" Astrid clapped and skipped back to the cabin.

Greta's gaze connected with Wyatt's again, and this time they shared a smile at Astrid's joy. Someday maybe they'd be sharing smiles over their own children.

They would have children, wouldn't they?

The very thought made her flush, and before Wyatt could read her wayward thoughts, she spun around. When she was inside the cabin away from his probing gaze, she pressed her hands against her cheeks and tried to still the erratic beating of her heart.

She'd grown to like Wyatt. And he seemed to like her. But she had to be careful. She couldn't let things move too quickly between them. She might have been hesitant at first about his three-month trial, but now that she'd had time to think on it, she realized that if Astrid didn't get better, she'd need to find a new way to help her sister, even if that meant leaving.

CHAPTER 13

Maybe the good Lord was smiling down on him after all.

Wyatt raised his arm and wiped the sweat from his brow against his sleeve. He peered back over the rows of gathered hay and then at the western sky before he released a breath. The scattered showers from earlier had moved on without drenching the earth. And he could almost allow himself to believe he'd finished the haying without any setbacks.

Roper Brawley had been madder than a hornet over losing more cattle sales and had threatened to burn the alfalfa field in retaliation. All the more reason Wyatt was relieved to get the haying done.

Not far behind him in the final row, Greta knelt next to a bundle, wrapping a piece of twine around the center, moving expertly as she had all week. Nearby, Astrid had abandoned her work and was cupping a caterpillar in her hand, jawing nonstop.

Somehow Greta managed to answer the girl's endless questions without breaking her concentration. With her head bent over the twine, he could watch her for a few seconds without her realizing he'd been staring. Why did she have to be so doggone pretty?

Despite the strain of the long days of late, she had a freshness and energy that was contagious. Not only had she worked with him in the alfalfa field from dawn till dusk since he'd started the haying, but once they finished for the day, she returned to the cabin and spent hours baking hand pies and making jam. He didn't know how late she stayed up, but every time he closed the barn door before bedding down, the light was still burning in the cabin.

Astrid helped her pick chokecherries in the mornings, and Judd had taken to bringing her huckleberries most nights after he returned from herding the cattle. Judd must've gone into the higher elevations to find the berries since the supply in the foothills was next to nothing.

Of course, Judd saw the value in Greta's hand pies and jams. It had been hard not to, after he and Greta had arrived home that first time with the two new cattle. After a second trip to town a week later, they'd both recognized Greta was earning more with her fixings than they'd panned in gold in a year.

Even so, Wyatt had the feeling Judd would have been gathering the berries for Greta regardless of whether she earned a penny for them. The older man had fallen for Astrid and Greta harder than a cowpoke getting grassed.

Wyatt's attention drifted over Greta and landed upon her lips. Fire blazed to life, sparking the need to kiss her again. A need that had simmered low and steady over the past few weeks since Steele had pressured him into kissing her in front of everyone.

Ever since, Wyatt had steered clear of taking her near the man. Thankfully, Steele had gone back to Denver and hadn't been around during the last visit to town.

As irritated as he was at Steele, he couldn't deny how much he'd liked the kiss. Maybe it had started as a show, but it hadn't ended that way. And now he couldn't put it out of his mind no matter how hard he tried.

And boy, had he tried. He'd nearly worked himself to death to get it out of his system. But against all his best efforts not to dwell on the kiss or Greta, he only seemed to think about it and her more with each passing day.

Her lips curved up into a half smile in reaction to something Astrid was saying. Lips that were pretty, soft, and responsive. Yep. She'd most definitely kissed him back, almost as if she'd wanted to kiss him—which wasn't possible, was it?

"Blast it all, McQuaid." He forced his attention to the bundle of hay in front of him. "Quit losing your mind."

They'd only been married a month. For now, he had to focus on friendship. That's all.

And as far as he could tell, their friendship was progressing real well. While they'd worked together with the haying, they had plenty of conversations. She shared about her life on the Illinois farm, explained how consumption had taken her stepmother and young half brother during the last two years. Greta had fought hard to save them, but in the end they'd gotten weaker and sicker until they died. Now she felt responsible for Astrid, and traveling to the West had seemed like her last option.

Not only did she share with him, but she was a good listener. She didn't poke or pry into his past but drew it out of him, and he'd found himself talking about his growing-up years and his family and how he was trying to make a new home for them.

He'd done more yammering with Greta in the little time he'd known her than he had with Judd in two years. There was just something right about her being here, and he was having a hard time remembering what life was like without her.

As he finished tying the twine, he stood and surveyed the land. He and Judd had already moved half the bundles into the barn. Tomorrow they'd transport and stow the rest.

Greta, too, rose to her feet and glanced around. Upon seeing their work completed, she arched her back and neck, giving him full view of her beautiful, womanly form.

His throat went dry. "Good Lord, help me."

She stretched her arms above her head and then yawned. Only then did she notice he'd been staring. She rapidly dropped her arms and gaze. At the same time, she cupped a hand over her yawn but couldn't hide the weary lines in her forehead.

"We're done," he called.

She fingered the hay standing tall in front of her. "I can help you carry these last bundles to the barn if you'd like."

He shook his head. "Nope. Let's go fishing."

Eagerness filled Astrid's pale face. Although she'd recovered from what Greta had called a "flare-up," the girl was still weak and tired easily. He heard her coughing most nights and knew Greta was up often with her. Wyatt doubted Greta ever got a full night's shut-eye and likely hadn't in years.

"Will you teach me how to fish, Wyatt?" Astrid moved the caterpillar from one hand to the other. "The way you do it, with the string and the fly?"

Since his move to Colorado, he'd taken to fly-fishing over regular line fishing. He hadn't had much time over the past month to fish, but he managed to catch enough to provide for a few meals a week.

"You told me you could teach me someday. And today is a good day, right?"

"Yep. And I'll teach Greta too."

"No." Greta smothered another yawn. "Astrid, you may go with Wyatt if you promise not to be a bother. But I have too many other responsibilities needing my attention."

"Always gonna be a heap of work," he said as they started back to the cabin. "And there will always be something pestering us for attention. But I reckon we oughta forget our cares for a spell."

Greta only resisted a little while longer, then gave in to both his and Astrid's pleading. Toting a couple of poles and bait, he led them to his favorite fishing spot upriver from the cabin. Greta spread a blanket in the shade of a cottonwood and sat down with a basket of mending. But Wyatt snagged her hand, pulled her up, and tugged her to the riverbank.

Though she protested, her eyes turned a light silver blue, the shade of the new needles on the blue spruce trees along the river, a shade he was learning reflected her happiness. After tying on the flies and readying their lines, he gave them each a rod and showed them how to overhead cast. Both were quick learners and soon had fish nibbling.

When Greta hooked her first trout, her delighted smile warmed him quicker than a swallow of hot coffee. He helped her net the catch. After he dumped it onto the bank, she wasn't afraid to remove the hook from the mouth and even asked him to show her how to tie on the next fly.

The fishing didn't hold Astrid's attention for long before she was busy collecting rocks. As Wyatt took up the girl's discarded rod and stood slightly upstream from Greta, his heart was nigh to full as he watched his two girls.

His two girls.

That was how he was beginning to think of them. They were his. His to care for and love and protect. While the realization was daunting, it was also gratifying to know he was accomplishing something worthwhile. He, Wyatt McQuaid, who'd never succeeded at anything, now had a wife and daughter he was providing for.

With the gurgling of water across the rocky bed and the rustling of the wind in the leaves overhead, he breathed deeply of the scent of damp pine needles and soil. The sunlight glinted off the water and their fishing lines, turning the spray of water droplets into sparkling diamonds. After so many doubts about his decision to try ranching, for the first time, peace wafted through him as gentle as the breeze in the branches.

"This reminds me of when Thomas took us fishing," Astrid called as she arranged her collection of rocks on a large flat stone nearby.

Greta nodded but didn't reply, concentrating on casting her line, her bottom lip captured between her teeth.

Was she thinking about how Thomas had died? Even though news of the war trickled into the mountain towns slower than molasses in January, they'd all heard enough to know the battles over recent months had been bloody and the death tolls too high to keep count.

"What was Thomas like?" His question tumbled out like the river water, flowing fast and unstoppable.

"W-e-l-l, he was always nice to me." Astrid picked another stone out of the water and added it to the others. "He bought me licorice."

Wyatt focused on Greta, gauging her reaction to his question.

As if sensing his gaze upon her, Greta glanced at him before she focused on her fishing line again, her brow furrowing. Was it still too painful for her to talk about her former fiancé?

"Forget it. It ain't none of my business—"

"He was a very good man." Greta tugged at her line. "I don't think he had a selfish bone in his body."

Greta's words of praise both comforted and riled him up. He liked knowing Thomas had treated Greta well. But on the other hand, Wyatt didn't want her to like anyone else . . . except him.

He waited for her to say more, and when she didn't, he resisted the strange need to probe further and find out about their relationship.

After Greta caught another trout, she retreated to the blanket with her mending. A short while later, Astrid curled up next to her, all tuckered out. The next time Wyatt glanced over at them, Greta had stretched out and fallen asleep too.

As he swallowed a yawn, he had the urge to lie down and rest. With half a dozen fish on a line in a shallow pool, why not give himself a break? After stowing the poles and bait, he lowered himself next to Greta. Careful not to disturb her, he crossed his arms behind his head, tugged the brim of his hat down over his face, and closed his eyes.

A tickle against his cheek startled him awake, and he tipped up his hat. For a second, he was disoriented and tried to gain his bearings. At the sight of the deserted riverbank and Greta and Astrid still sleeping next to him, he allowed himself to relax.

From the position of the sun, he guessed he hadn't slept long—maybe half an hour. There was still time to rest a spell longer, maybe catch a few more fish, before heading back.

As he shifted, he awakened to the pressure of Greta snuggled against him, her hand resting on his chest and her head on his arm. The wind blew wisps of her hair across his face. Her knot had come loose and now her hair spread out like newly harvested golden-brown strands of grain.

His entire body suddenly hummed and his every nerve tuned in to her nearness. He liked having her next to him but the second she woke, she'd probably pull away in embarrassment.

Though a warning went off inside him, reminding him he needed to be careful, he caressed the hair that lay on his chest. It was fine and glossy and cascaded through his fingers.

He had the overwhelming need to stroke her cheeks and chin and neck. He fought against his desire, but at her soft, sleepy sigh, one filled with contentment, his fingers moved from her hair to her face. Shifting enough to see her features, he caressed her cheek, down to her chin, and back up.

Her long eyelashes fluttered.

Even as the warning inside clanged louder, he ignored it and drew a line to her mouth, tracing the slight bow above her upper lip. His muscles tightened with the need to finish his perusal with his mouth.

Her fingers splayed across his heart, searing through his

vest and shirt. And when her hand slid up his neck as though testing the feel of him, he held his breath.

Was she awake? Or still partly asleep?

Her fingers roamed higher, moving to his jaw. Her touch was like fire, shooting heat through his veins. When she skimmed his lips, he couldn't stop himself—he captured her hand and pressed a kiss to her fingertips.

Her eyes flew open, flashing with confusion. Then, as she took in her position against him, she began to scoot away. He snaked his other arm underneath her, gently catching and kissing her fingers again.

As her gaze connected with his, the embarrassment faded, and she grew motionless, no doubt seeing the desire written in his eyes. He was certain of it when her lashes lowered and a flush rose into her cheeks.

The heat from his veins pooled in his gut. What would she say if he bent in and kissed her? Would she allow it? She hadn't resisted the last time, and he reckoned she wouldn't push him away now either. She was the kind of woman who expected to satisfy her husband's needs and bear him children without thought to herself.

He shifted his kiss to the thudding pulse in her wrist. Her lashes lifted to reveal curiosity and shyness. She'd accept him. He could sense it. All he had to do was bend in and kiss her.

His body tensed at the very thought of the pleasures that awaited him in her arms. And yet, even as he longed for her, he wouldn't use her. He'd told her three months, and as sure-as-crows-fly he wouldn't break his word. Besides, if and when they shared more intimacies, he wanted her to welcome his touch and invite him in to her arms. Not just endure it.

"Did you love Thomas?" he whispered, not sure why he couldn't be satisfied with her answer from earlier. But once the question was out, he was keenly aware that he needed to know how she'd felt about her fiancé.

As though sensing his need, she searched his face. "Yes, I loved him. . . ."

Jealousy cut a quick path through him. He released her and pushed himself up with the sudden need to wrangle something.

She scrambled to sit, positioning herself next to him but thankfully not touching him. He wasn't sure he could handle the merest contact without giving in to the need to gather her in his arms and kiss her until she forgot all about her former love.

From the corner of his vision, he could see her draw her knees up and wrap her arms around her skirt. Her hair still hung loose in beautiful swirling waves, waves that called to him.

He forced himself to stare straight ahead.

"I loved him," she said again.

"I only needed to hear it once—"

"Just as a friend."

"Just a friend?" His heartbeat stumbled. "Then you never—you weren't—together?"

"Wyatt!" she hissed, slapping his arm lightly and glancing at Astrid, who was still asleep. "We never even kissed."

"You didn't?" The tension eased from his body.

"Thomas wanted to kiss," she said hesitantly, almost as if she regretted her decision to hold back. "But to be perfectly honest, I wasn't attracted to him in that way."

"You mean the way you are to me?" He tried to keep his

tone light, but he hoped she'd give him a serious reply. Was she interested in him now that they'd had time to get to know each other?

"You're the first man I've kissed." As soon as her admission was out, she tucked her chin. It wasn't exactly an answer to his question, but it was telling.

"Good. I want to be the only man you kiss." A part of him couldn't believe they were sitting together having this kind of conversation. But another part wanted to connect with her more deeply, to earn her trust, and win her affection.

Out in the hay field, he'd told himself he had to keep things friendly-like with her. But he couldn't deny he wanted a whole lot more than just friendship. He wanted her to be his wife in body, soul, and spirit. Was that possible?

He tried to put together the right words to let her know he was aiming to have a good marriage. Before he could say anything, Astrid stretched and yawned noisily, and Greta turned her attention to the girl.

He stood and gathered the fishing supplies. Out of the corner of his eye, he watched her hug Astrid and then tickle her, earning giggles that filled the air, a sound sweeter than any other.

Sober reality settled around Wyatt. Greta had married him for one reason and only one—so Astrid could stay in the high country and have a chance at getting better. If the child didn't improve, what would Greta do? Would she stick with the marriage? Or would she be off trying to find the next best cure, leaving him and his cattle ranch far behind?

The honest truth was that even if Greta decided to stay,

he wasn't sure he'd be able to make a go of the ranch in the long run anyway. What if he failed at it? Failed her?

There was no sense blathering on about his feelings or carrying on with her. Not until autumn was over and she decided if she wanted to stay on with him. For now, he'd do well to keep busy and keep his mind from going where it didn't need to.

Chapter 14

After almost two months in Colorado, Astrid wasn't better. Not even a little bit.

With a huff of frustration, Greta pushed the basket of onions farther back in the new cellar Judd had dug out for her. She spread the hay evenly over the top of the onions. Then she shifted the bin of potatoes next to the onions, bumping her head against the low dirt ceiling supported by log beams.

The musty scent of earth mingled with that of the root vegetables she and Judd had harvested over the past few weeks since finishing the haying. Judd had done most of the picking and shelling, leaving the preserving up to her. And so far she'd canned tomatoes, beans, and beets.

Since Judd had been occupied with the garden produce, Wyatt had taken over managing the cattle. He was gone for hours a day in the pasturelands, corralling steers and keeping them from danger. He usually came back with game he'd hunted—rabbits, sage grouse, deer, and elk, storing up provisions since the game would soon be scarce once the colder temperatures and snow sent the animals into lower elevations or hibernation.

That meant he devoted every daylight hour to dressing the game, along with drying it in the smokehouse next to the barn. And that also meant she'd spent little time with him since their fishing expedition. They had the rare trips to town together when he took her to sell her baked goods and jams. Of course they were all together on Sundays, their day of rest, going to church and visiting in town. And he was always friendly and easy to talk to.

But she'd been waiting for another moment of closeness like that day by the river, and it hadn't come. Had he decided he didn't like her after all? Had she read more into his touch and their conversation that day than he'd meant?

Greta sat back on her heels, dusted her hands, and gazed around at the produce. She wanted to believe the busyness of preparing for winter was all that was standing between them. But as with other times, she sensed something more was holding him back.

Sunlight poured in through the hatch above, and she started up the ladder, forcing thoughts of Wyatt from her mind. Maintaining simple camaraderie was for the best. After all, she awoke some mornings in a near panic, wondering what would happen if Astrid took a turn for the worse during the winter months and needed a physician. Though a doctor lived in Alma, there was no guarantee he'd be available when they needed him.

Would she and Astrid be better off living in Denver? Should they be closer to physicians and the hospital that boasted of being able to help with consumption?

As Greta neared the top rung, a strange shout from the

front of the cabin stopped her. It was a man's voice that sounded nothing like Judd's or Wyatt's. Did they have visitors from town? Hopefully it wasn't Roper Brawley. Wyatt had indicated that if their neighbor came anywhere near, she was to stay in the cabin and not come out.

During Wyatt's last purchase of oxen a couple weeks ago, Brawley had threatened Wyatt as usual. Wyatt was getting tired of the harassing, especially because Brawley was already buying up livestock and leaving so few for him.

At another shout, Greta's pulse spurted with fear for Astrid, who'd been napping in the cabin. She scrambled the rest of the way up the ladder into the dirt surrounding the opening. Without bothering to shake out her skirt or shut the cellar door, she bounded forward and rounded the cabin in time to see an Indian duck inside.

She stopped short, dread driving into her chest.

Although Wyatt had spoken of seeing Utes passing through his land from time to time, he'd never mentioned having any problems. He indicated the Utes had made the mountains of Colorado their home for hundreds of years, but with the flood of miners arriving, they'd been giving up land and moving farther west.

Standing in the middle of the ranch yard were three mustangs with long manes and tails as well as muscular bodies of rich chestnut, black, and white. Without saddles, they were majestic and untamed.

And so were the Indians. She'd only glimpsed one, and he'd been young and tall with long braids, a buckskin shirt, and leather leggings. Her mind immediately filled with all the stories she'd heard during the stagecoach ride to Colorado—the atrocities committed by Indians against settlers moving west, the killing, torturing, and taking of captives.

With her heart beating fast, she started toward the door. Even if Astrid remained asleep while the natives were in the cabin, Greta refused to take any chances. She had to go inside and protect her sister, no matter the cost.

As she reached for the door handle, her fingers shook. She took a deep breath, shot a prayer heavenward, then swung the door open and walked inside.

"W-e-l-l, it's about time." Astrid knelt on one of the benches, slathering jam onto a biscuit. "I could use some help getting dinner ready for my new friends."

Two of the Indians were seated at the table on either side of her and the third, the tall one who'd just entered, was in front of the stove lifting a spoon from the pot of vegetable soup Greta had set to simmer.

They paused and stared at her, their dark eyes narrowing and seeming to assess every detail about her.

Should she grab Astrid and run, or should she join the girl in serving the men a meal? Astrid plopped a messy jam-covered biscuit onto the table in front of one of them, drawing their attention. She wasted no time in slathering another biscuit all the while chattering as though she made an everyday occurrence of visiting with Indians.

"Go on now." She motioned to the native who wore his loose hair cropped close to his shoulders. "Go on and eat it. I know you'll like it."

The man didn't move.

Astrid used her sticky knife to push the biscuit closer to him. "Eat it. It's real good. Greta makes delicious jam." At that, she flashed Greta a smile, one brimming with pride.

The Indian gingerly picked up the biscuit, examined it from all angles, and then licked the jam dribbling over the edge. His brows rose before he leaned in and took another taste. Soon all the natives were seated at the table, eating biscuits with jam and slurping vegetable soup.

While they ate, Astrid continued her one-sided conversation, only pausing whenever her cough racked her body. The Indians ate quietly and seemed to relish every morsel. When finished, they stood and exited just as silently.

Only the tall young one lingered in the doorway and looked at Astrid as she finished another burst of coughing. "Little girl sick."

At the sound of his stilted English, Greta fumbled with the plate in her hand and could only stare at him.

He, in turn, watched Astrid with concern in his eyes. "Waters good for sick and helping."

Greta nodded, trying to act as though she knew what he was saying but was anxious for him to take his leave with the others.

Thankfully, he didn't linger. As he strode out, Astrid followed close on his heels, her questions chasing him. Now that he'd revealed his knowledge of English, Astrid was all the more eager to talk.

Greta went as far as the doorway to keep an eye on Astrid to make sure she didn't do anything to irritate the Indians as they mounted their horses. The tall one spoke a few more English words to Astrid, pointed to the east, and then patted her head.

Only after they'd ridden away, leaving dust in their wake, did Greta's knees buckle. She sagged against the doorframe and then slid to the ground. While the natives had been polite, the relief pouring through Greta weakened her.

Astrid sat next to her and leaned her head against Greta's arm. Wheezing for breath, the child closed her eyes, her face pale and her chest rising and falling rapidly. Greta needed to carry her sister to bed and enforce rest time. But she was too weak herself to do anything but gather Astrid into her arms and kiss the top of her head.

A few minutes later, they were sitting in the same spot when the pounding of hooves alerted Greta to another visitor. Her body tensed, but before she could rise, Wyatt's outline came into view. He was riding hard and low, clearly in a hurry.

As he galloped into the yard and reined in near the cabin, she knew she ought to stand and greet him properly and offer him a drink and something to eat. But she wasn't sure if she could get her legs working.

He hopped from his horse and yanked down the neckerchief tied up over his mouth and nose to keep out the dust. His brow was creased and his jaw set. "You okay?" His dark brown eyes raked over both Astrid and her.

Greta nodded.

He crossed to them, his steps hard, his breathing labored. "The Utes let you be?"

"Then you saw them?"

"Yep. They passed through the east pasture from this direction. I rode like the devil for fear they'd stopped and harassed you."

"We fed them biscuits and soup," Astrid said sleepily, rousing enough to smile up at Wyatt. "They liked it, especially Greta's jam."

He dropped to his knees and brushed a hand over Astrid's loose hair. "Then they didn't hurt you?"

Greta squeezed his arm, his rigid muscles flexing beneath her touch. "We're fine. Really."

His hand covered hers, and he squeezed back, his eyes still filled with worry. "Were they here long?"

"Not overly so."

His attention shifted to the pasture, and he blew out a short, tense breath. "Thank the good Lord." His worry only confirmed the volatile nature of the situation with the natives and the dangerous reality of the ongoing conflict.

Astrid relayed a detailed account of all that had transpired before she yawned, reclining into Greta again and shutting her eyes.

Greta pressed another kiss against Astrid's head, sensing the child drifting to sleep.

"From now on, either me or Judd need to be here," Wyatt whispered.

"Of course not." The last thing she wanted was for Wyatt to feel as though he couldn't go anywhere because he had to stay behind and play nursemaid to Astrid and her. "You both have too much work to do. Besides, this kind of thing doesn't happen every day."

He situated himself next to her, extending his legs and leaning against the cabin. "Now that they know you're here, no doubt they'll be back."

"If they return, we'll just feed them again. That's what they seemed to want."

He was quiet a moment before he glanced at Astrid as though making sure she was asleep. "Last week, the Utes captured a couple of homesteaders to the south, stripped them, and made them crawl around on all fours like cattle and eat grass. They finally beat the living daylights out of the pair before they let them go."

She shuddered. "Have the Utes threatened you?"

"Not yet." Wyatt's handsome face remained a mask of frustration. "But reckon I oughta teach you how to use my rifle."

"I already know how to shoot. My stepbrothers taught me."

"You know where I keep my rifle in the barn?"

She nodded. "But I'm sure it won't come to that."

"I'm aiming to give you a lesson anyhow, just to make sure."

"Thank you, Wyatt." She squeezed his arm again, and this time, he captured her hand in his, threading his fingers through hers.

The intimate contact sent a fluttering of warmth through her. And when he rested their intertwined hands on his thigh, the warmth fanned outward.

Memories of their fishing trip rushed back, heedless of all her attempts over recent weeks to stave them off. With his hand securely wrapped through hers, suddenly all she could think about was how his feathery kisses had felt against her hand.

She had to put them from her mind and couldn't read more into his hand-holding. They were both just relieved nothing bad had happened. That's all.

She leaned her head back and tried to simply be content with the moment, sitting with him hand in hand and knowing he cared enough to rush home and check on Astrid and her. For now, that would have to be enough.

"Astrid's really something else, you know?" He peered down at the child, his eyes brimming with affection.

"Yes, she is." Greta's insecurities surfaced as they often did when she thought about trying to be a parent to Astrid. "I'm trying so hard to raise her right, but she's always taking risks—like today, just jumping in and serving the Indians biscuits."

"She's fearless."

"And often foolish."

"Maybe that comes from not knowing about her future. I reckon people staring death in the face ain't afraid of a little danger now and then."

Ever since Astrid had been a baby, she'd been willful and independent. But with the onset of the consumption, those traits had only seemed to grow more pronounced. Greta was thankful that since coming to the ranch, she had some help reining in the girl's antics. "You're good with her. And so is Judd."

"She's real easy to love." Wyatt reached across Greta to stroke Astrid's hair again.

Greta's heart softened as it did whenever Wyatt interacted with the little girl. He was always taking the time to answer Astrid's dozens of questions, allowing her to help, and showing affection for her in a brotherly way, like now.

"Being with her makes me miss my little sis a real lot." Wyatt's voice was wistful. "Sure as a gun miss them all."

"They must miss you too." How could anyone not miss a man like Wyatt?

He hesitated, then released her hand and stood. His hat shadowed his face, but she'd been learning that talking about his family and his past always brought out more shadows.

"I'd best be heading back. But I'll carry Astrid inside to bed first."

After Astrid was tucked under the covers, Greta watched Wyatt ride away and wished more than anything she could promise him that she and Astrid would be the family he longed for, that he'd never have to lose them. But as much as she wanted to reassure him, she couldn't. Not when he'd been the one to leave the door of their marriage open.

He'd left it wide open that first night she'd come to the ranch, and he'd given them both the option of stepping through it and walking away. As much as he might be growing to care about Astrid and her, he'd yet to make a move to yank the door closed and insist on keeping their marriage vows sacred. And the truth was, she couldn't yank the door closed yet either.

CHAPTER 15

Snow had fallen in the mountains.

Greta exited the church behind Astrid, her sights straying to the distant hillsides. The aspens had been changing, and the contrast between the evergreens and brilliant yellow never failed to take her breath away. Except for today. Not now that the highest mountain peaks wore new white crowns of snow.

Bad traveling. That's what everyone was saying this morning. Mrs. Mueller hadn't ridden down because of the ice. And though Greta missed seeing her, she was more worried about the mountain roads becoming impassable and cutting them off from getting help for Astrid should she need it.

"Can we go see the kittens again?" Astrid charged down the plank step and veered toward the livery, where last Sunday after church she'd happened upon a litter of eight-week-old kittens. "You said that I could bring one home."

"I said only if Wyatt was agreeable to it." Greta easily caught up with Astrid and snagged her hand. The child's pale complexion and the dark circles under her eyes testified to the strain of battling consumption. The last week especially had been difficult, with several nights of severe coughing. The sleepless nights and trouble breathing had taken their toll, not only on Astrid. Greta was wearier than usual too.

She'd worked well into the night making jam and hand pies to sell in town today. While the supply of chokecherries and huckleberries was gone, Judd had brought her wild plums from the foothills that she'd cooked up.

"Let's wait for Wyatt." She tugged Astrid to a stop beside her and glanced to where Wyatt stood in the doorway of the church talking with Reverend Zieber. In his Sunday church clothes, Wyatt was sharp, his crisp suit contrasting his ruggedness and making him more handsome.

Her stomach fluttered just looking at him, an ailment that was becoming commonplace whenever she saw him.

"If I can't have a kitten"—Astrid strained to keep walking—"then I want a puppy. Maybe Mr. McLaughlin will have puppies at the livery this time."

"Puppies?" came Wyatt's voice from behind. "What about puppies?"

"W-e-l-l, I was thinking a pet might be nice to keep me company." Astrid halted and gave Wyatt her most charming smile, one she'd learned could wrap the man around her pinky.

"A pet?" Wyatt's brows arched, and he glanced from Astrid to Greta, as though trying to gauge Greta's thoughts on the matter. After the visit last week from the natives, Wyatt had mentioned wanting to get a couple of cow dogs that would be able to cause a ruckus and alert them well in advance of any visitors.

While Greta agreed that having dogs couldn't hurt, she

wanted him to know he didn't have to give in to Astrid's whims. Before she could say anything, someone called out a greeting. They shifted to find Mr. Steele driving toward them in a bright yellow buggy with a single seat drawn by one horse. Greta had noticed the kindly gentleman in the service earlier sitting in the front row, back after his weeks in Denver.

Now she smiled a greeting.

As he brought his buggy to a halt next to them, he tipped his hat and smiled in return. "Lovely service this morning, wasn't it?"

For several moments they spoke of the message and made small talk about the harvest and cooler nights. Mr. Steele also mentioned to Wyatt something about being in touch with a cattle breeder in Missouri and that a payment was underway. And although the two didn't spell things out, Mr. Steele must have been helping Wyatt to get more cattle.

"I'm happy to say"—Mr. Steele focused on Greta again—"that by summer you might have more womanly companionship, as my wife is finally considering moving to Fairplay."

"That would be delightful, Mr. Steele. I would surely love the friendship."

"I told her we're attracting families with young children." Mr. Steele nodded toward Astrid, who was stroking his horse and talking to it as though she'd just made a new friend. "I also told her I'm planning to build a school and that I'm hoping we'll be able to fill it eventually."

He looked pointedly at Wyatt, who tugged at his shirt collar.

"I'm sure we will." Greta hoped someday Astrid would get well enough so she could attend school. In Illinois, the girl's illness had prevented her from going, and Greta had taken to teaching her at home during the winter months when she had more time to devote to it. But maybe things would be different here. She couldn't give up hope yet, could she? "I guess we'll know more in the spring."

Mr. Steele's countenance brightened. "Then does that mean what I think it does?"

"Of course," Greta said, even as Wyatt cleared his throat.

The older gentleman's smile widened. "I'm so pleased to hear the news, and my wife will be doubly so. Maybe she'll be here to help you by the time the baby arrives."

Baby? Greta's smile froze in place. Did Mr. Steele think she was expecting a baby? What had she said to give him that impression?

Again Wyatt cleared his throat. "Hold on a minute, Steele—"

"You're having a baby?" Astrid interrupted, her eyes clear and full of life in a way they hadn't been in weeks. She clapped and spun. "I'm going to have a niece or nephew. A brand-new baby!"

Mr. Fehling, the proprietor of Hotel Windsor, stepped out of the door of his establishment, wiping his hands on his apron and grinning from ear to ear. "Mrs. McQuaid is having a baby? How thrilling. The wee one'll have the honor of being the first baby born in Fairplay."

Several more passersby stopped to slap Wyatt on the back and offer Greta congratulations. As they did so, she couldn't seem to stop the current that was dragging her along. Though she made a few attempts to correct the misunderstanding, as did Wyatt, she felt as though she was grasping at a riverbank trying to find solid footing but was being carried too rapidly to change her course.

By the time they finished selling her goods to Mr. Fehling, word of her expecting a baby had spread to nearly all her patrons. She was downright mortified and had no idea how to explain she wasn't pregnant. She couldn't very well stand in the middle of Main Street and announce she wasn't with child because she and Wyatt had barely shared kisses, much less the marriage bed.

Wyatt's face was pale and taut by the time they made their way to the livery, and he seemed to be having as much trouble as she was in figuring out how to row upstream against the current.

"Hold on there, McQuaid." Captain Jim hurried down the sidewalk toward them.

Greta braced herself for more congratulations. But Captain Jim didn't make any mention of the baby and instead handed Wyatt a letter. "Came with freighters from Denver a few days ago."

Since Astrid had raced ahead to the livery, eager to see the kittens, Greta used the opportunity to escape from the public eye, slipping into the dark interior of the wide barn and its many stalls. On a Sunday morning, the place was quiet except for the soft nickering of the horses. Thin rays of sunlight slanted through the cracks in the walls, shining on the dust and warming the air with the familiar scent of horseflesh.

"Here, kitty-kitties," Astrid called as she probed the dark stall where the kittens had been last week.

Their trips to town on Sunday mornings always brought back the most remembrances of home. No matter how busy her pappa was, he'd always made time to honor "the Lord's day"—as he'd called it—and to attend church. The gatherings had been a place of community and friendship—and where she'd met Thomas during those lonely days after her mamma had died.

He'd been a true friend. Maybe she'd never felt warm flutters in her stomach at his touch the way she did with Wyatt, but she'd loved him. And he was the one she missed whenever she thought about home and Sunday mornings and church services.

"I can't find the kitties." Alarm laced Astrid's voice. "Can you help me find them, Greta?"

"Maybe the mother moved them to a new place." Greta made her way carefully through the hay, but before she could join the search, Wyatt stepped into the barn. His stricken expression and the open letter in his hand stopped her.

"What's wrong?"

"The letter's from Flynn."

Wyatt had shared enough about his brothers that Greta felt she knew them to a small degree. Two years younger than Wyatt, Flynn hadn't approved of Wyatt leaving the farm and had been angry with him ever since. During Wyatt's last visit home three years ago, they'd exchanged bitter words before parting. While Wyatt's mother had continued to write letters, Flynn had been silent.

Greta crossed to Wyatt and wasn't sure whether to take the letter and read it for herself or wait for him to elaborate.

He swallowed hard, his Adam's apple threading up and down his throat.

It couldn't be good news. She touched his arm, hoping he sensed her support.

"It's my ma." His voice choked, his eyes wide with heart-wrenching sorrow. "She died in childbirth."

"Oh, Wyatt." Without hesitating, she slipped her arms around him and drew him into an embrace. Maybe her own family had never been affectionate with her, but she'd learned from Thomas how to be a supportive friend. And right now, that's what Wyatt needed.

He gripped her tightly, almost as if he couldn't stand without her holding him up.

She wished there was some way to take away the pain, but just about the only thing she could do was be by his side through the grief.

"The babe died too," he whispered after a moment.

"I'm sorry, Wyatt." She pressed him closer.

"This is all Rusty's fault." His voice was hoarse. "He knew she couldn't handle having another babe, not after the way she almost died giving birth last time."

Wyatt didn't speak often of his stepfather, but whenever he did, he'd had nothing good to say, blaming Rusty for his mother's miscarriages in recent years along with a stillbirth that had left her in poor health.

"I should have sent for her—for them—sooner."

"You've been doing the best you could."

"I could've done more."

"You're the hardest working, most determined man I know. If there had been a way, you would have found it."

His chest shuddered as he drew in a deep breath. His nose burrowed into her neck, and for a long moment she simply held him. Thankfully, Astrid had gotten distracted by the horses and was busy feeding them handfuls of hay.

When he peeled away, she reluctantly released him but held on to his arm. She could feel the inner turmoil rippling through his muscles. With the length of time it took the mail to reach Fairplay, his mother had likely died weeks ago. There wasn't much he'd be able to do now, as much as he wished he could.

"She shouldn't have married Rusty. And it's my fault she had to."

"No, Wyatt. You did your best with the farm after your father died. You were only a boy—"

"To top it all, Rusty's saying my pa's farm is his." Wyatt spat the words. "Told Flynn he can stay 'til spring, but then he has to take everyone and get on out."

"Can Rusty do that? Don't you or Flynn have legal rights to the land?"

"Nope." The word contained a world of bitterness. "From what Flynn says, Rusty made Ma sign the deed over to him."

"That's awful."

"Guess I knew we'd lost the farm the day Ma married that fleabag." Wyatt hung his head, then took another deep breath before he lifted his chin, his features filling with the determination she'd grown to appreciate. "Don't matter. I was fixin' to have them come by next summer anyhow. Now this just makes it all the more certain."

On that first day meeting Wyatt during their time together in the cold cavern in the thunderstorm, he'd mentioned bringing his family west at some point. But the recollection was vague, and she'd put it from her mind.

"I'm gonna write to Flynn and let him know."

Her mind whirled with the implications. Wyatt had three brothers and a sister. Where would everyone stay? How would they feed and take care of additional people when they were already working long hours to get by the way it was?

Wyatt could do nothing less than offer them a home regardless of their insufficient quarters and provisions. If their situations were reversed, she'd do the same thing. Nevertheless, a boulder rolled into the pit of her stomach and lodged there. "Do you think Flynn will come?"

Wyatt's shoulders sagged. "I don't rightly know. But he says Brody's itching to join the war effort as soon as he turns eighteen, and Dylan's been talking about running away to join up too. I reckon Flynn'll jump at the chance to bring them west and out of the conflict, even if he'd just as soon jerk a knot in my tail."

If Greta could go back in time, she'd jump at the chance to avoid the war too and would have done anything to ensure that Thomas didn't enlist. He'd wanted to get married right away, had asked her if they could wed before he left for training. But, as with the kiss, she'd hoped the prospect of marrying her would bring him home quicker.

She'd been a fool. She should have told Thomas she'd marry him if only he'd go west with her. From what she'd heard, Colorado Territory's governor, William Gilpin, had formed several militia companies. But being so far away from the conflict, the infantry and cavalry regiments had only skirmished with Confederate Irregulars.

The fact was, most men in the mountains were too busy searching for precious minerals to think about the war. And neither the governor nor the United States War Department had pushed for the men of Colorado to enlist because the Union needed the gold and silver from the mines to help finance the war efforts.

Surely Fairplay would be a safe place for Wyatt's brothers to get away from the death and destruction of the war. "Why wait until spring? They should come now."

"I wish." The letter in his hand was now crumpled but still showed a brief paragraph in neatly slanted cursive. "By the time I get word to Flynn, it will be too late in the year to travel."

She nodded her understanding. But in her heart, the heaviness only sank deeper. As kind as Wyatt was and as generous as he'd been in providing for Astrid and her, he would need the space for his family. And after building an addition to the cabin, there still wouldn't be enough room to go around.

Also, Wyatt had no income yet from his cattle, at least not steady or reliable. Yes, they'd made a sizable amount today from Mr. Fehling. But this batch would be one of the last now that the fruit was mostly harvested. As usual, after replenishing baking supplies, she'd planned to give the left-over money to Wyatt so he had the cash to buy necessities for the ranch. But maybe he'd use it to help his siblings pay for their trip west.

Whatever the case, Wyatt didn't need to worry about her and Astrid too. Maybe, just maybe, it was time to get serious about planning to leave.

She took his callused hand in hers, trying to comfort him. "Let's get that letter to Flynn ready to post. He'll appreciate knowing he has a new place he can call home."

"I'll get some paper from Captain Jim and write it now."

"And we'll send him the earnings from today to help pay for their journey here."

"No how, no way. I ain't taking your money—"

She stopped him by laying a finger against his lips. "*Our* money, Wyatt." They'd had this argument before, and she never liked it.

Before she could drop her hand, he snagged it and pressed a kiss to her palm.

At the soft warmth, her breath hitched. The sadness in his eyes made them a rich molasses brown, and she found herself sinking into them, unable to look away.

"Looks like I have a knack for making a mess of things."

"Everything will work out," she whispered. But would it?

He brushed his lips against her palm again.

He'd rarely touched her in the weeks they'd been married, had stayed true to the boundaries he'd established from the start, had given them plenty of time to try out their marriage of convenience and see if it worked. With only a couple of weeks to go until the end of the three-month arrangement, it was safe to say they'd gotten to "liking each other."

Right now was proof of it, proof that more and more lately, this attraction was real. Her heart couldn't deny how much she liked him no matter how much her head warned her to be cautious.

As if reading her thoughts, he dropped his other hand to her waist, drew her closer, and placed a kiss on the inside of her wrist, his breath warm against her thudding pulse.

His fingers tightened and splayed over her hip, making her entirely aware of his searing touch and the power of his masculinity. His somber but beautiful eyes held hers, causing her heartbeat to sputter with strange need, although for what she didn't know.

"Better not bring your family here," came a voice from the livery door.

Wyatt stiffened.

Greta peered past him. Roper Brawley stood in the doorway, feet apart, hand on his gun. Wyatt stepped out in front of Greta, guiding her behind him while putting himself in the line of fire.

"You ain't gonna make it here." Brawley appeared calm, but his grip was tight against his gun. "Might as well admit it and stop wasting everybody's time."

"I ain't wasting time."

Though the sunlight filtered in from outside the livery, Brawley's face was shadowed beneath the brim of his hat, hiding his black eye patch. Seeing their neighbor never failed to make Greta shiver. Although most of the sightings had been from a distance, she had only to remember the first time he'd harassed her while she had been huckleberry picking for her to sense that this man was dangerous, perhaps even deadly.

Wyatt's fingers gripped the handle of his revolver too. "Last I checked, my mail and what I aim to do with my family is my business, not yours."

Brawley spat a stream of tobacco juice into the hay, his bottom lip bulging and his scraggly beard stained from the spittle. "No need to get all-fired up, McQuaid. Just doin' my civil-like duty to keep more people from being homeless than need to be."

"Hey there, Mister." Of course, Astrid had to choose that moment to decide she was done petting the horses. She skipped past Wyatt and would have gone straight toward Brawley if Wyatt hadn't grabbed her up and held her back.

She craned her neck to see Brawley regardless of Wyatt's hold. "What happened to your eye, Mister?"

"Astrid," Greta muttered. "Be polite."

"Just curious is all. Last time you came riding through town, I thought for sure you were a pirate, what with the eye patch and all."

"Good one, kid. Yep, I'm a pirate."

Astrid cocked her head and stared at Brawley. "W-e-l-l—"

Greta clamped a hand over the little girl's mouth. The situation was already tense enough, and they didn't need to add to the danger with Astrid's blunt remarks.

"Get on out of here, Brawley." Wyatt dropped his hand again to his revolver. "And you better not come anywhere near my place if you want to live a month of Sundays."

Brawley let out a barking laugh and then turned and sauntered away. Wyatt watched him go, his already-dark eyes turning murky. He passed Astrid over to her, told her to stay in the livery, and then left, his heavy-booted steps taking him in the direction of Simpkin's General Store. No doubt he planned to give an earful to Captain Jim for spilling the news about his family's predicament.

Whatever Wyatt might do, one thing was true. The West was no place for cowards. And Greta was fairly certain that with all her uncertainties, she was the biggest coward of all.

Chapter 16

Atop his horse, Wyatt patted his vest pocket underneath his coat and traced the outline of the ring. Had he been too rash in buying it for Greta? He reckoned it'd be the easiest way to let on that he wanted to keep their marriage going. 'Cause he did, didn't he?

At a wiggle in the small crate on his lap, he peeked inside, as he had dozens of times during the long day of traveling back from Mosquito Gulch. With the rough terrain, he'd been afraid he'd have trouble with his extra load. But thankfully, the ride toward home had been uneventful. Except for the cow having a hoof abscess and slowing things down, he hadn't had any problems.

The cow he'd bought with the earnings from Greta's plum jam.

Though she had encouraged him to use the money to help pay for his family's journey out here, he had to make sure Flynn agreed to moving first. And knowing his brother, he'd have a burr under his saddle and refuse to consider coming west.

Greta had easily accepted Wyatt's decision and instead asked for a milking cow she could use for butter making. He already had one pregnant heifer and hoped to breed more. So while tracking down the cow hadn't been easy, getting another for breeding was actually a smart plan.

Then again, just about everything Greta did was smart. She'd proven that her business efforts were worth the initial investment. No doubt she'd make just as much selling butter in town as she had with her jam and hand pies. She'd recently hatched chicks in her efforts to increase the number of laying hens. At some point, she'd have more than enough eggs to sell in town too.

She was as shrewd and savvy as the best businessmen he knew. Her suggestions regarding the farm and cattle were always intelligent. Her foresight was accurate. And her willingness to work hard was unmatched—except maybe by his.

As his horse reached the top of a rise, he reined in, sat back in his saddle, and swept his gaze over his land. The acreage spread out for as far as he could see, endless grass bending in the wind, as though kneeling in reverence to the white-capped mountains in the distance.

The sorrow that had been plaguing him since getting Flynn's letter a few days ago reared up and kicked Wyatt in the gut. If only his ma had been able to come and see all this . . . she would have loved it.

And now with the war dragging out, he was worried about all three of his brothers joining up. He was surprised Flynn wasn't fighting yet but was relieved that with Ma gone, he was still home taking care of things.

Wyatt reckoned he'd be fighting for the Union himself if he lived in the States. The honest truth was that he'd thought about going back a time or two and enlisting. He wanted to do his duty like the next man. But out here, they were too far away from the conflict. By the time they left and traveled east, the war would likely be over.

Even so, he should have sent for Ma—for all his family—sooner. He could have written to Flynn early in the summer, once the cabin was ready, and told them to come.

Wyatt swallowed hard and pushed down the guilt that came with the grief. He'd had years to make something of himself and to find a way to save Ma. And, blast it all, now he was too late.

A nip in the breeze slapped his cheeks. With November just around the corner, the days were not only growing cooler, but shorter, giving him less daylight for finishing all that needed to be done before winter set in.

His gaze snagged upon the cabin. At the sight of a thin curl of smoke coming from the cookstove pipe, his heartbeat gave an extra thump. He'd only been gone for three days, but with the eagerness driving him, anyone else would have guessed he'd been gone for three weeks.

He'd never felt this way after a trip. Then again, this was the first extended time he'd been gone since marrying Greta back in August. He could admit he'd been nervous about leaving her and Astrid behind, even if Judd had assured him he'd stick close to home.

His anticipation was mounting as he drew nearer. Anticipation for seeing Greta's beautiful smile and the sparkle in her eyes. Anticipation for hearing her voice. Anticipation for catching up on all she'd done the past few days.

More than that, she had unending confidence in his abilities in a way no one else ever had. She didn't flatter him or give him false hope. But because she believed he could do anything, he almost believed it for himself.

He nudged his horse forward, the movement shifting the direction of the cow and spurring her to move faster.

There was something satisfying in knowing he was returning home to someone and not just an empty house. He loved that whenever he came around, she stood in the doorway or sat back on her heels in the garden or paused in whatever task she was doing to watch him approach.

More and more lately, he'd been tempted to go right over and pull her into his arms. It was getting mighty hard to keep his hands and thoughts from her. He hadn't been able to stop himself from reaching for her in the livery. . . .

It was a good thing they had less than two weeks of their trial to go.

With everyone thinking they were expecting their first babe, maybe he oughta hurry on up and make their marriage official. If he did and she got pregnant, then he wouldn't have to worry anymore about how to explain she wasn't in the family way.

The very thought of holding her for as long as he wanted sent flames shooting through his blood. "Good Lord," he whispered, turning a plea heavenward. He threw open his coat to allow the air to cool him down, and he slipped off his hat to let the breeze ruffle his hair.

If only Steele had kept his big mouth shut and wasn't so doggone pushy. Yep, he understood Steele wanted to bring his wife and son west. Yep, he understood he'd shaken hands with Steele and told him he'd have a real marriage.

And yep, he understood Steele had already carried through on his part of the bargain by contacting the breeder in Missouri.

Trouble was, Wyatt couldn't rush Greta before she was ready, especially into having a babe. It wouldn't be right, no matter how much he liked her, and she liked him.

The big question was, did she like him enough to stay?

He patted his pocket and the ring again. It was about time to find out.

The last hour of the ride seemed to take days. By the time he drove the cow into the yard between the cabin and barn, his chest was near to hurting with the need to see her. Judd had heard him coming and was already limping toward the corral gate.

By the fading light of the evening, Wyatt watched the cabin door, waiting for Greta to make her appearance. She'd likely be wiping her hands on her apron, busy with another one of her projects.

But as he moved the new cow into the corral, the door remained closed.

"First calf heifer?" Judd gave a curt nod toward the new milking cow.

"Yep, she oughta have some good breeding years left." Wyatt's sights again strayed to the cabin, and he waited for the door to open, warm light to spill outside, and Greta to welcome him with one of her heart-stopping smiles.

But the cabin was quiet, almost too still. If the curl of smoke hadn't been rising from the stovepipe, he would have assumed no one was inside. Maybe she wasn't as excited to see him as he was her.

"How'd things go?" He followed the cow into the corral.

"Astrid's been in a bad way." Judd's voice was low, and the grooves in his leathery face cut deep.

"Worse than usual?"

Judd closed the gate and took his time latching it. "Not much."

Greta must have heard his arrival by now. What was wrong? He studied the lone square window next to the door and wanted to ply Judd with a dozen questions. But Judd wouldn't say much more than a rock buried in dirt.

When Wyatt had told Judd that everyone thought Greta was pregnant, all his friend had said was, "*The more you pile on the manure, the harder it'll be to come clean.*"

Maybe Judd was right. Maybe he should have come clean and been honest with Greta from the start. She was an understanding woman. With her business sense, she might have even approved of the bargain he'd struck with Steele in marrying her for the cattle.

He was in too deep now to know where to begin shoveling himself out of the heap.

Judd took the crate, peeked inside, and cracked a crooked smile.

Wyatt dismounted his horse, and after a few more minutes of relaying news about the cow purchase, Wyatt moseyed toward the barn, unable to keep his shoulders from sagging with weariness.

Judd grabbed the lead line away from him. "I got this. Go on now."

"You sure?"

"I ain't the purty one you're dyin' to see."

"You're a *little* purty," he teased.

Judd released a stream of spit that shot hard and straight

into the dirt yard. "Get on. You're gonna be as useless as a dead pig in the sunshine until you see her."

Wyatt glanced toward the house and scrubbed a hand down his grin. "You're probably right."

"I'm near always right." Judd moved on without missing a beat in his lopsided gait.

Fortifying himself with a lungful of crisp evening air, Wyatt grabbed the crate and headed to the cabin. Everything was just fine. But the minute he stood in front of the door, all his doubts crowded around him.

Why hadn't she come to greet him? What if he'd read the signs wrong and she didn't like him after all? What if he was imposing on her?

He lifted his hand to knock, but then, as with other times, he opened the door without announcing himself. After all, it was still his home, and he wasn't about to get permission to enter.

As he slipped inside, the front room was in immaculate order, the way he'd come to expect from her. Bunches of drying herbs and other vegetables hung from the rafters, filling the air with an earthy scent that made his stomach rumble with hunger. Several new shelves Judd had added were lined with jars of canned goods. The table was half filled with shucked corn waiting for preserving.

Even with signs of her all around, she wasn't in sight.

He peeked through the bedroom door to find the windowless room was dark. But the faint light from the front room gave him a view of Greta sitting on the bed with her back against the wall and Astrid curled up next to her.

Were they both asleep?

He tiptoed through the cabin until he stood in the doorway.

Sure enough, Greta's eyes were closed, and her chest rose and fell in slumber. As far as he could tell, Astrid was asleep too.

Best thing was to leave them undisturbed for a spell. If Greta was tuckered out at this time of the day, then she probably wasn't getting much shut-eye at night.

Her hand rested against Astrid's hair, her fingers motionless.

Wyatt's chest squeezed with a strange tenderness. Greta was always putting the needs of everyone else above her own, especially Astrid's. She deserved to have someone look after her once in a while. Someone like him.

After setting the crate on the floor, he silently crossed to the bed. He'd help take off her shoes and tuck her in next to Astrid. Then maybe he'd sit in the other room and listen for Astrid to stir so he could give Greta a break.

Upon reaching her, he hesitated. He didn't want to chance waking her.

Her bun was loose, strands having escaped to curl around her chin.

Rather than go for her shoes, his fingers had a mind of their own and stretched toward her chin and the stray hair. He caressed the piece back behind her ear and admired the way her lashes fanned against her cheeks. He wanted to stroke her high cheekbone down to her lips. But he forced himself to straighten.

As he took a step back, a sigh escaped from her lips. "Wyatt?" Her lashes lifted. "You're home?"

In an instant he found himself right where he'd wanted

to be all day, lost in her beautiful silver blue eyes. "Didn't mean to wake you."

Her lips curved into a sleepy smile, and she captured his hand, cutting off his breath. "Did you have a good trip?"

"Got you a milking cow." He could hardly think of anything with her warm hand wrapped in his.

"I like you, Wyatt." Her voice was still groggy. She'd said those words to him before, and they never failed to stir him. But this time, he wasn't sure if he was satisfied with just the liking and her sweet way of expressing her appreciation.

He rubbed his thumb over her hand, relishing the rare contact with her.

She tugged his arm. "Sit for a minute and tell me about your trip."

"Naw, I want you to sleep. We can catch up later."

"I missed you." Her words came out like a plea. But in the next instant, she dropped her gaze to Astrid, as if mortified by her declaration.

She'd missed him. That was something more. He lowered himself to the wooden beam that formed the edge of the bed frame. He was afraid that in her embarrassment, she'd pull her hand from his, so he tightened his hold.

"Hey." He caressed her hand again with his thumb. "I missed you too."

Her lashes flew up, and her eyes widened. "You did?"

"Yep. A whole lot." He might as well spill the truth. "I was mighty ready to be home again."

She lifted her free hand from Astrid and cupped his cheek. "And I was mighty ready for you to be home."

He suddenly couldn't think of anything but the fact that

she was touching his cheek. He was scruffy and unshaven and dusty, but her fingers felt as smooth and soft as a newborn calf's hide. He leaned in to her, giving her permission to stay there, to caress him, to hold him, to do whatever she wanted.

As though sensing his offer, her hand skimmed his jaw. A charge of pleasure shot through him, making him conscious of their proximity. Before he could stop himself, he caressed her cheek the same way she had his.

At her quick inhale, he froze. He didn't want to scare her or push her away. But as he looked into her eyes, he didn't see any fear, only welcome. And desire?

A low burn started in his gut and spread into his blood. Would she let him kiss her? Right here? Right now?

He rubbed his thumb from her cheek to her lips. As his callused pad brushed against her soft fullness, she sucked in another breath, staring straight at his mouth in return.

When she imperceptibly moved toward him, he closed the distance, letting his lips touch hers and drink her in like water from a crystal-clear mountain brook. She responded with a thirst that matched his, and she slipped her hand behind his neck as though to urge him to get his fill.

Her lips were sweeter than anything he'd known, but rather than sating him, the kiss made him thirstier so that he delved deeper, needing more of her. She arched up, giving him more, her hands moving from his neck to his shoulders and down his arms, as though she needed him too.

The pressure in his chest tightened. This woman. His wife. Greta. Was he falling in love with her?

The very thought brought him to a halt, and he broke the kiss. Her soft gasps brushed his lips, the warmth, the sweetness, the pleasure overwhelming him but also settling fear deep into his bones and digging up all the doubts that had been lingering.

What if he couldn't be the kind of husband she needed and he ended up letting her down? What if his attempt at ranching didn't work out? What if he had to move on again?

Chapter 17

Greta hadn't been ready for their kiss to end and wanted to press into Wyatt, showing him he didn't have to stop, that he could go on kissing her for as long as he wanted.

Her cheeks heated at the prospect. She had a feeling such kissing would lead to more. Much more. And was she really ready for that?

Of course, not now. Not with Astrid here.

But surely there was no question she cared for him. She'd been able to feel it swelling within her over the past few days of his absence. She'd missed him more than she could explain—even to herself. And now that he was here, she didn't want him to leave.

Next to her, Astrid coughed—just lightly—but enough for Greta to know her sister would soon be fully awake.

As if realizing the same, Wyatt started to back away. Before he could get too far, she gripped a fistful of his shirt and tugged him closer. With the momentum, she pressed forward and lifted into him, letting her mouth touch his.

At her offering, he faltered. Had she been too rash in seeking out another kiss? She started to back away, but he released a soft groan and let his lips fuse with hers, moving against her hungrily and without restraint.

The passion stirred a hunger inside her as well as a realization that this intimacy with her husband wasn't merely a duty she had to endure. She longed to be with Wyatt, wanted to be closer, desired him.

At a giggling from Astrid beside her, Greta toppled from a world of bliss back to reality. She wrenched away from Wyatt, trying to put as much distance and dignity between them as possible, especially when Astrid propped on her elbow and stared up at them.

"It's okay," Astrid remarked happily. "You don't have to stop on account of me."

Wyatt shot up from the edge of the bed, rubbing his hand across the back of his neck and clearing his throat.

Greta's face burned, and she had the urge to step outside and cool off. She opted for pressing her hands against her cheeks.

"If you keep kissing," Astrid continued, "maybe we'll have two babies instead of one."

"Astrid," Greta reprimanded. "Polite young ladies don't talk about such things."

"I'm not polite. I'm a rancher."

Through the dim lighting, she could see Wyatt's lips quirk into a half smile as they usually did at Astrid's bold statements. The comments only served to remind Greta of the uncomfortable predicament she and Wyatt had gotten themselves into with the false pregnancy news. She still hadn't figured out how to graciously unravel the misunderstanding.

At a soft whine from a box on the floor, Astrid sat up. "What's that?"

"Got something for you." Wyatt stepped out of the room and returned a moment later with a lantern. After hooking it on a nail in the rafter, he bent over the crate and picked up a furry bundle.

"A kitten?" Astrid's voice rose with excitement.

"Nope. Couldn't find any kittens." Wyatt approached the bed, petting the creature in his arms. "But I did find this little fella."

He lowered the bundle into Astrid's lap, and a black-and-white puppy stared up at her with innocent and curious black eyes, his tiny nose sniffing the air, as if trying to discover his whereabouts and who Astrid was.

"Oh my." Astrid's eyes widened.

"He's adorable." Greta stroked the puppy's head and earned a lick.

Astrid followed Greta's example, and the puppy licked her too. "I think he likes us."

"I'm sure he'll love you." Wyatt reached down and scratched the dog's back.

"I hope so." Astrid did the same. "I know I'll love him."

Wyatt smiled, and his gaze flitted up to Greta's as if he wanted to share the precious moment with her. Her heart swelled with a sense of contentment and joy she'd never known before.

"What's his name?" Astrid asked.

"He ain't got one yet." Wyatt straightened and crossed his arms, which emphasized his muscles and the broadness of his chest.

"He needs to have a name." Astrid grew braver and scratched at the puppy's neck.

"Then you oughta pick one. A name fit for a mighty fine cow dog."

"He's a cow dog?"

"Yep. He'll help us with herding and chasing cattle down and keeping 'em from wandering off."

The puppy stood on wobbly legs, his ears perking and his snout lifting. Astrid touched the puppy's nose and earned another lick. "Won't he get hurt by the cattle?"

"Nope, he'll be faster than greased lightning."

"Good."

The pup wagged his tail and watched Astrid expectantly, as though ready for her to give him a name, but he was more likely waiting for her to feed him.

For a few seconds she stroked the pup, and Greta's heart ached at how thin and pale Astrid was getting. Though Greta tried to ply her sister with food, nothing appealed to the girl. Her appetite was gone, and she was losing weight at a frightening pace.

Greta had wanted so badly for the Colorado air to provide the cure for the consumption. But after the past months of mountain living and an only worsening condition, she finally had to accept that the climate wasn't helping Astrid. The move had been useless.

"What if I call him Chase?" Astrid asked.

"Chase. Sounds about right." Wyatt scratched the pup and was rewarded with a happy yip.

Astrid laughed. "I think he likes it."

The puppy yipped again, earning more of Astrid's laughter, ending in a fit of coughing that left her breathless.

As Astrid lay back, weak and pale, Greta smoothed her sister's hair off her face and pressed a cool rag on her forehead. Astrid pushed Greta's hand away and struggled to sit back up.

"Don't overdo it."

Clearly sensing her worry, Wyatt scooped up the pup. "I'll take Chase out to do his business and let him run around."

Greta smiled her thanks, but Astrid protested. "No. Please don't take him from me."

"Don't you worry none." Wyatt repositioned the squirming pup. "He'll get tuckered out and be ready for some shut-eye in no time."

While Wyatt was gone with the new puppy, Greta tried to feed Astrid a little supper and made her drink some tea. But Astrid was distracted and wouldn't rest until the puppy was back on the bed snuggled up against her. When the two were asleep, Greta crept from the room, hoping to see Wyatt one last time before he retired to the barn.

Her heartbeat sped at the sight of him sitting at the table, whittling with his pocketknife. At her appearance, he looked up at her and let his knife grow idle. For the first time since he'd returned, she let herself get a good look at him.

He was oh-so-handsome. With his hat off, she could see his dark hair was cropped short after a recent cut Judd had given him. His face was bronzed and in need of a shave. And his dark brows furrowed over his rich brown eyes. "She's getting worse, ain't she?" he asked softly.

Greta didn't want to burden him with Astrid's health, especially first thing after getting home from a long trip, but she had to say something. "She's having another flare-up."

Wyatt studied her face as though seeing past her answer to the truth. "What more can we do for her?"

She hesitated and then sighed. "I don't know." To avoid

his probing gaze, she headed to the stove, where she'd left a pot of soup simmering. She ladled out a bowl and brought it to him along with biscuits and a jar of plum jam.

She spun away to pour him a mug of coffee, but he snagged her hand and prevented her from going. "Wait."

For a second, she didn't want to face him, too afraid he'd ask her more questions and discover just how bad Astrid's consumption was. But when he laced his fingers through hers, his solid hold seemed to reassure her that everything would be alright, that he would be here to support and help her, that she wasn't alone.

Slowly, she turned to face him.

He focused on their intertwined hands. "I brought something back for you."

"I saw the plums." She glanced by the door to the basket filled with the wild fruit. "Thank you for finding them for me." Maybe this time she'd have to save the profits for herself . . . just in case she took Astrid to the hospital in Denver.

He shrugged. "I found a couple of trees, and it didn't take long to pick 'em clean."

"And thank you for the puppy for Astrid. I know she's been wanting a kitten, but I think the dog is actually a better pet for her right now."

"I'll get her a kitten too. But she might have to wait 'til spring."

"You don't have to—"

"Every barn needs a cat or two."

"True enough."

His fingers tightened against hers, sending a shiver down her backbone. When he rubbed his thumb over her hand, all she could think about was the kisses they'd shared in the bedroom and how much she liked them. Did he want to kiss her again?

Her breath stuck in her throat at the possibility. If he made the least move to do so, she wouldn't resist.

"It's not the plums or the puppy. It's something else." In the next heartbeat, he tugged her down. She shifted to sit on the bench next to him, but he guided her so that she found herself on his lap, her shoulder brushing his brawny chest. Her fingers tingled with the memory of running her hands so boldly over his shoulders and arms. Being so near only made her want to do it again. Yet she didn't dare do something so brazen and held herself stiffly, uncertain what to expect.

He dug into his inner vest pocket and pulled out a small item. "I had a last little nugget of gold I've been hanging on to. And I finally figured out what I wanted to use it for."

Her pulse pattered to a stop and a sputter of worry took up rhythm instead.

"I was planning on waiting a couple more weeks to give it to you. But now's as fitting a time as any." He lifted her left hand and slipped off the wedding band Mr. Steele had given to them. Wyatt's expression was grave, his concentration intense, which made the drumbeat of worry inside pound louder.

He placed the old band on the table. Then he held her hand and slipped on the new.

"Oh my." She took in the gold band engraved with twisted leaves that alternated green and yellow gold. "It's beautiful."

"Are you sure? The store in Leadville had slim pickings, but I was hoping it'd be alright."

She held out her hand and examined it, marveling at the intricacies of the engravings and the beauty of the colors together. It was perfect, and she couldn't have chosen anything better or more fitting. In the same breath of delight, she shook her head. "I love it, but I can't accept it. It's too nice. Much too nice."

"I want to—"

"And I'm sure it was too expensive. You need the money for other things."

"Nothin' that can't wait."

"No, Wyatt. I don't deserve something like this. Really, I don't—"

He silenced her by leaning in and covering her lips with his. As before, the touch was tender and made her forget about everything but the connection with him—one that plied open her lips as much as her heart.

This man . . . Who would have guessed how swiftly and completely she'd come to care about him? Not only was she attracted to every aspect of his good-looking body, but she loved everything about him from how sweet he was to Astrid to how hard he worked on the ranch. He had so many good qualities and was a better husband to her than she could have dreamed of having.

She suspected she never would have had this kind of relationship with Phineas Hallock had she married him, especially this kind of attraction, passion, and desire. She didn't know much about marriage, but she knew these feelings for Wyatt and this bond developing between them were special.

Just how special was it?

The question startled her enough that she pulled back. He didn't press in and attempt to continue, but his lips brushed her cheek, then her chin line, then the tender spot where her neck met her jaw.

She gasped and shifted to give him all the room he needed. His arms slid around her as though he couldn't bear to let her go. She wanted to assure him he had nothing to worry about, that she'd never leave. But how could she make that promise?

As his kiss moved to her ear, his breath, his presence, his power seemed to surround her, and she closed her eyes as heat swirled inside. He placed a kiss into the hollow of her ear before grazing downward. She clutched his shirt, trying to keep from drowning in the sensations his touch was awakening inside her.

At a rattle of the door, she released him. In the next instant, Judd stepped into the cabin, and she jumped up from Wyatt's lap, forcing him to let her go. For a second, she stood motionless attempting to gain her bearings.

Judd's bushy white brows arched high as his gaze swung between Wyatt and her. "Came to get grub. Guess I can wait."

"No." Greta rushed to the stove, mortification pummeling her. "I have soup and biscuits ready." As she stood in front of the stove, she pressed her hands against her cheeks, feeling the warmth radiating from her skin.

Behind her, Judd's boots thumped in an uneven gait across the floor. He paused halfway in.

She reached for a bowl from the shelf next to the stove, then scooped soup inside. His steps resumed until he reached the table and pulled out the bench with a scrape.

At the *oomph* he made sitting down, she released a shaky breath. Once the bowl was full and the plate piled with biscuits, she twirled the ladle in the pot. Wyatt's slurp filled the silence.

Why was she so embarrassed? She hadn't done anything

wrong by kissing Wyatt. And it didn't matter that Judd had seen them. They had every right to be kissing if that's what they wanted to do. Didn't they?

Straightening her shoulders, she breathed in and then turned, walked across the room, and placed the bowl and plate in front of Judd, all the while avoiding looking either of the men in the face.

Wyatt didn't pause in his eating, and Judd mumbled his thanks as she scurried back to the stove. She picked up the mug but then almost dropped it.

"Fixin' to head out tomorrow and cut more timber."

"Good idea," Wyatt said through a bite of biscuit. "We'll be needing the fuel come winter."

"Not for fuel. For another room."

Greta started to pour the coffee but then halted. Wyatt grew abruptly silent. And, of course, Judd didn't elaborate.

What was he implying? That she and Wyatt needed their own room now?

Oh my. Her hand shook and coffee sloshed over the rim. She set the mug down and wiped her hand on her apron, a flush rising into her face once more.

Wyatt cleared his throat. "Reckon we'll need the space come summer when Flynn and the kids get here."

His words sent an icy splash against Greta, causing a chill to skitter over her skin. Wyatt's family was coming.

"You'll be needin' a room long before that."

Greta had no doubt now what Judd was referring to, but the warmth from moments ago had dissipated, leaving confusion in its place. She couldn't allow these feelings for Wyatt to deepen, not when he had his family to think about. She wouldn't add to his worries and responsibilities, not when he needed to be there for his siblings in their time of greatest need.

Besides, she had to keep Astrid her priority. Greta had come west to save her little sister, and she couldn't forget that. No matter the personal sacrifice, she had to do whatever she could to save the child's life. And what other option did she have but to take Astrid to Denver and seek additional help?

Chapter 18

Wyatt shoveled another forkful of hay into the loose net hanging from the wall. At the sound of childish laughter outside in the corral, he paused and glanced through the open barn doors to where Judd was leading Astrid around on their mare, the gentlest of their horses, a bay Morgan crossbreed named Dolly.

The new pup raced after the horse, scampering and falling and getting right back up. Although Astrid had wanted to carry Chase in the saddle with her, Judd squashed that idea faster than a bug, explaining how the pup wouldn't turn into a good cow dog if she took to coddling him. So he'd doubled the horse lesson with dog training, and now the pup's antics were making Astrid laugh.

Astrid's laughter—along with the fact that she was out of bed—eased the tightness from Wyatt's chest. She was still pale and thin and delicate, but the coughing had lessened, and she was eating more.

Yesterday, after he and Judd had arrived home from cutting

timber, she'd been sitting outside in the sunshine braiding the cornhusks Greta had saved and dried. When Wyatt asked what she was making, she proudly displayed the round braided mat Greta had finished and placed just outside the door.

Today, when he and Judd had ridden in with the two teams of oxen dragging another batch of trunks, Astrid had already saddled Dolly and pleaded with Judd for another riding lesson. She hadn't needed to plead since Judd would have pushed her to California in a wheelbarrow if she'd have asked him.

Wyatt had gladly taken over the responsibility of unhitching the teams, stacking the logs, and now taking care of the evening chores so Judd could spend time with Astrid. They'd both learned to take advantage of her good days, because they were infrequent and didn't last long.

From the way she was riding Dolly, she probably didn't need any more lessons. In fact, from the first time Judd had hoisted her up, she'd been a natural. But with her being sick and weak, Judd was only right to be cautious.

Wyatt cast a glance to the sky. The sun hung low and the shadows were long, meaning daylight would give way to night soon. The air contained a dampness that hinted at colder weather moving in.

Was it wrong for him to wish for rain so tomorrow he could stick closer to the ranch? While he and Judd had felled a decent number of trees, they had several more days of hard work before they'd have enough to add a second level to the cabin.

He let his gaze stray to the cabin, hoping for a glimpse of Greta, but she was avoiding him and had been ever since the night he'd arrived home and kissed her. Steele hadn't been around to force him into it. The honest truth was that he'd done it of his own will and had enjoyed every sweet second. And sure as a gun, if Judd hadn't come in, he wouldn't have stopped.

Maybe he'd rushed her that night, pushed for more than she was ready to give. Now he'd gone and made things awkward between them. Sure, she was busy making the last batch of jam from the plums he'd brought her, but she was also hiding.

Pursing his lips to refrain from cussing himself out, he shoved his fork into the hay mound, lifted the brittle pieces, and stuffed more into the net. If only he could find a moment alone with her to apologize and somehow reassure her that she could have all the time she needed. And he'd also reassure her that adding on to the cabin didn't mean things between them had to change. Not until she was ready.

With the hay nets full in each stall, he set to work mucking the floors, his thoughts alternating between Astrid and Greta, and most often landing on the beautiful woman he'd married but whose heart he'd yet to win.

She'd liked the wedding band, and she hadn't taken it off once since he'd slipped it on. He'd caught her admiring it a time or two with the awe that had been in her eyes when he'd first given it to her.

At least he thought she'd liked it, the same way he thought she'd liked kissing him. But what if he'd been wrong about both?

"Can't be wrong," he muttered. She'd told him she missed him. She'd wanted him to sit with her. She'd touched him of her own free will. Fiery sparks struck to life in his gut just thinking about the way she'd kissed him back.

Astrid called out a greeting, and Wyatt looked up to see Greta striding across the yard, twin pails swinging from her hands.

He stepped into the shadows of the stall. She must be coming to do the milking. His pulse tottered like a colt learning to walk. Should he use the opportunity to talk? Or would doing so make the awkwardness worse?

She'd taken to milking the new cow three times a day. He had to hand it to her. It was a smart move to increase the cow's milk supply if she hoped to produce butter to sell. It would take some time, but eventually the cow would give her more.

For now, she was storing the churned butter in a shallow pan of cold river water in the cellar. By the time they went to town by the week's end, she'd have not only her jam to sell, but a fair amount of butter as well. It was a heap of work, but like always, she didn't shy away from it.

As she entered the barn, her footsteps crunched in the hay with the confidence of someone who knew what she wanted and wasn't afraid to go after it. He liked that about her. If only she wanted *him* . . .

He waited until she reached the cow before he let his shovel bang against the stall and alert her that she wasn't alone. He stepped into the open and waited for her to adjust to the dim barn interior.

As her eyes locked on him and rounded, he guessed she'd thought he'd gone out to check on the herd, likely hadn't expected to find him there. When she took a quick step back, he held out a hand. "Greta, hold on."

She glanced at the double door.

"I'm sorry." He had to get at the heart of what he wanted

to say before she ran off. "Sorry for the other night and getting carried away with—well, you know . . ." He pointed his finger back and forth between them, hoping she'd catch his meaning.

She watched him, her eyes rounding further. "You're sorry you kissed me?"

"Yep." He breathed out a sigh, but it caught in his throat at the dismay that flashed across her pretty features. "I mean, nope. Nope, I ain't sorry about the—" Again he waved his finger between them. "Ain't never gonna be sorry for that."

She placed the pails on the ground on either side of her and cocked her head. No doubt he sounded like a blathering idiot. "What I'm trying to say is, I'm mighty sorry for rushing you. I meant what I said on our wedding day—that I ain't a brute and won't be pushing you for anything you're not ready for." The words tumbled out awkwardly, and he shifted the shovel around, needing something to do with his hands.

After a moment, her shoulders sagged. "You don't need to apologize, Wyatt. You're not rushing or pushing me."

His head snapped up. "I'm not?"

It was her turn to duck her head. "No. I'm not sorry about kissing you either."

The heavy load he'd been carrying seemed to slip from his back. His chest felt suddenly lighter, as though he could breathe again.

She started twirling a lock of hair around one of her fingers. It was a nervous habit she had, one that was endearing.

He braced the shovel against the stall with the sudden intense hankering to hug her. Even as he took a step forward, he hesitated. "If you ain't mad about the uh—kisses"—his voice cracked, and he cleared his throat—"then why are you avoiding me?"

She wound the strand around her finger higher before unraveling and starting again. She opened her mouth and started but then stopped. Finally, she dropped her hand. "Astrid and I are only going to be a burden to you once your family comes. And I don't want that, Wyatt. I really don't." The anguish in her tone spoke of past hurts that had yet to find healing.

This time he crossed to her, praying she wouldn't bolt. As he reached her, he lifted a hand and touched the same silky pieces she'd just been fiddling with. "Listen, you and Astrid are my family now too."

"But you didn't have to take us in." Her voice was still raw. "You did it because you're a good and kindhearted man who was trying to help out and do the right thing."

Her words pricked at the guilt he'd tucked far away. He'd gotten good at stashing it into the back corners of his mind and telling himself that his deal with Steele didn't really matter. That if he'd known then what he knew about Greta now, he'd have dropped to his knees and proposed to her on the spot that first night he saw her.

"You're already working so hard to make ends meet, and you'll have to work harder when you start to support your brothers and sister."

He stroked her hair back. "We'll make do—"

"Even with the addition on the cabin, there won't be enough room. We'll be short on plates and cups, and we'll have to stretch the food—"

"We'll figure it all out. Might not be easy, but together we'll make it work."

Her brows furrowed.

He stroked at the worry lines on her forehead. "If anyone can make it work, you can. You're one of the smartest people I know."

Her features softened. "You think so?"

"Yep. You've got a real good sense for business, better than anyone I know."

"Now you're just flattering me."

"No way. Wouldn't say it if I didn't mean it." He reached to pull her into his arms, but she took a step back and braced a hand against his chest.

"There's one more thing." Her brow wrinkled again.

He slipped his arms around her anyway, fitting his hands at the small of her back and drawing her closer, intending to break down her resistance and prove that nothing else mattered except her.

At his touch, her hand dropped away from his chest, and she relaxed into him.

He enveloped her more completely, tucking her head under his chin. This was what he wanted, and he could go on holding her like this all night.

"I'm taking Astrid to Denver," she mumbled against him.

The air seized in his lungs. "What?"

"Please try to understand, Wyatt." She started to tremble in his arms. "She's not getting better here, so I have to try the hospital in Denver, the one known for helping people with consumption."

"She's better today." His voice held a note of desperation, but he didn't care. A part of him had known her leaving was coming, and now that it was here, he didn't want to face it.

"For today, but what about tomorrow?"

He followed her reasoning. Astrid wasn't improving. Lately, the girl was having more bad days than good ones. But, blast it all, that didn't mean they had to leave, did it?

Greta pulled away, and he didn't stop her. "I'd like to go before the snow in the mountains makes travel impossible." She hugged her arms around her middle but still shook.

His muscles tensed with the need to hold her close. But hadn't he promised he'd let her go if things didn't work out for her on the ranch? He couldn't go back on his word no matter how much he might want to.

And yet, if she cared about him—as she seemed to—maybe they didn't have to let the separation be permanent. Maybe they could figure out a way to stay together.

"I'll take you and Astrid to Denver. We'll go together and stay there until she's better."

"No, you can't. You're needed here. There's so much that has to be done before your family comes."

She was right, but he didn't know how to wrap his mind around letting her go. "Judd'll take care of things over the winter, and I'll hire someone to help him."

She didn't reply except to bite her lip, knowing as well as he did they didn't have a single cent extra to hire on help.

He didn't want to lose Greta. Maybe he'd once been hesitant about taking her for a bride. But now that he had her, he wasn't willing to give up without a fight. He was falling in love with her, for crying-in-the-rain. Did he dare tell her that?

"Wyatt!" Judd called from the corral. "We've got visitors."

He had half a mind to tell Judd to inform their guests he wasn't home, but the low warning in the older man's tone set him on edge.

He squared off with Greta. "We ain't through talking about this."

"I refuse to let Astrid and me be a burden to you." She straightened her shoulders.

"It's Brawley and his men," Judd said more urgently.

Wyatt's hand went to his pistol at his belt as he strode over to the rack on the wall where he kept his rifle. What did Brawley want? It couldn't be good. It never was.

"Get on," Judd said to Astrid as he deposited her into the barn doorway. The girl was concentrating on holding the wiggling pup and didn't seem to notice the seriousness of the situation.

Greta's face, on the other hand, had lost its color. She wasted no time in crossing to Astrid and drawing the girl farther into the barn.

Wyatt peered out, taking in three riders approaching the cabin, then he glanced over his shoulder to where Greta huddled with Astrid. "Stay in and don't come out for any reason, ya hear?"

She nodded, her eyes wide.

With Brawley and his men bearing down, he took an extra few seconds to swing the barn doors closed behind him and whisper a prayer that God would keep Greta and Astrid safe.

Chapter 19

Greta pressed a finger to her lips, warning Astrid to be silent. But her sister was too busy playing with Chase in a pile of hay. The pup was trying to get away, clearly not ready to put an end to his training lesson.

"McQuaid!" Brawley's voice carried over the pounding of horses drawing near.

"What do you want?" Wyatt shouted.

The stamping plod of the hooves tapered to silence and was followed by a whinny and a snort of protest.

Astrid lost hold of Chase, and the pup bolted across the barn and managed to squeeze through a crack in the door. She jumped up and raced after the dog. "Naughty puppy!"

"Astrid, no!" Greta lurched after her sister, but Astrid was already opening the door and darting through. With her heart pounding, Greta followed her sister outside. Astrid reached Chase quickly, scooped him up, and scolded him again.

Greta rushed toward the two, but Astrid was waving a greeting at the newcomers. "Hi there, Mister."

Brawley had reined in a dozen paces from Wyatt, who clutched the handle of his revolver but hadn't drawn it. Yet. Judd leaned casually against the corral post, but his hands rested on his revolvers too.

Wyatt didn't take his sights off Brawley but gestured toward her and Greta. "Doggone it. Both of you get back in the blamed barn."

Before Greta could reach the child, Astrid bounded closer to Brawley. "Mister, look, I got a puppy. Do you like him? Isn't he a sweet little thing?"

Brawley dropped his gaze. "Sure, kid. Real sweet."

Greta crept up behind her sister, wishing she could thrash the little girl.

Astrid tilted her head and stared hard at Brawley. "I figured it out finally. You sure sound a lot like—"

Greta cupped a hand over Astrid's mouth and began to drag her backward toward the barn. Thankfully, Astrid was growing too tired and weak to fight.

Once they were safely back inside the barn, Greta took the pup from the girl. He wiggled only a moment before the energy left his body, and he released a noisy half yawn, half whine. Astrid, too, stifled a yawn. The horse-riding lessons had taken their toll, and she needed to lie down.

Greta tugged her sister toward a shadowed corner where a mound of hay could provide a cushion and hopefully a place to remain safe during Brawley's visit. She bit her cheek to keep from scolding Astrid and pulled her sister down next to her.

"Greta," Astrid said through another yawn, "Brawley sure

sounds an awful lot like the fella who robbed our stage-coach."

"Hush now." Greta pressed a finger against Astrid's lips. It was pretty clear Brawley wasn't part of the Crooked-Eye Gang. How could he have been with his missing eye? None of the gang members had been wearing eye patches. At least not from what she'd seen through the slits in their sacks.

"You're not welcome here." Wyatt was responding to something Brawley had said about the nature of his visit. "It's late. Go on home."

"Heard about your bargain with Steele." Brawley persisted, his tone hard, almost bitter.

"That ain't any of your business." Wyatt's voice was just as hard. "I said to go home."

Stroking the pup, Greta lifted a silent prayer for Wyatt and Judd's safety. She'd seen the way Wyatt could shoot, and he claimed he'd learned from Judd, who was even better. Regardless, she didn't want a gun battle tonight or the chance of anyone getting hurt.

Brawley released a short laugh. "Reckon if Steele's willing to give you a loan on a herd of Shorthorns in exchange for you marrying and starting a family, he'd do the same for me."

Greta sat up, and her fingers stilled. What had Brawley just said? That Mr. Steele had given Wyatt a loan for cattle in exchange for marrying her?

She swallowed hard against a sudden tightening in her throat. It couldn't be true.

"That ain't how it is," Wyatt said.

"I'd have done the same thing in your place. Might as well get a wife and cattle all in one deal."

Deal? The knot inside slipped lower into her stomach and cinched hard. Was that what she really was to Wyatt? A part of some kind of deal?

Her thoughts returned to the night she'd first met him, how reluctant and nervous he'd been to propose. He mentioned that Mr. Steele had been the one to suggest he approach her. But he never indicated he'd done so to gain the cattle deal.

"What do you want, Brawley?" Wyatt asked. "Why are you here?"

"Tell Steele to offer me the same thing."

"Go on and ask him yourself."

"I did, and he said no."

"Then there ain't nothin' more to be done."

Greta shut her eyes to fight back sudden tears. It all made perfect sense now. The wedding at Mr. Steele's house. Mr. Steele's insistence that they share a wedding kiss. Even the kiss that day in the Hotel Windsor when she'd sold her first batch of hand pies to Mr. Fehling. Mr. Steele had all but ordered Wyatt to kiss her, and he'd gone along with it.

And the news of the baby? Was that why Wyatt hadn't been more forceful in correcting Mr. Steele's false assumption? Because Mr. Steele expected him to have a family as part of the bargain?

Maybe Wyatt's kisses this past week had been nothing more than his attempt to woo her into bed and get her pregnant. His apology from before—was it part of his selfish scheming?

Greta pressed a hand against her mouth. She'd easily fallen into Wyatt's arms just minutes ago and believed he didn't want to lose Astrid and her after he'd offered to accompany them to Denver. But it had all been a farce, just his way of trying to keep her so Mr. Steele didn't cancel his loan.

What about the wedding band? She fingered it as she had dozens of times since he'd slipped it on. It was exquisite, the most beautiful ring she'd ever seen. She'd thought he'd given it to her because he truly cared. But had it been one more part of a ploy?

The ache in her heart swelled so swiftly and painfully that it pushed for release. She managed to capture a half groan, half cry in her hand.

"What's wrong?" Astrid peered up at Greta.

Greta could only shake her head and blink back tears. She couldn't concentrate on the rest of Brawley and Wyatt's argument—just more of the same threats.

"First you steal my land." Brawley's voice had risen and was taut with anger. "Then you steal my business buying up cattle from the miners. And now you're stealin' my right to be the first to bring in a herd."

"Ain't no one stealing nothing from you. Go find your own investor."

"Or maybe I oughta do what I've been aiming to do all along. Run you out of here."

At the clicking of hammers on the guns, Greta tensed. No matter how angry she was at Wyatt, she didn't want the brawl to end in someone's death.

"Go on now." Wyatt's voice was low and menacing. "Time for you and your men to be on your way."

The silence lengthened until at last the jangle of spurs and harnesses mingled with the thud of horses galloping away.

When silence settled over the barn and outside corral, Astrid pushed up. "Are we gonna be okay now, Greta?"

She wanted to nod and assure her sister everything was fine. But the ache in her chest hurt too much and was growing more painful with each passing moment.

As the barn door swung open and Wyatt stepped inside, he searched the shadows for them, his brows slanted with worry. Astrid stood, drawing his attention. "Are those mean guys gone now, Wyatt? Is it safe for us to come out?"

"Yep. You're safe."

Greta rose more slowly, and as she stepped forward, she wasn't sure she'd be able to walk, at least not without shaking.

Wyatt took his time replacing the rifle on the rack. When he turned, he removed his hat and stared at the ground in front of him, his head hanging and his shoulders sagging, leaving Greta no doubt of his deception.

Astrid took Chase from Greta's arms and set him down. He sat and stared up at Greta with cute black eyes, as if waiting for her to say something.

What should she say? Could she even speak without crying?

"I'm sorry, Greta."

"I don't want to hear it. Don't apologize to me again."

"This ain't what it appears—"

"It appears you married me in order to get cattle. A wife for cattle. Isn't that right?"

Wyatt jammed his fingers through his hair and blew out a loud breath. "I asked Steele if he'd be willing to invest, to give me a loan, and he said he'd do it if I married you."

Though Brawley had said the same thing, the words straight

from Wyatt's mouth pierced her. "And he expects you to have a family?"

Wyatt shifted and kept his gaze trained on his boots. "You heard him yourself. He's fixin' to make the town a place with other children and families. Figures if he does, then his wife and son will come live here with him."

"So that's why you don't want me to leave and take Astrid to Denver?"

"Take me to Denver?" Astrid said from where she knelt stroking the puppy. "Why are you taking me there?"

"Nope," Wyatt said. "That ain't why—"

"Tell me the truth, Wyatt." Greta stepped forward, the pain radiating into her limbs and somehow giving her the strength she needed to confront him. "If Steele hadn't offered you the cattle loan, would you have married me? Simply to help me out?"

He twisted at the brim of his hat.

"Why are we leaving, Greta?" Astrid stood, her thin body rigid. "I don't wanna go."

Greta put her hand on the little girl's head, trying to comfort her but unable to reassure her of anything, not when the world was crumbling beneath their feet.

"I don't want you to go either," Wyatt said.

"Answer my question, Wyatt. Would you have married me without Steele's loan?"

He was silent for several heartbeats. Then he shook his head, almost sadly. "I don't rightly know."

"Probably not?"

This time he didn't reply, which gave her the answer she didn't want. Wyatt hadn't intended to marry her to help her out or for his old friend Phineas's sake or even because he wanted the companionship. He'd done it for one reason and one reason alone—for cattle.

Tears stung her eyes. She had to get out of the barn now, before she lost control of her emotions and started sobbing. She didn't want Wyatt to see how much he'd hurt her.

"Come on, Astrid." She reached for her sister's hand. "We need to go pack."

"No!" Astrid held her arms stiffly at her sides.

"Wait and hear me out." Wyatt started toward her.

Greta held out her arm to halt him.

He stopped, his beautiful brown eyes tortured. "You gotta believe me, Greta. Things might've started out for the wrong reasons, but it ain't like that anymore."

She blinked to hold back the tears threatening to spill out.

"I like having you and Astrid around." His tone was low and sincere. "I like it a real lot."

Deep inside she sensed the honesty of his confession. He couldn't have pretended everything.

Even so, how could she trust his motives again? How would she know if he truly cared about her or whether he was trying to win her over to keep Mr. Steele happy?

"It doesn't matter anymore," she said more to herself than Wyatt. "I told you I need to take Astrid to Denver, and now knowing you never really wanted us just makes it easier to go."

"Greta, please." His expression radiated anguish. "I don't want to lose you or Astrid."

"Why?" She forced the question through her tight throat as she slipped off her wedding band. "So you don't lose your cattle deal with Mr. Steele?"

Without giving him time to answer, she marched to him and thrust the ring into his hand. Then she grabbed Astrid's arm and headed to the barn door.

Though Astrid struggled against her, Greta held on tightly as she exited and started across the yard. Judd stood silently next to Dolly holding her lead line, no doubt having heard every word of her argument with Wyatt. She could feel him watching Astrid and her with troubled eyes. She suspected he'd known all about Wyatt's dealings too, and part of her wanted to blame the old ranch hand for staying silent. On the other hand, knowing Judd, he'd likely been an unwilling participant in the whole scheme.

"Wait!" Wyatt strode out of the barn. "Please, Greta, let me say more."

She picked up her pace, practically dragging Astrid along. She couldn't fall prey to Wyatt's charm. If she let him get anywhere near her, he'd sweet talk her into doing whatever he wanted, just as he'd been doing all along.

"We're leaving tomorrow," she called. "Please don't try to stop us."

Distant gunshots echoed in the stillness of the evening, causing her to stumble to a halt a few paces from the cabin with Astrid bumping into her from behind. Who was shooting and why?

Wyatt and Judd had both grown motionless as well and were staring toward the north pasture behind the barn.

More gunshots resounded in close succession.

Wyatt exchanged a glance with Judd. "You don't think it's Brawley, do you?"

"Yep. Has to be."

"Tell me they're hunting."

"More like rustling." Judd's lips formed a grim line beneath his bushy white mustache.

Wyatt spun and stalked back into the barn. The moment he disappeared, Greta's legs turned as wobbly as jam, and she had to hold on to Astrid for balance.

"What's rustling, Greta?" Astrid stared at the horizon as more gunshots filled the air.

"Stealing." As upset as she was at Wyatt, she didn't want him to lose his cattle, not after how hard he'd worked to build up his small herd.

"They can't just steal them, can they?" Astrid bent and picked up Chase. "They'll get in trouble if they do."

"Let's pray that's the case."

As Judd limped into the barn after Wyatt, Greta's muscles tightened with dread. A moment later, Wyatt emerged atop his horse with Judd following on his mount, both carrying their rifles.

They weren't thinking of riding out to the north pasture and fighting Brawley over the cattle, were they? Brawley's parting words echoed in her head: *"Maybe I oughta do what I've been aiming to do all along. Run you out of here."*

Wyatt reined in his horse near them. "Take Astrid and stay in the cabin." His eyes flashed with anger, and his jaw was set with determination.

She wanted to tell Wyatt not to go, that it was too dangerous, that she was afraid of what might happen to him. But she bit back the words that weren't hers to say anymore. Even if such a warning had been within her rights, he wouldn't listen anyway. He was the kind of man who did hard things, who didn't shrink from danger, and who wasn't afraid to protect what was his.

As much as she admired those qualities about him, she didn't want him to go out and fight Brawley, not with the angry threats still ringing in the air.

"Don't come out until we get back!" Wyatt called, and then without another glance, he slapped his horse into a gallop.

Chapter 20

Wyatt's pulse pounded with fury. Riding low, he nudged his heels into his horse and urged it faster. Behind him, Judd's steed kicked up grass too.

He wasn't about to let Brawley drive his cattle off his land. No how, no way. He'd paid for each of the steers, branded them, and invested hours into fattening and watching over them. Brawley couldn't get away with this. And he had to know it. Anyone with eyes in his head would see Wyatt's brand, the block *Mc* seared into the hide, and sort out which cattle belonged to him in no time.

Wyatt just prayed his pesky neighbor was doing nothing more than riling up the cattle and driving them into the foothills.

The setting sun cast shades of pink and purple all across the mountain peaks. Daylight was fast fading, and he and Judd wouldn't have much time to round up the spooked herd before darkness fell.

"There!" Judd pointed to the northeast.

Wyatt squinted where Judd indicated, but he couldn't make out anything but grassland, brush, and boulders. Doggone it all. He should have figured with the way Brawley was all-fired up that he'd find a way to make trouble.

When Judd pulled ahead and veered toward one of the boulders, Wyatt followed, only to have his heart plummet when he realized it wasn't a boulder.

It was one of the steers. Down. On its side.

With growing horror, he glanced around to the other forms that at a distance had looked like large stones. Now up close he recognized them for what they were. His cattle.

Judd reached the nearest steer first and was already hopping to the ground by the time Wyatt stopped next to him. Judd knelt and placed a hand on the steer's flank. But Wyatt didn't need to dismount and examine the animal. The blood trickling out of the bullet hole in its head told Wyatt everything he needed to know.

Brawley and his cowpokes had killed his cattle. Every single one.

The prostrate bodies were scattered over the grassland. None of them moved, not even to twitch. The rage that had been rampaging through Wyatt's veins faded away to nothing, leaving him strangely empty, except for the haunting chant: *You were a failure, and you'll always be a failure.*

Ever since Greta's arrival, he hadn't been setting store by his past mistakes. He wasn't exactly sure what about her caused the chant to disappear. Maybe her confidence in him and her confidence in herself made him believe everything would end up alright. Or maybe it was their partnership and the way they worked so well together in running the ranch.

But he'd gone and lost Greta and had only himself to blame. He should have done the right thing and made sure she knew from the start exactly what kind of deal he'd made with Steele. Instead, he'd walked a mile around the issue, hoping it would go away on its own. Now she was the one going away.

And the voice was back, yelling at him louder than ever that he didn't have what it takes to be a rancher. He scrubbed a hand over his mouth and down his bristly chin.

Maybe all this time he'd been fooling himself into believing he'd be able to build a livelihood on the land that could eventually become self-supporting. But this place was too untamed. His enemies were too unyielding. And his luck was all used up—if he'd ever had any to begin with.

Judd stood, removed his hat, and peered around at the needless carnage. His leathery face was grave.

The despair inside Wyatt burrowed deeper. On top of all his other shortcomings, he'd also let down Judd. When he'd asked Judd to stay and help him build the ranch, he promised him a new and exciting opportunity along with the chance to put down roots here in this land of beauty. But now, what was the point in staying? Their herd was dead. And his deal with Steele was dead too.

All along, a part of him had known the deal wasn't right, that he shouldn't have bargained over a woman's life. He should have called things off and figured out another way to build the herd.

A gust of cold wind whistled low against the earth and rustled the dry grass, as though calling him to mourn. The coldness reminded him of winter's approach and the bleakness of the months ahead. Wasn't much he could do now.

But come spring, he could claim a homestead on the plains and give farming a try. At least he had the know-how.

Judd held his hat over his heart and bowed his head, no doubt praying.

Wyatt expelled a tight breath. He wasn't sure he wanted to pray any more. Not when God didn't seem to care a lick about helping anything in his life to go right.

After several more moments of silence, Judd replaced his hat and then stood back to take in the scene again.

Another gust of cold air buffeted Wyatt, taunting him about everything he'd lost. "Not every day a man loses both his wife and his livelihood."

Judd turned to his mount and retrieved the rope from the saddle. "You ain't lost either yet."

Wyatt snorted. "I know you ain't deaf or blind. You heard Greta and you see this." He waved toward the dead cattle. "I'm done."

Judd knelt and wrapped the rope around the hind legs of the steer. "You can walk away every time the flies start bitin'. Or you can swat 'em until they're gone."

"Huh?" Wyatt was used to Judd's adages and respected him for his experience and wisdom. But sometimes, he wished his friend would just come out and say what he meant.

Judd knotted the rope and then sat back on his boot heels. "Problem with you young pups is that you expect things to be easy, and then the minute they're not, you pack up and hightail it out."

"I ain't expecting nothin' to be easy. You've seen how hard I've been working for months." Wyatt couldn't keep the frustration from rising with his voice. "Poured my heart and life into this ranch. And for what? What do I have to show for it? A herd of dead steers, that's what."

"Quit your blubbering," Judd muttered, standing up.

"I ain't blubbering."

"Could have fooled me."

"Things are always going wrong for me. Can't seem to make a go of anything I set my hand to."

"Things always go wrong. Just the way it is in a broken world." Judd shot a stream of spit straight into the dirt. "We can call it rubbish and throw it away. Or we can pick it up and fix it as best we can."

Wyatt shook his head. Judd didn't understand what his life had been like, all his efforts to make a way for himself so he could build a new home for his family. Something always put a hitch in his plans and kept him from succeeding.

"Been hanging my hat on something my ma taught me from the Good Book," Judd continued, jawing more now than he had in a month. "She always said, we ain't supposed to be surprised when we come against fiery trials. If the Lord suffered, then we gotta expect the suffering too."

Wyatt wanted to respond that he wasn't surprised by fiery trials, but as he glanced around the growing darkness at the dead steers, his inner dickering fell silent. Had he expected the good Lord to take away his problems and make everything work out? What if he'd been pulling away from God and blaming Him when things didn't go the way he wanted?

Fiery trials. Reverend Zieber had recently preached about the three men who'd been thrown into the fiery furnace for not worshiping a false god. The onlookers had seen not three men in the fire, but four. God hadn't taken them out of the fiery trial. He'd walked with them through it.

Was that what God promised? Not to pluck him out of difficulties but to be there in the midst of them?

"So"—Wyatt tried to make sense of everything—"you think I need to stay put instead of walking away?"

"Yep. Instead of seeing dead steers, it's time to see beef." Judd started toward the next steer.

Beef? The cattle hadn't nearly reached the weight and size he'd hoped for. But Judd was right. If they butchered them before the meat turned rancid, they could salvage this mess and sell off the beef. Their profit wouldn't be hefty, but it would be something.

"Time to pick up your suspenders," Judd said, "slap 'em over your shoulders, and get to work."

Wyatt hopped down from his mount and retrieved the rope from his saddle, guessing that Judd planned on moving the steers closer together for the night so they'd have a better chance at keeping bloodthirsty wild animals away while they worked.

It would be a long, hard night ahead. And an even longer few days to come. But instead of calling it quits and moving on, maybe this time he'd learn to pick things up and fix them as best he could.

At some point, Judd returned to the homestead for more supplies, including lanterns. When he returned, Wyatt was surprised to see Greta with him. From where he knelt in a puddle of blood, he had half a mind to stand up and shout at her to go back to the cabin, that she shouldn't be here.

At the sight of the dead cattle, she cupped a hand over her mouth, and he thought she'd be sick to her stomach. But then she straightened her shoulders and dismounted. She emptied the contents of her saddlebag, including knives, a sharpening stone, and bone saw. Once she'd stacked them, she approached, carrying a skinning knife.

"If you sever the head and feet and slit the breastbone," she said, standing over him, "I'll start skinning."

He jabbed his blade farther toward the spinal cord, rocking it back and forth. "You shouldn't be out here. Go back with Astrid."

"Astrid's just fine. She's asleep." She jutted her chin. "I'm staying and helping."

"Judd and me, we can take care of things."

"We'll have a better chance at saving the meat if we work together."

He'd already bled several of the steers, but he had a dozen left to go. Dusk had fallen, and though the moon above was full and bright, the lanterns Judd and Greta had brought along would be real helpful.

She would be real helpful too. After growing up on a farm, no doubt she had plenty of experience butchering pigs and chickens, maybe even a cow. Fact was, he couldn't turn down her offer. At the same time, he didn't want to subject her to the hours of bloody work ahead.

"Let me help you, Wyatt," she said softly.

When he glanced up, her beautiful eyes were filled with compassion. Even though she had every right to be angry and hurt, she didn't have a spiteful bone in her body.

"Fine. Bring me the bone saw, and I'll get one of the steers ready for skinning."

Throughout the long hours of the night, they worked ceaselessly—bleeding, skinning, and cutting the cattle. As they did so, his attention kept straying to Greta. She scraped the hides, never stopping to rest, working as efficiently with the cattle as she did with her jams.

Had he been as wrong about giving up on her as he'd been with the ranch? Did he need to find a way to hang on and fight for her, for them?

He had to convince her to stay a few more days, at least until he was done with butchering and selling the beef. He couldn't do anything or go anywhere until he salvaged what he could of his herd. But after that, he'd travel to Denver with her and Astrid for the winter. Now without the cattle, Judd could more than handle the ranch by himself.

First he had to persuade her to give him a second chance, and he prayed to the good Lord she would.

CHAPTER 21

Greta awoke with a start. At the sight of sunlight pouring through the windowpane in the front room, she bolted upright in bed. The movement shot fire through every muscle and brought back the memory of the long night.

Before dawn, Wyatt had insisted she return to the cabin and asked Judd to take her back. Though they still had over half the cattle to finish butchering, she'd been too tired and cold to protest.

They'd stopped by the river to wash the blood from their hands. She'd already been frozen down to her bones from the frigid temperatures. And the iciness of the river had confirmed the urgency of making it out of the high country to Denver before it was too late.

Even so, she couldn't leave Judd and Wyatt in such desperate straits. Though they hadn't said so, she guessed they'd work through the day and again into the night until they finished the job.

After packing up a basket of food and coffee, she'd given

it to Judd with the promise to bring more at noontime. She fed the chickens, milked the cow, and watered and fed Dolly and the four oxen that hadn't been out in the pasture with the others. Then she'd fallen into bed next to Astrid.

Greta shoved the covers away and glanced again at the bright sunshine, attempting to gauge how much time had passed. She sensed it was later than she'd anticipated.

"Astrid?" she called as the cold of the cabin enveloped her and sent chills across her skin. She'd shed her garments from last night, and now they sat in a heap next to the bed, the blood splatters turning brown and crusty as they dried. Did she have time to scrub out the blood to prevent staining? She had so few garments and couldn't abide losing an outfit.

Attired in only her shift, she touched her feet to the cold floorboards and shivered. "Astrid?"

When the little girl didn't answer, Greta pushed all the way up and shuffled out of the bedroom, her muscles protesting each step. She glanced out the window, expecting to see Astrid with Chase. The chickens roamed the yard, but otherwise it was deserted without a sign of the girl or the pup.

Frustration pooled inside Greta. Before climbing into bed, she'd stressed to Astrid the need to stay in the cabin for the morning, explaining what had happened to the cattle. The girl had been sullen and quiet and had rolled over, ignoring Greta. At the time she'd been too tired to reprimand Astrid.

Returning to the bedroom, Greta heaved a breath. Hopefully, Astrid was just in the barn and hadn't decided to go fishing. Greta didn't have time this morning to track her down.

She dug through the trunk to find her oldest skirt, trying not to disturb her packing from the previous evening when her anger at Wyatt had given her all the energy she'd needed to place everything she and Astrid owned back into their trunk and bags.

Astrid had tried to stop her but had been too tired and resorted to curling up next to Chase in the bed and crying. "Please, Greta," she'd pleaded through her sobs. "Please don't make us leave."

"We have to go." Greta knelt in front of the trunk, folding another of Astrid's skirts. Although she wanted to gather the girl in her arms and comfort her, she stiffened her backbone in order to make herself stand firm against Astrid's pleas and wiles.

"Wyatt's real sorry. Real sorry. I could see it. And he said he wants you and me to stay."

"It doesn't matter what Wyatt thinks." Greta continued arranging the garments into a neat stack. "What matters is that you get better. And since you're not getting better here the way I thought you would, now we need to try the hospital in Denver. Now before snow covers the mountain passes."

Greta would probably earn enough for the stagecoach fare once she sold the butter she'd churned with cream from the new cow. But she didn't know how she would afford the care or the lodging after they arrived in Denver. All she knew was that she had to get Astrid the help.

"I don't want to go to a hospital." Astrid hiccupped through her sobs.

"We have to try it. It's all we have left."

"I want to die here." Tears streamed down the girl's cheeks. "Please, Greta, let me die here where I'm happy."

Greta's heart, already aching from Wyatt's betrayal, couldn't hold any more pain. "You're not dying, Astrid."

"I am, and we both know it."

"We can't give up yet."

"I'm not giving up; I'm just being realistic." Astrid sounded much too grown-up.

Greta shook her head, unwilling to listen to the child's gloomy predictions any longer. "I'm taking you to Denver tomorrow. So please resign yourself to leaving."

She'd turned her back and held herself together until Astrid's sobs had given way to slumber. Only then had she broken down and let the tears flow—tears for Astrid, for Wyatt, and for broken dreams. She'd still been crying when Judd had galloped into the yard and delivered the news that Brawley had slaughtered the cattle.

After that, she hadn't had time to grieve. She'd been too consumed with helping Wyatt and Judd to feel sorry for herself and Astrid. Now, by the light of day with the trunk and bags staring at her, Greta's heart grew heavy again.

She dressed quickly and then put a pot of coffee on the stove before starting her search for Astrid. As she crossed to the barn, the late-morning sunshine bathed her and brought warmth to her aching body. She glanced to the distant north pasture and pictured Wyatt as he'd been all night, bent over the dead steers, working feverishly to butcher them.

Deep inside, she knew she couldn't remain angry at Wyatt for what he'd done. The truth was, she would have entered into the marriage of convenience even if she'd known fully about his cattle deal. She'd been too desperate to care.

And as much as he'd used her in an attempt to get what he needed, she'd used him to be able to stay in Fairplay and take care of Astrid. How, then, could she condemn him for being selfish when she was equally so?

At least he'd been honorable in keeping their marriage chaste. He could have taken advantage of her and used her in other ways, but he'd had the decency to give her a way out if that's what she wanted.

Maybe he should have been more up-front with her about his arrangement with Mr. Steele, especially once they'd gotten to know each other better. But Wyatt had probably been worried about her reaction—and last night she'd proven he had reason to worry.

Now after losing his herd, he needed the loan from Mr. Steele if he had any chance of making it. Yet, once she left, Mr. Steele would pull out of the deal, and Wyatt wouldn't be able to get the new herd.

Was there any way to help him keep the loan? Could they pretend to remain married for Mr. Steele's sake? She gave a quick shake of her head. No, they'd already let the news of the pregnancy linger all week, and she couldn't lie about anything else.

She lifted her gaze beyond the north pasture to the mountain peaks, including Kenosha Pass. The jagged rocks above the tree line were snow covered. And the snowfall would continue to accumulate. Her time was running out. All she had was today. She'd help Wyatt today, and then she needed to leave tomorrow.

Shoving aside her tumultuous thoughts, she picked up her pace. "Astrid? Come out, please." She opened the barn doors and let the scent of the recently cut alfalfa greet her. The new dairy cow bleated, letting Greta know she was ready for her midday milking. But otherwise, the barn was silent and the shadows within were motionless.

After spinning on her heels, Greta retraced her steps to

the cabin and then veered to the path that led down the embankment to the river. She called Astrid's name and searched along the bank, checking the usual fishing spots.

With mounting irritation, Greta returned to the cabin and searched the perimeter of the barnyard, hoping to find Astrid playing with Chase or lounging in the shade taking a nap. Finally, Greta returned to the barn, climbed to the loft, and searched the stalls only to realize that Dolly was gone.

She breathed a sigh of relief even as she wanted to throttle the child. No doubt Astrid had taken the puppy and ridden out to see Wyatt and Judd and offer to help with the butchering.

While doing the milking and then cooking up a simple meal to take out to the pasture, Greta rehearsed the scolding she planned to give Astrid for disobeying and leaving in spite of the strict instructions not to go anywhere. She could only pray Wyatt would have the foresight not to let Astrid stay out in the pasture overlong.

When the noon hour passed, Greta's insides stretched thin with impatience, even as she kept herself busy with the laundry. By midafternoon, she stood in the yard and peered into the distance toward the north pasture, fuming at Wyatt and Judd for not being stricter with Astrid and insisting that she come home.

As Greta paced back and forth, she made up her mind to set out by foot. It was a long walk, especially carrying food. But they'd left her no other choice. The moment she stepped out of the cabin with her bonnet securely in place and a basket in hand, she caught sight of a rider approaching.

She hoped to see two horses but realized Wyatt was returning without Astrid. She released an exasperated breath.

The child had likely twisted Wyatt's arm into staying. She lost sight of him when he reached the river and waited for him to cross over.

When minutes passed without sight of him, she set the basket down and hurried along the dirt path that led to the river. Upon reaching the bank, she stopped short at the sight of him stripped to his waist and kneeling at the water's edge.

She hid behind a bush, though the branches with their dried leaves could hardly conceal her. Her mind traveled back to the first time she'd happened upon Wyatt at the river, how he'd been in his union suit. She had been embarrassed to see him in such scant attire and also reluctant to disturb his morning routine. Since then, she'd refrained from going to the river until he had time to groom and bathe.

Now in full daylight, his sculpted chest and arms and shoulders were fully visible. As he splashed water over his arms and scrubbed away the blood, she couldn't make herself look away. She knew she ought to. She was leaving the ranch and couldn't let herself admire this man, not when she'd never see him again.

She took a step back, but then he straightened and she froze again. The sunlight glistened off the water that ran down his arms and chest into the trousers that sat low on his hips. He'd discarded his hat in the grass next to his shirt, and his hair was damp and slicked back. His handsome features were made darker by the unshaven stubble that covered his jaw and chin.

He was the handsomest man she'd ever seen. She'd known it the day she'd first watched him saunter down the street toward her in Fairplay. And it was truer now seeing him this way.

She'd once marveled that he'd been interested in her since she wasn't anyone special and didn't have the ravishing beauty of some women. Now, after knowing about the cattle deal, she realized he hadn't had any initial feelings of attraction.

Even if his interest had developed over the past few months, she no longer knew how to interpret his intentions.

"And it doesn't matter," she whispered to herself sternly. It didn't matter what Wyatt thought about her. She was leaving, and he'd be free to find a woman of his own choosing when he was ready rather than having a stranger foisted on him.

"I can see you, Greta." Humor laced his voice.

She pulled herself up tall, trying to retain some dignity. "I'm sorry. I didn't know you'd be bathing, or I wouldn't have come."

"Didn't think you'd want me walking into the cabin full of blood and guts."

"True." Although, after today it wouldn't matter. The thought filled her with wistfulness. "I'll let you finish and meet you at the cabin."

Without waiting for a response, she started back up the path and was surprised a moment later when he caught up with her, leading his horse. Although he'd put his hat back on, he was still bare chested.

As he fell into step next to her, she couldn't stop from ogling him once more. Up close, his body was more beautiful, the muscles in his arms taut and bulging, his chest smooth and corded.

He slanted a glance at her and cocked a brow.

Heat infused her cheeks, and she picked up her pace. "You really should put your shirt on."

"I reckon you're right, and I apologize." He kept stride

with her. "But figured you wouldn't want to see me decked out in this." He held up his balled-up shirt, which was damp with sweat and blood and all manner of filth.

She was acting like a prude when there was no reason to. "I should be the one apologizing. You have every reason to go shirtless, and I shouldn't even be thinking about such things at a time like this."

"What things?"

"Your bare chest." The moment the words were out, she flushed again. "I mean, I shouldn't be thinking about how you look without a shirt—" She cut herself off. The more she talked, the more awkward she was making the situation. She'd do better to say nothing more about it, to change topics entirely.

"How do I look?"

"I'd rather not say." As they crested the rise, the cabin came into view, and she was suddenly anxious to disappear inside and put a safe distance between herself and Wyatt.

"Hopefully, better than I feel." He released a weary sigh, one that stirred her compassion. After all that had happened and the long hours of work, he had to be weary and hungry and frustrated.

"You look good," she conceded, hoping to encourage him but once again feeling as though she'd overstepped herself.

"Good? That's all?" His tone contained a note of teasing that helped ease some of her discomfort.

"I refuse to say anything further." She lowered her head, letting the brim of her bonnet shield her embarrassment.

He reached for her hand and stopped abruptly, tugging her to a halt next to him and twisting her until she was facing him. He stood an arm's length away and examined her from her head to her toes, the light in his eyes making her skin tingle with strange anticipation.

She waited for him to say something, but he dropped his gaze and let it wander again. "What are you doing?" She was surprised to find herself somewhat breathless.

"You got to stare at me. Figured it's only fair I get to do the same to you."

"There's nothing to stare at." She tried to tug her hand free.

He held her fast. "From where I'm standing, there's a whole lot to stare at. You're the prettiest woman I ever did see."

The tingles changed to hot streaks that raced along her limbs. Even so, the insecurity of moments ago came back. "You're just being nice."

"Nice? I ain't in the habit of saying things to be nice." His fingers tightened against hers, and with his other hand he reached up and skimmed her collarbone.

The touch was so light and unexpected and exquisite she forgot to breathe.

For a moment his fingers stalled, then he captured the fluttering ribbon of her bonnet and tugged it, loosening first one side and then the other. Before she knew it, he pushed her hat back so she was left defenseless without anything to hide behind.

As she allowed herself to meet his gaze, she lost herself in the heartache and desperation in the dark, vast woodland of his eyes. She could read there his keen disappointment in losing his cattle and now possibly having to give up on his ranch. She could read the frustration and understood it well after how hard they'd worked all autumn. And she could sense his disappointment in himself for not finding a way to make his dreams come true.

He lifted his hand, and this time he caressed her neck starting by her earlobe and ending at the hollow of her throat. Again, she couldn't breathe, could only watch the murky brown of his eyes and feel his pain deep within herself.

"I'm sorry," he whispered hoarsely. "I never meant to hurt you. And now that I've lost everything I've been working for, I realize you're all I really want."

His words, his touch, the honesty—it reached deep inside and stirred the emotion she'd been trying so hard to ignore, an emotion she could no longer deny. In spite of everything, she was without a doubt falling in love with Wyatt.

"With all that's going on," he continued, his voice still hoarse, "I know this ain't the best timing. But I had to see you and ask you to wait to go—at least 'til we can talk. I kept thinking I'd ride back today only to find you and Astrid long gone."

She started to nod, but then froze. "Hasn't Astrid been out working with you and Judd?"

"Nope." His brow shot up, and his eyes clouded with confusion.

"You're sure?"

"I'm sure as a gun."

Greta's world crumbled in one swift fell. And she knew exactly what had happened. Astrid had run away.

Chapter 22

Greta's face lost all color, and she swayed as though her legs might give out. Wyatt grabbed her arm to keep her from toppling.

"What's going on?" He tried to steady her even as his own exhaustion took a slug at him.

Her eyes widened and filled with horror.

"Calm down and tell me what's wrong."

Her fingers shook, and her silver blue eyes brimmed with tears. "Astrid's gone."

"Where'd she go?"

"I don't know. She's been gone since I awoke this morning. I thought she rode out to work with you and Judd. . . ."

"She took the horse?"

"And the pup."

His mind spun as he tried to digest the news. "She might be fishing—"

"I've checked everywhere. She's nowhere near."

He scanned the river, the banks, and the distant bends both ways. Where would a little girl like Astrid go? And why?

Greta closed her eyes and wavered again.

He slipped his arm around her, and thankfully she leaned into him, his lack of shirt no longer of concern. "Hey now. Maybe with the loss of the cattle, she decided to go to Fairplay to hunt for gold again."

"No. This time she's angry at me. She pleaded with me last night to be able to stay here. She doesn't want to go to Denver, even if the hospital there can make her better."

"So she reckoned if she ran away, she could get out of leaving?"

"It's possible. Especially since she knows that if we don't go soon, we won't be able to travel through the mountain passes."

Did Astrid think she could hide for a few days? Out in the wilderness? By herself? Wyatt's blood turned cold. Not only were there wild animals to think about, but the weather was unpredictable and the temperatures most nights fell below freezing.

"We need to find her." He started toward the cabin, guiding Greta.

"Where do you think she went?" Greta picked up her pace to keep up with him.

"I'll ride to town first and check if anyone's seen her."

"I'll go. You have to sleep."

"I ain't gonna be able to rest until she's found."

"Please, Wyatt—"

"I'm going, and nothin's gonna stop me." He'd failed his family when they needed him most, and he wouldn't fail Greta now.

When they reached the cabin, she made him sit down for coffee and a meal while she fed and groomed his horse. He and Judd had worked all night and all day, butchering each steer and then lugging the slabs of beef to the river in the north pasture so the freezing water would keep the meat fresh until they carted it to the surrounding mining towns to sell.

Judd was still at it and had finally ordered him to go. Even though Wyatt hadn't said anything, Judd had probably sensed the anxiety growing within him all day. Either that or he'd noticed the frequent glances Wyatt had cast in the direction of the homestead.

He'd expected Greta to ride out and finish helping them long ago, especially with the way she'd protested when he'd made her leave earlier. As hours passed without her showing up, he'd worked himself into a frenzy and almost hadn't stopped to wash himself up at the river before riding on to the cabin.

At the sight of her on the river path, he'd nearly wept with relief to see she hadn't left him yet. And now all he could do was pray that once they found Astrid, Greta would give him a chance to speak his piece.

By the time he was done with the meal and changed clothing, he had a fresh burst of energy and was ready to head to Fairplay.

"I want to go with." She held the reins as he climbed up into his saddle.

"I'll be able to ride a whole lot faster and search more places by myself." He settled himself and adjusted his hat. "Besides, someone's gotta stay and let Judd know what happened."

As she passed the reins up to him, he wrapped his hand around hers.

Tears pooled in her eyes, and she glanced away, blinking rapidly.

"And I reckon you need to be here if she comes back."

Greta nodded and bit her lower lip.

He squeezed her fingers, wishing he could reassure her that everything would be okay. But he'd lived in the mountains long enough to know the wild land sometimes demanded a steep payment for living there. And he just hoped this wasn't one of those times.

"Pray." He released his hold and slapped the reins. "Pray hard."

Greta watched the horizon until the sun dipped behind the mountain peaks and the chill of darkness crept in around her. Even then she sat on a bench outside the cabin, wrapped in her shawl, and refused to go inside. The lantern on a stump next to her allowed her to work on the mending, but she couldn't concentrate, her heart aching too much at the thought of Astrid being somewhere cold and alone and in danger.

She tried not to think about the cougar poised above Astrid, ready to pounce, and how Astrid had been unaware of the danger so close. But the image kept surfacing nonetheless. Astrid was foolishly fearless at times and was just a child who couldn't possibly survive on her own.

"Oh, God," Greta whispered, lowering an old pair of Wyatt's trousers to her lap, the ripped knee only halfway patched. Her prayer stuck in her throat as it had since Wyatt had ridden away urging her to pray.

God was surely weary of all her problems. Why would He want to hear from her again, with one more trouble?

At the opening of the barn door and the sight of lantern light, she shook off her melancholy and stood. Judd was awake and would need supper. When he'd ridden in from the butchering during the late afternoon, he'd been almost too weary to dismount from his horse. After she explained what had happened with Astrid and where Wyatt had gone, he nodded gravely.

Though he'd wanted to ride out and search, she encouraged him to rest first. He barely made it to the barn before he collapsed into a mound of hay and fell asleep.

Now as he limped toward her, his steps were hurried, his horse saddled and in tow.

She wasn't about to let him go anywhere without having something to eat. Before he could say good-bye, she picked up the lantern, entered the cabin, and headed straight to the stove, where she'd kept a pan of fish and potatoes on the back burner.

A moment later, the door opened and his uneven steps thumped against the floor. "I'm heading out."

"No." She hurriedly scooped a spoonful of potatoes onto a plate. "Sit and have a meal first."

He hesitated.

She crossed to the table and put the plate down, then returned to the stove and poured him a mug of coffee. When his footsteps resumed and the bench scraped, she breathed out her relief.

"I've already made enough extra work for Wyatt." She brought him the coffee. "I don't want to cause trouble for you too, not after last night."

He paused, his spoon halfway to his mouth. His white hair stuck on end and his clean shirt was buttoned haphazardly. And although his forehead was creased with extra worry lines, his eyes regarded her as kindly as always. "Ain't no trouble."

She laughed lightly, almost bitterly, at his statement. "I've been nothing but trouble to everyone, even to the Lord himself."

Judd studied her face for a moment before resuming his meal.

The weight of Astrid's running away pressed upon her again, and she wanted to go back outside where she could take up her vigil for Wyatt's or Astrid's return. Instead, she found herself in front of the window, staring through the dusty pane to the dark grassland.

"The way I see it," Judd said after the scraping of his plate turned silent, "a team of oxen can carry more together than apart."

"That's true." She kept her focus on the west, her body aching for the need to see Wyatt galloping home with Astrid trailing behind.

"We all got troubles we're carrying."

She shifted her attention back to Judd. "You have troubles?"

"Yep. Too many to count." He took a swig of coffee.

"I didn't know. I'm sorry."

He set his cup down on the table and twisted it around.

In all the weeks she'd known him, he never complained about anything. And though he was the quiet sort, she hadn't taken him for a man with a broken past. But maybe she'd been wrong. Now she waited, hoping he sensed that she cared enough to listen if he wanted to talk.

"Being here and having a family again—" he wiped his sleeve across his mustache—"it's like having an ox by my side."

Had he lost his family? She assumed he'd lived a wanderer's life and moved around too much to settle down, but maybe he'd once had a wife and children.

"With Wyatt and now you and Astrid—" his voice cracked and he cleared his throat—"the load's lighter."

"Not with Astrid and me. We're bound to make things harder, not easier."

"Nope. From where I'm sitting, that little girl is the good Lord's gift to every person she meets."

"Really?"

"Yep." He lifted his mug and took another swig, the swallow slow and pronounced.

Astrid did have a special way of bringing joy to people with her enthusiasm, optimism, and unconditional love. Perhaps that easy acceptance had been just what Judd needed to ease the burdens he was carrying from his past, whatever those might be.

"And from where I'm sitting," Judd said, "God don't consider us trouble any more than you consider that girl trouble."

"Astrid can be quite the handful."

"But I reckon you'd rather she come to you with her problems than run away."

"Very true."

"The good Lord wants us to do the same. He says: 'Cast thy burden upon the Lord, and he shall sustain thee.'"

Was it true God wanted her to come to Him with her concerns rather than keeping them to herself or trying to solve the problems on her own?

For so long, every time she prayed, she'd felt like she was disturbing God. Maybe He was waiting—even wanting—her to come to Him and let Him bear the burdens with her.

At the sound of pounding hooves, Greta flung open the door and stepped into the doorway. She strained to see through the blackness until a rider's form came into view.

Wyatt.

She searched around and behind him, desperate to see Astrid. But he was alone.

Chapter 23

At the first light of dawn, they headed toward the eastern foothills.

Wyatt pulled in a deep breath, his thoughts stuck on Astrid and where she might have gone. He hadn't witnessed any evidence of her riding to Fairplay. No one in town had seen the little girl, and none of the men in the mining camp had come across her.

He'd been mighty grateful when Steele and a dozen others had offered to form search parties and head out at daybreak, one group heading north toward Alma and another aiming for Buckskin Joe. Wyatt had promised to send word if Astrid came back during the night. And all the ride back to the homestead, he'd prayed she'd be there, that she'd gotten cold and hungry and decided to come home.

But only Judd and Greta had greeted him with disappointment because he was alone. He'd had a hankering to pull Greta into his arms and comfort her right then and there, but he'd been too blamed full of frustration at himself for failing her, for not protecting Astrid, and for not being able to keep their family together the way he should have.

Ahead, the eastern sky was a rust-colored red along the fringes of the mountains where the sun was gaining momentum. Though he hadn't ever taken Astrid to the hills east of his land, she'd heard him and Judd jawing about that area plenty enough to know what it was like. Maybe she'd gone into the woods where she figured she'd find shelter for herself and the horse.

With the cold nights, miners weren't prone to roam away from their campfires, and wild animals would wait to forage until the warmer sunshine of daytime. Even so, desperation nagged him worse than a rattler in a woodpile.

Greta was pale and silent behind him as he led the way, riding hard across the pasture. He wanted to reassure her that with everyone searching, they'd find Astrid. But he couldn't promise her that any more than he could promise her that taking Astrid to the hospital in Denver would help.

The honest truth was that nothin' was certain. Like Judd said, they lived in a broken world and hardships were a part of life. About the only thing they could do was persevere, stick together, and pray for the good Lord to make them stronger through it.

And even if he was still tempted to throw his hands up and admit defeat—the way Brawley wanted him to—he reckoned he oughta practice some of Judd's wisdom and stop walking away every time the flies started bitin'.

He tossed another glance over his shoulder to Greta and tried to fight against the old insecurities crowding in—thoughts that she'd be better off without him, that he'd never be able to provide for her the way she needed.

If only he had the know-how on what to do to make things better.

As the sun rose higher and added light to their search, they slowed down and spread out so they could cover more ground. He kept Greta always within his sight, unable to shake the fear that he was losing her and there was nothing he could do to slow down the process.

All morning and afternoon they combed the foothills, checking every last place he'd ever talked about, hoping Astrid would show up somewhere. They continued searching and calling for her into the evening. And they didn't start back toward the homestead until after darkness, silent and somber, but secretly holding out hope that maybe Astrid would be there waiting for them.

But Judd met them outside the barn with slumped shoulders and a shake of his head. He offered to ride to town to sell some of the beef and check with the other search parties. While he was gone, Wyatt tried to keep himself busy with chores and tending the remaining livestock.

By the time he headed into the cabin, he was as weary and low as a snake's belly in a wagon rut. At the sight of him, Greta pivoted to face the stove, but not before he caught sight of the tears streaking her face.

"I've got supper ready for you." She swiped at her cheeks.

Supper didn't matter a lick right now, not when she was crying. He set his hat on the table and crossed to stand behind her.

She sniffled and wiped at her face again.

Blast it all. He hated seeing her in so much pain. He hesitated a moment and then reached for her, slipping his arms around her waist, drawing her backward, and embracing her from behind.

She grew rigid.

He stilled. Had he made a mistake in trying to ease her misery? An instant later, when her body softened and melded against him, he allowed himself to relax. And when her hands came up and folded over his where he held her, he released a slow breath.

She sniffed, this time louder.

He wanted to offer her encouragement of some kind, but he couldn't formulate any words. He tugged her closer and prayed she sensed that he cared.

She leaned her head against his shoulder, her hair brushing his chin. And for several heartbeats, she let him hold her, resting against him as if that's where she wanted to be.

But then she wiggled, trying to free herself. "I'm sorry, Wyatt. I want to stay strong so I don't bother you."

"Hold on now. You're not bothering me—"

"You've got enough to take care of with the beef, and instead you spent your entire day searching for Astrid." She reached for a spatula and the pan, but he stopped her by turning her around so she was facing him.

"Listen to me." His tone was stern but soft, and he held her upper arms so she couldn't escape. "Nothin', and I do mean nothin', is more important than finding Astrid, ya hear?"

Biting her bottom lip, she refused to meet his gaze.

"The beef'll be fine. And even if it ain't, we'll figure out how to get by."

Her beautiful eyes welled with tears. "I hate that I'm causing you so much trouble."

It was nearly the same thing she'd said to him that afternoon in the barn before Brawley's visit. "You're not causing trouble."

"That's not true. Since you brought us here, Astrid and I have only made your life more complicated and worrisome."

"You've made my life better and more bearable."

She shook her head, and tears spilled over and down her cheeks. "You're too nice, Wyatt. But I know how much of a hassle we are, especially with Astrid being sick."

"Ah, darlin'." The word of endearment slipped out before he could censure it. And with it said, he threw the rest of his caution away, wound his arms around her, and pulled her close.

She pressed her face into him, her tears dampening his shirt.

How would he convince her she wasn't a hassle? "I'm mighty glad I was there in town at the right time to get you. I'm the lucky one."

He meant every word he said, and he hoped to reassure her. But a sob escaped, and she buried her face deeper into his chest, muffling more sobs.

For crying-in-the-rain. He brushed his hand over her back. "I'm sorry, darlin'. I don't want to hurt you, but it seems that's all I'm good for."

She pulled back then and half laughed through her tears. "Oh, Wyatt. I like you."

"Then you'll forgive me for using you to get the cattle deal?"

"Yes, but only if you'll forgive me for using you to have a safe place for Astrid."

"There ain't nothin' to forgive. You were desperate."

"So were you." Her cheeks were splotchy and her eyes red, but she'd never looked more beautiful as she peered up at him, her lashes still wet but her eyes filled with—love?

Was it possible she *loved* him? Not just *liked*?

His heartbeat stuttered forward, picking up its pace. Now wasn't the time or place for making a declaration of his own love for her. But he needed her to understand that he didn't want her to leave.

Maybe if he reassured her he was serious. "I'm gonna tell Steele to call off the cattle bargain and let him know we're not having a babe—"

"No." She grabbed his shirt. "You can't do that, Wyatt. You need the cattle now more than ever."

He straightened and stood taller. He'd already made up his mind and wasn't about to let her sway him. "I need to be a man of truth more than anything."

Her fists tightened in the fabric. Her lips pursed as though she wanted to protest but was holding herself back.

"Come what may, I gotta set things right. I've been deceiving Steele, and I need to come clean with him. And this way, you won't ever wonder if I'm saying or doing something because of the deal. You'll know you can trust me."

Finally she nodded. "I understand. And I respect you all the more for what you need to do."

He let himself relax, and for the first time since holding her, he took notice of the softness of her body pressing into him, along with her warmth and nearness. The way she clung to his shirt and the intensity of her gaze sent a surge of heat through him. Doggone, he needed to kiss her.

His attention dropped to her lips. Would she welcome him? Somehow the thought of kissing and holding her seemed right, another way to offer comfort and support in the difficulties of life . . . during this difficulty of Astrid being gone.

As if coming to the same conclusion, her fingers released his shirt and glided up his torso to his shoulders. The caress sent more heat through him and slung his self-control out the window. If he kissed her tonight, he was only asking for trouble. He'd end up sweeping her into his arms, carrying her to the bed, and lying down next to her.

Although every muscle in his body tightened with his desire, tonight wasn't the right night. Before he could change his mind, he took a step back and broke their connection.

She dropped her hands, her expression chagrined.

He had another urge, almost overwhelming, to pick up her hands and kiss each of her fingers. "I'm going now," he whispered, "before I do something I might regret come morning."

"Regret?" Her eyes rounded with confusion.

"Yep. I'm aiming to talk to Steele and call off the deal before I kiss you again."

"You don't have to." As soon as her words were out, her cheeks turned pink.

With a suppressed moan, he forced himself back another step. "Yep, I have to. 'Cause next time I kiss you, I ain't gonna stop."

She dropped her attention to the floor, her pretty lips turning up into a shy smile.

He forced himself to turn and walk to the door. For tonight he had to be satisfied with her smile and the realization that when he did get around to kissing her again, she'd be good and ready. He'd see to that.

CHAPTER 24

Astrid had been gone for two full days and two full nights. And with every passing day and night, the chances that something dire had happened to her increased. Greta didn't want to think about all the scenarios, but her mind flashed with scenes of Astrid lying injured at the bottom of a ravine or lost somewhere in the mountains.

Unfortunately, Judd brought back only bad news from his trip to town. Neither of the other search parties had located a trace of Astrid anywhere, and no one in any of the mining communities had seen her.

Judd had borrowed a horse from Mr. Steele, and with his mount weighed down with more beef to sell, he left to ride up to Tarryall, looking for Astrid along the way.

As with the previous morning, Greta had the saddlebags packed with food and supplies before dawn. Wyatt decided they'd head south toward a couple of the lakes he'd mentioned to Astrid, lakes with good fishing. Greta didn't think

Astrid would attempt any fishing since she hadn't taken fishing equipment with, but they had to explore every option.

All the while they rode, Greta's thoughts replayed the conversation she'd had with Wyatt the previous evening. *"I'm mighty glad I was there in town at the right time to get you. I'm the lucky one."*

His humbleness in asking for her forgiveness had touched her deeply. As had his desire to approach Mr. Steele with the truth. Wyatt was willing to lose the cattle deal because he wanted to prove he was truthful and trustworthy. Without the cattle, what else could he do with his land? Certainly not farming. The land was too dry and the growing season too short.

He needed cattle.

If—when—they found Astrid, she needed to take the girl to Denver. But surely if Wyatt cared about her the way he seemed to, they could work out the situation. She didn't know how, but she wanted to believe there was something they could do to save the ranch.

In spite of another day of sunshine, the wind blowing from the north was cold and nipped at her ears, cheeks, and nose. The grass was covered with hoar frost, sparkling in the sunshine and crunching under the horses' hooves. She pulled her cloak around her and was thankful for the warm mittens she'd donned.

Slightly to the east of her, Wyatt scanned the ground they were traveling. In an overcoat, he held his reins with one gloved hand and braced the other against his thigh, looking every inch a rugged cowboy. His profile was etched with determination, made stronger by the set of his jaw and mouth. The shadows of his hat made his facial hair seem darker, lending him an intensity that caused her heart to sputter.

As if sensing her gaze, he glanced at her, his brows rising above his rich brown eyes, eyes that could draw her in and make her forget about everything but him. Like last night when he'd focused on her lips as though he might kiss her again. Under the spell of his beautiful eyes—and his calling her *darlin'*—she'd nearly risen on her toes and kissed him first. She'd wanted to kiss him more than anything else, had wanted to be in his arms, had wanted to lose herself with him and forget about their troubles.

She'd all but flung herself at him and invited him to stay and kiss her.

As though remembering the same, Wyatt shifted his attention to her mouth. *"Next time I kiss you, I ain't gonna stop."* The memory of his low voice rumbled through her and stoked the embers inside her. How long did she have to wait for the next time?

Embarrassed by her eagerness, she dropped her gaze to the ground, which she should be examining with as much care as he was. According to Wyatt, they had to scrutinize every detail, every turned stone, every footprint, every broken blade of grass.

The problem was, it all looked the same to her and had for miles—treeless land, the grass now brown, almost gray, with a lone prairie dog popping up once in a while to scold them as they passed.

Nevertheless, she had to focus. Astrid's life was at stake.

"Hold up." Wyatt's tone was taut and filled with warning. "Utes to the west."

In the distance, a dozen Indians rode single file, heading

to the north. They traveled briskly without wavering from their course.

Wyatt drew his horse next to hers. Only then did she realize he rested his rifle across his lap in one hand and his pistol in the other. He sat tall in his saddle, his focus intently upon the Indians. Though the natives hadn't harmed her or Astrid that day they'd visited the cabin, this party might not be as kind as the men who'd visited.

The Indians huddled in their deerskin shirts, fringed buckskin leggings, and buffalo robes, the wind rustling their long hair intertwined with beads, feathers, and bones. Men at the forefront were followed by a few women and children riding their beautiful mustangs.

Her body tensed as she waited for them to notice Wyatt and her and steer toward them. But the party rode onward without a glance in their direction. "They must not see us."

"Oh, they see us alright." Wyatt's fingers grazed the triggers of his guns. "They probably saw us long before we spotted them."

"Then why aren't they coming over?"

"I don't rightly know, but I reckon they sense a change in the weather and are in a hurry to get someplace."

A change in the weather? The wide expanse of the cloudless sky was as beautiful and blue as always in the morning. Perhaps a change was moving in later in the day.

From a distance she couldn't make out the faces of the Indians, but the tall, young Ute who'd been kind to Astrid came to mind. He'd even seemed concerned about her coughing. What had he told Astrid? Something about water being good for the sick?

Greta's pulse slowed. At the time, she'd been too afraid to

consider the Indian's suggestion, assumed he was alluding to drinking water. But what if the Indian had been referring to specific water that could help the sick? And what if Astrid remembered what the Indian said? After all, she conversed with him longer, and maybe she questioned him more about it.

"Wyatt." A trembling started in her stomach and spread to her limbs.

He remained focused on the backs of the Indians as they rode into the distance.

"Wyatt," she said again, this time more urgently.

His attention finally shifted to her.

"Do you know anything about water that might be helpful to someone who's sick?"

He relaxed his hold on his rifle. "What kind of water?"

"The day the Indians came to the cabin, one of them heard Astrid coughing and told her that water was good for the sick. Maybe there's a well? Or a pond? Or a lake with especially clear water?"

For a long instant, Wyatt remained motionless, as if trying to make sense of what the Indian had said. Then he sat straighter and tipped up the brim of his hat. "Or maybe a hot spring?"

"What's a hot spring?" she asked.

"From what I've heard, they're pools of water that stay warm all year round."

"The water never gets cold?"

"Nope. The Indians use the springs for bathing, but I ain't heard nothing about the water helping someone who's sick."

"Is there a hot spring in the area?"

Wyatt's eyes narrowed with sudden intensity. "It's a real

small one. Judd's been to it. Says it's tucked away in some hills southeast of the ranch."

"What if Astrid went to the hot spring thinking she could get better there?"

"It's about as good a guess as any that's where we're gonna find her." Wyatt started strapping his rifle back onto his saddle. "Let's pray to the good Lord you're right."

Since they were already well south of the ranch, they shifted their direction and rode hard toward the east. While they galloped, Greta alternated between pleading with God for help and silently chastising Astrid for being so foolish to believe a hot spring would help her—if that's what the Indian had told her. It was just as foolhardy as thinking that panning for gold in the river in Fairplay would recoup the money they'd lost in the stagecoach robbery.

Astrid had never been an easy child, not even when she was younger. But Greta never imagined taking care of Astrid would only get harder—nearly impossible. With the difficulties, who else would love and care for Astrid? Certainly not the stepfamily they'd left behind in Illinois. Certainly not an orphanage.

Astrid had no one left but Greta. And in spite of how hard and complicated her half sister made life, Greta loved her and wanted the best for her.

When the grassland began to rise into the hills covered in ponderosa pine, Wyatt slowed his horse. He led her for a distance along a winding creek until the vegetation on both sides became so overgrown that they were forced to ride through the water itself. After a dry summer, the creek was low and sluggish.

When they stopped to allow their horses a drink, a moose

stepped out of the brush a dozen paces away on the opposite bank. Enormous, with antlers spanning six feet across, the magnificent creature took its time drinking, its large muzzle and the furry flap of skin underneath dipping into the creek.

She and Wyatt remained motionless to avoid drawing the moose's attention. Though it seemed peaceful enough, Wyatt explained that the creature would charge at them if it felt threatened.

After the moose wandered off, they resumed their hunt for the hot spring. Wyatt didn't speak as they rode, and he paused frequently to listen, the trickling of the creek the only sound along with the rustling of aspen and cottonwood leaves.

Finally, after passing a bend in the creek, Wyatt stopped and held out his hand toward Greta in a signal to halt. He pressed a finger to his lips and pointed ahead to a clearing. Tied to a tree and grazing in the long, dry grass was a horse. Their horse. Dolly.

Swift relief clogged Greta's throat, making speech impossible. She swept her gaze over the rest of the open area in a frantic attempt to find Astrid. But except for the horse, the area seemed deserted. What if a group of Indians had come to the hot spring for a bath, found Astrid there, and had taken her captive?

Wyatt slipped down from his mount and tied the lead line around a nearby aspen. Greta wasn't sure her legs could hold her, but she dismounted too, forcing herself to remain strong.

Wyatt hiked through the brush away from the creek, and Greta trailed him. They passed several boulders, until at last she caught a glimpse of steam ahead. It was like the steam that wafted from a bubbling pot of soup on a cold day, with translucent fog swirling upward and disappearing into the air.

She wanted to shout out Astrid's name and tell her to come to her immediately. But she continued behind Wyatt, who didn't make a sound as he crept closer. The steam grew thicker, rising out of the tall grass. Behind the grassy area, the hillside was covered with more ponderosa pine, providing a shelter of sorts to the hot spring.

At a sudden chorus of barking, Wyatt paused. Was that Chase? Had he sensed their approach?

"Chase, come on, boy," came Astrid's worried voice. "Stay by me."

Wyatt started forward, striding too fast for Greta to keep up. An instant later, he was holding a wiggling puppy.

"Chase!" Astrid called. "Come back here now."

Carrying the puppy, Wyatt pushed through the grass toward the steam, breaking through and reaching what appeared to be a pond. Beneath the cloudy vapor, the water was clear and shallow, showing the rocks that formed the basin.

And there on the opposite side, submerged in water up to her shoulders, was Astrid.

Greta pressed a palm to her chest, the relief so staggering she wanted to sit down and cry.

"Hey there," Wyatt said calmly, stroking Chase. "I think this little guy misses home."

Astrid pushed up until she was sitting cross-legged. "W-e-l-l, he might've missed it, but I don't, and I'm not going back."

Emotion pressed for release, and Greta couldn't hold back. "Oh yes, you are!"

Wyatt's hand encircled hers, and his gentle squeeze stopped

her tirade. He'd discarded his gloves and left them with his horse, and now his skin was warm against hers. "We sure did miss you and Chase."

Astrid's lips faltered at Wyatt's declaration. Her hair was unbound and hung in wet, tangled waves over her shoulders. She wore only her shift, which revealed her pale, skinny shoulders and arms.

From what Greta could assess, the child was unharmed and hadn't suffered in any visible way from being out in the wilderness by herself. In fact, her face had more color to it than Greta had seen in months, if not years—likely from the heat of the hot spring.

"Since we realized you took off," Wyatt continued, "we've been looking for you night and day."

"You shouldn't have looked." Astrid lifted her chin stubbornly.

Greta started to reprimand her, but again, Wyatt's fingers pressed hers. When she glanced up at him, his eyes implored her to let him do the talking. She hesitated. She'd never had anyone to help her with Astrid before. She was used to shouldering the discipline and parenting all on her own. What if she let Wyatt share the burden, only for him to discover he didn't like carrying the load?

On the other hand, Judd had told her that a team could carry more together than apart. Did she need to trust Wyatt to bear the care of this child with her rather than pulling away and trying to do it all on her own?

His warm brown eyes waited for her permission to continue. Her heart quivered, but she gave his hand a squeeze back. He nodded, then repositioned his hand, lacing his fingers through hers. The connection told her more than words could, that he wasn't afraid to stand beside her and hold her up during this trial.

"It ain't just been me and Greta looking." His tone turned serious. "It's been Judd and half the town of Fairplay. We've all been worried near to death about you. Thought something bad must've happened."

Astrid had the grace to drop her eyes, her expression turning remorseful.

"'Cause you know this mountain land ain't an easy place to survive." He released Chase, who meandered along the edge of the hot spring, rooting among the weeds, no doubt hungry. "Especially for someone trying to make it on their own. We've got to stick together. We're better together."

When he shifted his gaze to Greta's, she sensed he wasn't just talking about Astrid but was also referring to himself and his desire for them to remain a family.

"I wanna stay together." Astrid's eyes flashed with defiance. "Greta's the one who wants to leave. Not me."

"I just want to save your life. You know that's all I've ever wanted to do."

"My life is saved." The little girl skimmed her hands across the steaming water. "The waters have made me all better. And now we can stay with Wyatt and Judd on the ranch. We don't have to leave and go to a hospital."

Greta's heart dropped. Of course Astrid, in her simplistic view of life, would think she was miraculously cured and that their problems would so easily go away.

Before Greta could figure out how to respond, Wyatt shrugged. "If you have to go to the hospital, I'm aiming to be right alongside you and Greta. And then when you're better, I'll bring you back."

"Greta's mad at you, and she won't want to come back." Again, Astrid glared at her, as if she blamed Greta for all their problems.

"I hope she'll want to stay with me." He tightened his fingers against Greta's and tugged her closer. "'Cause, the truth is, I love your sister and want her to be my wife. Forever."

At his bold declaration, Greta's breath got lost somewhere inside her. When he gently turned her to face him, he tipped her chin up, giving her no choice but to meet his gaze, which was brimming with love and longing and a plea to stay. "I mean it," he whispered. "I love you."

The words to respond got lost inside too. Instead, she reached up and cupped his cheek, hoping he could read her love in return.

"I'm glad you love Greta and want us to stay." Astrid stood and let the water drip off her bony body. "But I've decided to live here at the hot spring."

"Astrid!" Greta released Wyatt. "Don't be silly."

"I figure I'll be better out here where I won't be causing trouble for anyone."

Greta held in her exasperation. "You can't live on your own—"

"Just admit it. You'd be lots better off without me." Astrid balled her fists at her sides as though daring Greta to walk over and make her leave. "So why do you care where I live?"

Greta hoped Wyatt would step in and take over the conversation again. But this time, he was silent, and rightly so. This was between her and Astrid, and there wasn't anything he could say to make the problem go away.

"Of course I care where you live." She tried to stay calm like Wyatt had done moments ago.

"All I've ever been to you and to everyone is a burden!" Astrid's eyes were glassy with tears. "And now I don't have to be anymore."

"You're not a burden." But even as Greta spoke, the truth barreled into her. Astrid was simply following her example. She'd always considered herself a burden to everyone she'd lived with, and now Astrid was doing the same.

Regret welled in Greta's chest. "I never meant for you to feel like you're a burden to me, because you're not."

"I am." Tears rolled down her sister's cheeks. "You wouldn't have had to move here if not for me. If not for me, you'd be able to sleep better at night. And you wouldn't have so much work and worry."

With her heart breaking, Greta started forward through the tall grass, winding her way around the hot spring. Everything Astrid said was true, and yet Greta didn't care. Astrid was more important than all the inconveniences and sacrifices and work. And somehow, she had to convince the little girl of that.

As Greta approached, Astrid lifted her chin but couldn't stop the tears. Greta's own tears began to slide down her cheeks. Though her sister started to back away, Greta pulled her into an embrace, wrapping her tightly. "Oh, Astrid."

The child held herself stiffly for only a moment before she hugged Greta in return, releasing broken sobs. They held each other for a while, until Astrid's sobs tapered to sniffles. Greta knelt, pulled the girl down onto her lap, and kissed her head.

Wyatt was leaning against one of the boulders and had Chase in his arms. He seemed in no hurry, willing to give her the time she needed to make things right with Astrid.

"I haven't been a very good example to you," Greta whispered. "I've been worrying for too long about burdening everyone around me, and all that's done is made you worry about the same."

As Astrid snuggled in closer, gratefulness welled up within Greta. *Help me, Father in heaven, to do better in the future and show Astrid that she isn't a burden.*

She lifted her prayer hesitantly and then caught herself. She had to stop believing she was a burden, especially to God with her prayers.

"You know what?" She combed the wet tangles away from Astrid's face. "Being your big sister and taking care of you has made me into a better person."

"It has?" Astrid's voice wobbled.

"Yes, all the hardships we've faced have made me stronger. Watching you fight your sickness with such courage inspires me to be braver. Seeing you live with such joyfulness makes me appreciate each day all the more. I wouldn't be who I am today without you in my life."

"Really?"

"Really."

Astrid released a sigh.

Greta's eyes welled again with tears. "So don't think I'd be better off without you. Because that's not true at all."

"Okay."

She couldn't keep from smiling at Astrid's easy acceptance of the truth. Why couldn't it be as easy for her to have such childlike faith that everything would be alright?

"Maybe we can help each other," Greta suggested.

Astrid pulled back. The anger was gone from her silvery blue eyes, and they were filled with hope. "How can I help you?"

"Whenever we start to feel as though we're bothering someone, Judd told me to think on the Scripture that says: 'Cast thy burden upon the Lord, and he shall sustain thee.'"

"Cast our burdens on the Lord? Like casting a line when we're fishing?"

Greta brushed Astrid's hair again. "I guess it's a little bit like that. We toss our burdens way out into the deep flowing waters, and let Him carry them."

Astrid smiled. "I like that."

"Good." She kissed Astrid's head again. "Now let's go home. Okay? A lot of people are searching for you, and we need to let everyone know you've been found."

She nodded and stood. "I guess I won't live here at the spring after all, 'cause I need to do my part in helping you be stronger. But I want to come back. It's a real nice place, Greta. And I think you'll like it."

As Astrid started talking about all she'd done during the past few days, Greta whispered another prayer of thankfulness and then met Wyatt's gaze across the distance. His brows rose, as though he was making sure everything was alright.

She smiled her reassurance, praying everything would be okay. But a part of her couldn't keep from wondering how she'd be able to make things work out for everyone when there was still so much at stake.

CHAPTER 25

He'd told Greta he loved her and she hadn't said anything back. Sitting at the table, Wyatt took another sip of his coffee and tried to douse the sourness in his gut.

"I'm not too tired," Astrid said through a loud yawn in the other room where Greta was tucking her into bed. "I want to go with you."

"You need to sleep," Greta insisted.

During the ride back from the hot spring, Astrid had chattered about her time away, how she'd slept very little at night because she'd been cold and afraid. She'd packed enough food for her and Chase to last a few days, so at least she hadn't gone hungry. Regardless, when they arrived home, Greta made a meal of eggs, bacon, and roasted vegetables—enough to feed a dozen starving cowpokes. Then she dunked Astrid in a bath, scrubbing away the sulphur from the springs.

Judd had shown up midafternoon. From one of the peaks overlooking the valley, he'd seen the curl of smoke rising from the homestead and had figured there was news or no one would be home. When he'd galloped in and barged into the cabin, Astrid had thrown herself into the old man's arms, and he held her for a full five minutes before finally letting her go.

When Judd had stalked out of the cabin to the barn, Wyatt was pretty sure he'd seen dampness on the old man's cheeks. Although Judd rarely spoke of his past, Wyatt knew Comanches had attacked his home, burning down his house with his wife and children locked inside, while making him listen to their tortured screams. Finally, they'd beaten him and left him for dead.

Neighbors had found him and nursed him back to health, but his hair had turned permanently white and his leg had never healed right. Worse were the internal scars.

For a long while, Judd had lived a wild and restless life . . . until he'd made his peace with the good Lord. Even so, Judd had been a wandering soul for years, and Wyatt feared one day Judd would get fed up and have an itching to move on. If he did, Wyatt wouldn't blame him, especially since failure seemed to follow Wyatt around like stink on a pig.

Wyatt prayed Judd would practice his own preaching and stick with the ranch rather than walking away. On the other hand, this wasn't Judd's problem to fix. It was Wyatt's. And he didn't rightly know how to save the ranch.

All he knew was that he had to get to town and alert everyone they'd found Astrid. While there, he was fixin' to cash in on more of the beef. More than anything else, he had to talk to Steele and tell him he wanted out of the deal—and that Greta wasn't in the family way and never had been. The very thought of having to eat crow made him squirm right down to his boots. But he was determined to do the right thing, especially for Greta.

Judd opened the front door a crack and peeked through. "Not interrupting anything, am I?"

Wyatt grinned. "Nope. But wish you were."

Judd grunted, then shuffled inside and made his way to the stove and the coffeepot. "Get a hotel room tonight."

In the process of taking a sip of coffee, Wyatt choked and sprayed out the liquid. As he cleared his throat and wiped at his mouth, he glanced to the bedroom and prayed Greta hadn't heard the comment.

The older man poured himself a cup of coffee as calmly as if he'd just told Wyatt to go fishing. When he turned and limped to the table, his thick white brows rose. "Stop being so blamed afeared to make her yours."

"For crying-in-the-rain, Judd." Wyatt shot another glance toward the bedroom. Greta's head was bent, and she didn't seem to be paying attention to their conversation.

Judd sat down and slurped from his mug.

Wyatt was afraid his friend would yammer on some more, but thankfully he was a man of few words and seemed to have said all he had to say.

A few minutes later, as Greta stepped into the main room, Wyatt took a final swig of coffee and then rose from the bench. She walked straight to her cloak hanging on a peg on the back of the door and started to put it on.

"You don't have to come." He stuffed his fingers into one of his gloves. "I can handle everything."

"I want to ride with you." She lifted her chin and tied the string on her cloak, giving him a glimpse of the determination in her eyes and the firm set of her lips.

Did she reckon if she tagged along, she could somehow wrangle Steele into giving him the loan anyway? Wyatt wasn't going that route. After the lying, no doubt Steele would rather see him tarred and feathered than give him a loan. "Promise you won't try to convince Steele of anything?"

She finished with the ties and then swung open the door. "I'm not making any promises I can't keep." She bounded outside before he could respond.

He expelled a sigh, then strode after her to the horses Judd had already groomed as well as weighed down with beef to sell. Wyatt caught hold of her waist before she could climb into the saddle. At his touch, she halted but didn't pivot.

He moved in closer, and before he could stop himself, he tugged her back against his chest, hugging her from behind. She was probably getting mighty tired of him reaching for her.

"Hey," he said softly, starting to release her. "Don't know why I can't keep my hands off you."

"It's alright, Wyatt," she replied just as softly, leaning into him and letting him bear her weight.

Her words were all the permission he needed to wrap her up more fully and bend in and press his face into her hair, breathing her in. Oh Lord help him, he loved this woman.

The words felt like they needed to be said again. But he held them back, uncertainty poking at him.

"When we get with Steele, let me do the talking first," he murmured against her hair. "Can you promise me that?"

"I guess so."

He forced himself to release her and assisted her into the saddle, all the while too doggone aware of how soft and womanly she was.

During the ride to Fairplay, his thoughts locked in on

Judd's suggestion to get a hotel room. He sensed the wisdom in his friend's request. He oughta make their first night together special. Greta deserved that. But was it still too soon? And did he need to cool his heels?

She hadn't been pushing him away, but she also hadn't given him any notion she'd welcome him into her bed. She was unusually quiet during their ride into town, and he guessed her thoughts were focused on Astrid.

As they reached the outer limits of Fairplay, she slowed her horse. "I know you'll want to sell the beef, and I've got an errand to run while you do that."

When she refused to look at him, wariness prodded him like a hot branding stick. He didn't know what she was up to, but it wasn't good.

He swept his sights over Main Street. The traffic was light for the late-afternoon hour. Most miners were still at work. The taverns were silent. And the stragglers lounging around the other businesses were sparse.

Steele's yellow buggy was parked outside Hotel Windsor, and a sudden desperation welled up within Wyatt to put things right between him and Greta once and for all. "Before we do anything else, I reckon we oughta let the fellas know Astrid's safe."

"You're right." Greta tore her attention from McLaughlin's Livery and the stagecoach parked in front, the driver still unloading bags and trunks for the few lingering passengers, including a stout woman wearing a fancy red gown.

Was Greta remembering the day she'd arrived and regretting her decision to travel to Fairplay? Or was she figuring out how to leave?

Wyatt urged his horse toward Hotel Windsor and was

relieved when Greta did the same. As they dismounted and hitched their horses to the post, Wyatt noticed through the window that the dining room was crowded.

All the better. The more fellas hanging around when he delivered the news about his and Greta's marriage and the false pregnancy, the less gossip would go around later.

"Ready?" He halted in front of the door.

She nodded.

After drawing in a deep breath and whispering a prayer for strength to do what he needed to, Wyatt swung open the door and stepped inside behind Greta.

The place grew silent and every eye turned upon them. Likely every man in the room had noticed them outside and now was waiting anxiously for an update on Astrid.

What should he share first? The news about Astrid or the news about him and Greta?

Steele was at his usual spot at a center table, attired in a suit and smoking a cigar. As the door closed behind them, Steele pushed back and rose, his face a mask of concern.

Wyatt swallowed his reservations. Steele was a good man. Maybe his cattle deal had been manipulative and pushy. But he'd meant well, had Greta's best interests at heart. Now it was past time for Wyatt to be honest with him.

"Greta and me ain't having a babe," he blurted out. "And that's 'cause we haven't been living as man and wife. I've been staying in the barn."

Next to him Greta stiffened. From the murmurs rippling around the crowded room, he guessed he'd surprised everyone. The empathy on Steele's face faded as confusion rolled in.

Wyatt reckoned he should have shared the good news about Astrid first, but what was done was done. And he may as well finish saying his piece. "I know I broke our part of the bargain, Steele. But that's okay. I'm putting an end to it today. I'll figure out another way to get my cattle without using Greta as part of the deal."

Steele's expression didn't transform into anger or indignation. Instead, the gentleman glanced to his companion at the table. In a stovepipe hat and dark suit, the other fella sat with his back toward Wyatt. Something about the newcomer seemed familiar, but Wyatt couldn't focus on anything else but making sure Steele understood the truth.

Steele's attention returned to Wyatt, his eyes narrowing. "So if you haven't been living as man and wife, does that mean you didn't consummate your marriage?"

Greta sucked in a mortified breath.

"Blast it all, Steele," Wyatt hissed, cocking his head at Greta. "Now ain't the time to get vulgar, not with a lady present."

"But if she's been living with you more like a boarder and not a wife, then there's still hope for me to rectify my mistake."

A lasso wound around Wyatt's middle and cinched tight. "What mistake?"

"The mistake of giving away Mr. Hallock's bride."

The gentleman in the chair finally stood and turned. Wyatt took a rapid step back. The balding man with his vest stretched taut over his well-rounded midsection was none other than Phineas Hallock.

Greta swayed and would have collapsed if Wyatt hadn't grabbed her arm and held her steady.

"Hallock?" Wyatt took in his friend's kind face—a face he hadn't seen since late last autumn when he'd ridden away to

California to make purchases for his bride. His mail-order bride, Greta.

"Hello, Wyatt." Hallock fumbled for a handkerchief from his vest pocket, pulled it out, and then blew his nose with the loud honking Wyatt remembered.

Greta's arm started to shake beneath his hand, and her face was pale, making her eyes wider and more beautiful. She could only stare at Hallock as though seeing a ghost.

"Mr. Hallock arrived on the stage," Steele said. "And I was just explaining to him that since we'd believed he was dead, we had no choice but to find an alternative for Miss Nilsson."

Wyatt opened his mouth and tried to tell Steele that Greta wasn't Miss Nilsson anymore. She was Mrs. McQuaid. But he couldn't get the words out.

Hallock made thorough work of wiping his nose before he stuffed his handkerchief back into his vest pocket.

Steele clamped Hallock on the shoulder, making him flinch. "I was just apologizing profusely to Mr. Hallock and attempting to figure out how I could rectify the situation. Now it looks like I can do so by annulling your marriage to Miss Nilsson so Mr. Hallock can have his bride back."

"Now, hold on, Steele," Wyatt managed. "Who said anything about annulling the marriage?"

Steele pulled himself up taller. "You just came in here, canceled our deal, and admitted that you've been living in the barn. Since you don't want her—"

"I never said I didn't want her."

"Looks that way to me." Steele's tone hardened and his eyes flashed with the anger Wyatt had been expecting. "And since she's never really been yours to begin with, you need to do the right thing by Mr. Hallock and give her back."

Next to him Greta was openly trembling.

Steele gentled his expression and finally spoke to Greta. "Is everything McQuaid said about your arrangement true?"

"Yes." The word was a constricted whisper.

"You've been living as his housekeeper and not his wife?"

"Now, come on, Steele—"

"Let her answer."

Wyatt rubbed the back of his neck, frustration and fury rising to tighten his muscles. This wasn't working out at all the way he'd intended. In fact, it was going by the way of the boneyard fast.

"Have you been living as his housekeeper or his wife?" Steele said again.

She stared at the floor, her expression still mortified. "I guess it's been more like a housekeeper."

"There." Steele smiled at Hallock. "See? It'll all work out for the best after all."

"Maybe so." Hallock peeked shyly at Greta before he focused on his hands folded in front of him.

Wyatt had the sudden need to drag Greta out the door and home to the ranch as fast as he could. Greta was his. He loved her. They belonged together.

But what about Hallock?

Wyatt's mind jumped back to the previous summer when the sluice box had been as empty as his belly. He'd been down in the mouth, sitting outside his tent taking off his wet socks and airing out his sore feet when he noticed several miners laughing and pushing someone around. Of course he hadn't been able to sit idly by. He jumped up and elbowed his way into the fray, rescuing Hallock and in the process gaining an unlikely friend.

After that, Hallock had taken to inviting him to dinner at his newly constructed house several times a week. While they were complete opposites in nearly every possible way, Wyatt had come to see the good in the gentle-spirited man. He made sure the fellas gave Hallock the respect he was due. And Hallock made sure Wyatt had enough grub to fill him.

While Wyatt didn't want to give up Greta, how could he keep from hurting this kind and trusting man?

"Don't forget." Steele narrowed his gaze upon Wyatt again. "Mr. Hallock's the one who paid for Greta and Astrid to come to Fairplay. They're indebted to him, not you. And if anyone deserves to have her as a bride, Hallock's first in line."

Steele was right. Wyatt wouldn't have been able to afford their passage, not in a hundred years. But Hallock would be able to give Greta everything she needed and more. He'd find the best care for Astrid this side of the Mississippi. He could take her to Denver, pay for her treatment, and even hire a physician to come to Fairplay.

Sure as a gun, Greta and Astrid would be better off with Hallock.

Wyatt's shoulders slumped. He couldn't promise them anything, especially not after losing his herd as well as the cattle deal with Steele. As much as he loved Greta—in fact, because he loved her—he had to let her go.

How could he do anything less than release her from their vows and give her the better life she deserved?

CHAPTER 26

Greta was frozen in place. She wanted to run from the dining room and escape to some place far away, but she couldn't make her feet or voice work.

Phineas Hallock wasn't dead. He was very much alive and standing less than a dozen paces away.

He shifted, rubbed a hand across his nose, and then pulled out his handkerchief again.

Beneath her hand, she could feel the tension radiating from Wyatt's arm. Although she'd expected him to speak with Mr. Steele at some point, she certainly hadn't been ready for him to be so candid about the true nature of their relationship the moment they walked into the hotel.

During their exchange, she'd been ready to crawl underneath one of the tables. But then Mr. Hallock had spun around. It had only taken a moment for her to place his face with the picture he'd sent her, a daguerreotype she still had at the bottom of one of her bags.

While he appeared older in person, his kindness remained

constant. She could immediately sense in him a gentle spirit, one that had come across in his letters and convinced her to accept his marriage proposal.

It was the same one now that told her she couldn't spurn him, that to do so would be too cruel after all he'd done for her. Yet how could she leave Wyatt? How could she live without him?

Those same questions had been plaguing her during the entire ride into town. Even if they'd forgiven each other, and even after all the things he'd said about loving her and wanting her in his life, she'd known deep inside she still had to do the right thing for Astrid.

And that meant going to McLaughlin's Livery to purchase two stagecoach tickets for Astrid and her to ride back to Denver.

As hard as it was to imagine leaving Wyatt, she had to persist in her plan to get Astrid more help. She guessed Wyatt had every intention of accompanying them to Denver. But he belonged here working his land, buying more steers, and building the addition onto the cabin for his family. While she wanted to promise him she'd come back from Denver, she couldn't guarantee that either, not without knowing how Astrid would fare.

Pain had wedged into each part of her heart during the ride into town. She'd decided to make the arrangements for the ride back to Denver before she could change her mind—or Wyatt convinced her otherwise.

But now . . .

She glanced from Mr. Steele back to Phineas, who lifted his curious gaze to her once more, then rapidly dropped it and shifted his feet.

She couldn't do as Mr. Steele suggested and marry Phineas in place of Wyatt, could she? But she certainly couldn't just walk away, not after Mr. Steele's reminder of how much Phineas had paid for Astrid and her to travel to Fairplay.

With all eyes suddenly focused upon her, her face heated. "I'd like the chance to talk with Mr. Hallock privately. If that's agreeable to him and everyone else."

Wyatt's features hardened. "Nope, it ain't agreeable to me, but I'm guessing I don't have much say in the matter."

As conversations erupted around them, she squeezed Wyatt's arm and leaned in. "Please try to understand, Wyatt."

"Understand what?" His voice was low and his eyes filled with hurt.

"I won't let Astrid and me be the reason you lose your ranch."

"Without cattle, I'm bound to lose it eventually anyway."

"No." She shook her head, refusing to believe he'd have to give up everything he'd worked so hard for. He couldn't. She wouldn't let him.

Determination surged and chased away the embarrassment that had been strangling her. "Mr. Steele, you were wrong." Her voice drowned out the commotion in the room.

At her accusation, Mr. Steele's conversation with a man next to him stalled. He shifted his attention to her, his mouth half open and his brows lifted.

"You were wrong," she said again, as silence descended. Her nerves quivered, making her legs weak, but now that she had everyone's attention, she had to speak. "The day I arrived in Fairplay destitute and homeless, I realize you were trying to help a desperate lady out of a desperate situation.

And I do appreciate your concern. You were kind to both Astrid and me."

At the mention of Astrid's name, more brows rose.

"Astrid is just fine," she assured them. "We found her this morning at a hot spring. She is unharmed and as well as can be."

Some of the men nodded, their expressions relieved.

"And I thank each of you for your help in searching for her. Your kindness means more than you will know."

Again the men began to speak, and Greta was afraid that she was losing her opportunity to try to help Wyatt. And once lost, she doubted she'd regain it. "You've all been kind." She raised her voice again. "And Mr. Steele in particular."

The gentleman shifted his attention back to her, his expression wary. No doubt he was wondering where she was going with the conversation.

"Mr. Steele, I know you were looking out for Astrid and me when you brought up marriage to Wyatt. But you were wrong to make me a part of the cattle bargain."

"Greta, don't," Wyatt softly pleaded.

"I don't think you understand," Mr. Steele said.

"Maybe not everything. But I do know Wyatt's one of the hardest-working men I've ever met. He's got more willpower in one finger than a lot of men have in their entire bodies."

Wyatt tugged on her. "It's alright. Let it go."

Mr. Steele's gaze shifted to Wyatt, frustration flashing across his suave face. "That might be true, but—"

"He deserves a deal of his own, for being a man of integrity as well as for being so hardworking. The fact is, if you loan him the money he needs to invest in a herd, you'll be the one who stands to gain a profit off his hard work. And if I'm not mistaken, the profit on beef will only increase as the access to eastern markets gets easier with the building of more railways."

Wyatt released an exasperated breath, but she kept her attention fully upon Mr. Steele. She couldn't show any signs of weakness or hesitation now, or she might lose his interest. "As a matter of fact, any mine owner in the area willing to invest in the cattle will stand to earn a hefty profit."

If no one else took the bait, she'd plead with Phineas to loan Wyatt the money. It was the least she could do for Wyatt after everything he'd done for Astrid and her.

She lifted her chin. "If you don't want to give Wyatt the loan, then he'll need to start asking around for another investor. And I have a feeling that someone else, perhaps Mr. Hallock himself, would be more than eager to invest."

"Indeed, indeed," Phineas said in a high, shaky voice. "I should very much like that."

The men began to talk again, throwing out suggestions for other wealthy mine owners who might be willing to help Wyatt out.

"Be quiet, everyone!" Mr. Steele waved a hand for attention. "I never said the deal is off. I've already contacted the breeder in Missouri, and I'm not planning to bail out now."

Next to her, Wyatt tipped up the brim of his hat, his expression guarded.

Mr. Steele locked glares with Wyatt. Silence filled the space between the two. Finally Mr. Steele picked up his hat from the table, settled it on his head, then pushed in his chair. "McQuaid, I'll meet you in my parlor in thirty minutes. We'll talk cattle, and I'll also have my assistant draw up annulment papers."

Annulment. The word hit Greta like a blast of winter air, just as it had the first time he'd mentioned it.

Mr. Steele stalked past them without waiting for a reply.

Wyatt stood rigidly as the other men milled around the room.

"You'll get your cattle, Wyatt." She forced the words past her tight throat. "And your ranch is going to grow and become very successful. I just know it."

His beautiful brown eyes studied her face, as if searching for something. His expression was somber but still oh-so-handsome, so much that her heart hurt just looking at him.

As much as he might think he wanted to stay with her, in the long run he'd realize the wisdom of investing in his ranch instead. She had to stay strong and push through her need to throw her arms around him and beg him not to end their marriage.

"This winter you'll be able to construct the new addition onto the cabin, work on expanding the irrigation ditches, and start building fences in the pastures. By the time summer comes, you'll be ready for your family and the cattle." She hoped what she left unsaid came across—that he couldn't give up all that to be with Astrid and her.

"Let's just go on home, and we'll figure it all out there. Please, Greta."

"I have to speak with Mr. Hallock first."

Before Wyatt could respond, some of the men who'd been helping search for Astrid approached and wanted to know more details about her condition. As Greta filled them in on the details, she was keenly aware of Wyatt next to her, the way he took off his hat, dug his fingers into his hair, and then expelled a taut breath. Finally, he jammed his hat back on, pivoted, and walked out, letting the door slam behind him.

An ache rose swiftly into Greta's throat. She'd just cut him loose from his obligation to her and pushed him away. It was for the best, but she resisted the urge to run after him and tell him she didn't want to lose him.

"Miss Nilsson?" A man cleared his throat.

She forced her attention back to the conversation at hand to find that Phineas had approached her. He was twisting at the buttons on his vest. Already stretched to the limit, the buttons looked as if they would pop off at any moment.

"Mr. Hallock," she said as graciously as she could, finding that she was almost peering down at him since he was a good two inches shorter than her five-feet-five inches. While he'd mentioned that he wasn't a tall man, she hadn't expected to stand above him.

"I do apologize for my delay," he said with a squeak.

What could she say, especially after all that had transpired over the past three months since her arrival in Fairplay?

With the others pushing in around them and growing louder, she glanced at the door. "Perhaps we could step outside to talk?"

"Indeed, indeed." He bolted to the door and held it open for her. As she exited, her heart dropped. Wyatt had already unloaded the beef from her horse and was gone, with no sign of him or his steed anywhere along Main Street.

For a moment, panic seized her. Then she gave herself a mental shake. Surely, she'd see him at least one more time when she returned to the homestead to gather Astrid and their belongings. Even so, her limbs were weak as she lowered herself onto the bench in front of the hotel.

"Miss Nilsson, thank you for speaking with me." Phineas sat beside her, perching gingerly on the edge as though he might jump and flee at the slightest cause. "I regret the inconveniences and hardships my delay has cost you."

He went on to explain that he'd gotten a much later start leaving San Francisco than he anticipated. When the stagecoach had reached Salt Lake City, he'd been delayed indefinitely due to trouble with Indians on the trail. Apparently, he'd written to her regarding the setback, but the letter had gone to her home in Illinois, and she never received it because she'd already departed for the West.

Whatever the case, Phineas hadn't died. And the murdered and mutilated body discovered in the mountain pass that spring obviously belonged to some other unfortunate soul.

"The delivery of everything I purchased will be postponed until next spring." He shook his head, his fleshy forehead wrinkled in consternation.

"Please don't trouble yourself on my account." She couldn't keep herself from searching every horse and rider that rode past. Hopefully, Wyatt was only selling the beef and hadn't left without her. No matter his frustration, he was a man of too much principle to make her fend for herself.

Phineas's attention kept flitting to the livery and several passengers still waiting by their luggage. He had to be relieved to be back in Fairplay.

He toyed with his buttons again. "I just never expected the additional delay out of Salt Lake City."

"I'm sure you didn't." She couldn't rouse the enthusiasm he deserved. Back in August when she'd arrived, she would have been excited to meet him. Of course, she would have been nervous too, but ultimately she would have made the best of their marriage of convenience.

She had to muster the same resolve now. But how could she, not when she cared so deeply for Wyatt? When he was all she could think about? When he was the only man she wanted?

"Then you won't mind living in the house without all the furniture and decorations?"

Could she really live with Phineas? Marry him? Be his wife? She swallowed hard, gripping her hands tightly together in her lap. Maybe once a loveless marriage would have been enough. But it wasn't anymore. Not after all that she'd experienced with Wyatt.

She didn't know how she could go through with marrying Phineas, but she couldn't tell him that. At least not yet. Not until she had a chance to figure out what to do. For now, it was best if she didn't hurt his feelings or cause him undue stress. "No, I'm sure we'll be fine without furniture and decorations."

His shoulders slumped, almost as if he'd hoped she'd say otherwise.

"And you won't mind—not getting into the house?" His voice squeaked again as the words tumbled out haltingly. "I need to give the renters plenty of time to find other arrangements."

Maybe that's what she needed. Plenty of time. She could try to get him to postpone marriage plans since she was taking Astrid to Denver for further treatment. That would give her more time to figure out how to repay him for the cost he'd invested in her travel to Fairplay.

"Mr. Hallock, about Astrid . . . She hasn't been getting

better. Her condition, in fact, has worsened. As a result, I've decided to take her to the hospital in Denver. I've heard good things about what the physicians there are doing for consumption patients, and I'm hoping they can help Astrid."

He didn't reply.

She chanced a sideways glance to find that he was staring at the passengers near the livery, his face a mask of sadness and despair. She waited for him to say something, perhaps protest her desire to leave so soon after his arrival. But he remained silent, which made her heart sink farther.

"I'm sorry to disappoint you," she said quietly. "I know that's not what you were expecting after arriving home."

He shifted his attention to her, his brow creasing. "Not what I was expecting?"

"Yes, I'm hoping to leave on the stagecoach tomorrow."

He sat up, his girth straining against his vest. "I don't understand. Why are you leaving?"

Hadn't he been listening to what she'd just said? "I'd like to take Astrid to Denver."

His face remained blank.

"For further treatment."

"Then she's not getting better?" He glanced away again, clearly distracted.

Greta paused.

He wiped at his eyes.

Was he crying? And if so, why?

"Mr. Hallock? Is something wrong?"

"What?" He blinked rapidly. "No, no, no. Of course not."

"Are my plans to leave hurting you—?"

"That's not it at all."

Was it because of Wyatt? Was Phineas upset she and Wyatt

had lived together and grown close? Her throat clogged again just thinking about losing Wyatt.

She twisted her hands together tighter and fought against her longing for Wyatt. She didn't want to love him. But the simple truth was that she did. She loved Wyatt McQuaid, and the need for him welled up so strong and hard she could barely breathe.

"I'm sorry, Mr. Hallock." She couldn't go through with marrying Phineas. It wouldn't be fair to be with him when she was in love with another man, even if he was a man she couldn't have. "If I'd known you were still alive, I never would have married Wyatt, never would have allowed myself to care for him. I know it must hurt to think about me being with him—"

"That's not what's bothering me."

"It's not?"

"No, no, no. Indeed not. Wyatt's a good man for his willingness to take care of you in my stead." He removed his handkerchief from his vest and blew his nose, the noise loud enough to catch the attention of people passing by.

"What is it then, Mr. Hallock?"

He tucked the cloth back into his pocket and stared at the stagecoach for a long moment before he dropped his head. "It's nothing, Miss Nilsson. Nothing at all. We shall get married as planned."

Chapter 27

Wyatt's boots slapped against the plank sidewalk as he exited the general store. At the sight of Greta's horse still tied outside Hotel Windsor, his hands closed into fists. The thought of her sitting with Hallock made him so mad he wanted to knock someone or something into next week.

He'd gone out to the mining camp, sold the beef, then come back into town. And she was still yammering away with Hallock. He had half a mind to go over and interrupt them.

Halting at the edge of the sidewalk, he glanced in the direction of Steele's house. He'd put off going for as long as possible. The thirty minutes had turned into close to an hour, and Steele was sure to be blazing mad at him by now.

Yet at the prospect of meeting with Steele, past insecurities rolled through him like tumbleweed blowing down the street, tempting him to turn tail and run off after the next big dream.

But he wasn't that man anymore, was he? He couldn't

quit just because the going was getting real tough. He had to stick to his guns and learn to persevere. But at what cost? Would he have to let go of Greta in order to stay at the ranch and see it through?

Giving her up would be a fiery trial. The hardest yet. But through it, he couldn't forget God would be walking beside him and helping him to the other side.

With a silent prayer for strength and wisdom, he forced himself to start toward Steele's house, but then he halted in the middle of the street, turning and staring straight at Hotel Windsor.

What if he only had to release her temporarily? Their parting didn't have to be forever, did it? He wanted Greta to do anything she could to save Astrid's life. He'd support her and provide as much as possible to help her. And when she was done fighting to cure Astrid, the two of them could come back. He'd be here waiting for them. For her. For as long as it took.

Could he wrangle her into considering that option?

With his pulse picking up speed, he aimed for the hotel, jogging the last few steps. He threw open the door and spoke the first words that came to mind. "I'm sorry, Hallock. I love Greta. And I'm not giving her an annulment."

Silence descended over the room, and every man present halted midmotion to gape at him.

With all the attention upon him, his insides curled up with embarrassment the same as the first time he'd barged into the hotel today, but he spoke again anyway. "I'll help you find another bride. We'll write letters and get someone else to come west for you. But the fact is, Greta is my wife, and I'm aiming to keep her." He glanced at the corner tables, looking for Hallock and Greta.

"They're not here." Mr. Fehling stood in the middle of the dining room, coffeepot in one hand and a mug in the other. "They were sitting on the bench out front, and then the next thing we knew, they were walking down the street toward Mr. Steele's house."

Panic twined around Wyatt's middle. There was only one reason the two would have gone to Steele's—to get the annulment papers so Greta could sign them.

Wyatt spun, a fresh sense of urgency prodding him forward. He raced out the door and down the street. If she signed for an annulment, he wouldn't touch a pen to the paper.

As he arrived at the front door of the modest two-story clapboard home, Wyatt stopped short. What if Greta didn't love him enough to fight for their marriage through the obstacles and hardships? He hadn't been wrong in sensing her attraction or that she cared about him. But did she care enough? After all, she hadn't said anything about loving him.

Drawing in a steadying breath, he opened the door and stalked into the hallway. At the sound of voices coming from Steele's office located in the room across from the parlor, Wyatt crossed to the doorway.

Surrounded by a haze of cigar smoke, Steele sat at his desk with his assistant next to him. The young man was bent over and writing something on an official-looking document. And Greta and Hallock stood on the opposite side, watching him while Steele instructed his assistant.

"Might as well tear that thing up," Wyatt said.

Everyone swiveled in his direction, including the assistant, who straightened, ink dripping from his pen and leaving splatters across the sheet.

"I'm staying married to Greta. And that's all there is to it." He crossed his arms and spread his feet, daring anyone to defy him.

Greta stood stiffly, her shoulders straight, her chin high. And though her eyes flashed to him for an instant, she focused back on the sheet on Steele's desk. The flash was long enough, however, for him to see her inner turmoil. He still had time to sway her.

If only he could get Hallock to understand and accept his marriage to Greta, then Wyatt might have a fighting chance of keeping her. "I'm mighty sorry things had to turn out this way, Hallock. But what's done is done. I love Greta. She's my wife. And I ain't giving her up."

Hallock released a long exhale, and his shoulders seemed to relax.

At the unexpected reaction, Wyatt paused for a second but then pushed on. "I'm fixin' to reimburse you for everything you paid for Greta and Astrid to come west. I might not be able to right away, but you know I'm a man of my word and I'll do it."

"Indeed you are." The worried lines in Hallock's forehead smoothed away. "But it isn't necessary."

"Sure as a gun is."

"No, Wyatt. I'm the one who started this whole process of sending away for Miss Nilsson. It's my responsibility to cover the costs."

"Listen, Hallock, I don't care what you say. I ain't signing an annulment."

Thankfully, Steele was staying out of the conversation. He leaned back in his chair and took a puff on his cigar, his gaze bouncing back and forth between them.

Wyatt chanced a look at Greta. She was staring at the sheet on the desk and twirling a strand of her hair around her finger. She might not be jumping up and down at the sight of him, but she hadn't objected.

Before he could formulate the words to convince her not to give up on their marriage, insistent knocking at the front door interrupted them. Wyatt wanted to ignore the pesky intrusion until he was sure Greta was safely still his wife.

But at the increased pounding, Mr. Steele took out his cigar and pointed it in the direction of the door. "Answer that, will you, McQuaid?"

Wyatt had no choice but to backtrack to the door. As he swung it open, he was surprised to find the stout woman in the red gown from the stagecoach standing there. She held a red-and-white-striped parasol above her, shielding her from the sun and casting a shadow over her face. Even so, Wyatt could see she was a middle-aged woman, and her frizzy graying hair surrounded a stern countenance.

"Mr. Steele?" She eyed Wyatt with an air of mistrust.

"Nope. I'm Wyatt McQuaid. Steele is busy at the moment. You'll have to come back later—"

"Henrietta?" Hallock spoke from behind him.

The woman's expression softened as she peered at Hallock standing in the hallway just outside the office door. "Phineas, I know I said I'd wait for you to figure things out. But when I saw you walking down here with a woman, I had a very bad feeling about it."

Hallock gazed at the newcomer with such longing that a hopeful current zipped through Wyatt. Who was this woman and what did she mean to his friend?

Before Hallock could answer, Greta stepped into the hallway.

Henrietta turned her full attention upon Greta as though sizing up her competition. But there wasn't any competition as far as Wyatt was concerned. No woman could ever compare to Greta.

"Miss Nilsson?" A note of despair colored Henrietta's tone.

Greta hesitated. "No, actually, I'm Mrs. McQuaid."

At her announcement, Wyatt's heartbeat ticked up a notch. Did that mean she wanted to stay with him? He tried to catch her gaze, but she kept her attention riveted on the newcomer. Why? Because she might give in and allow herself to care about him?

"You're Mrs. McQuaid? His wife?" Henrietta nodded at Wyatt.

"Yep. She's my wife," he answered before Greta could deny it.

The relief that transformed the woman's expression was almost comical. "Oh, I beg your pardon. I assumed she was the mail-order bride Phineas had sent away for. And I had a terrible feeling he wasn't going to sever ties with her, as he assured me he'd do, so he could marry me instead."

"What?" Greta asked the question at the same time as Wyatt.

Hallock ducked his head and stared at his shoes.

Henrietta twisted the handle of her parasol. "We've been traveling companions since leaving San Francisco. And during the few months we were delayed in Salt Lake City together, we developed affection for one another. I'd made arrangements to become a teacher in Denver, but Phineas assured me Fairplay could use a teacher too."

The tension in Wyatt's muscles eased, and he allowed himself the first full breath since walking into Steele's house. "So the two of you are hoping to get married?"

The woman nodded. "Being such a man of principle, Phineas wants to make arrangements for Miss Nilsson first. And when I saw him walking with so pretty a young woman, I assumed he'd changed his mind."

"No, no, no." Hallock's face turned red. "Indeed not. I haven't changed my mind. I just haven't yet figured out how to change Miss Nilsson's."

"Let's talk to her together, Phineas. If she's as kind as you indicated, then when she sees us together, she'll surely give us her blessing."

"Of course I give you my blessing," Greta said.

Henrietta's eyes rounded, and she glanced at everyone as though trying to make sense of who belonged to whom.

"I'm the mail-order bride." Greta smiled gently. "And since Phineas wasn't here when I arrived on the stagecoach, Wyatt offered to marry me."

"I see." Henrietta smiled back. "Then nothing is preventing Phineas and me from getting married?"

Wyatt shook his head. "Nope—"

Hallock cut him off. "If Wyatt promises to take care of Greta for the rest of her earthly days—then I will, with good conscience, release her from any obligation to me." Hallock met Wyatt's gaze. Friendship and goodwill radiated from Hallock's face just as it always had.

"You have my word. I love Greta more than my own life. And as much as I respect you, I wouldn't have been able to let you have her. So thank the good Lord He's provided a solution."

"Indeed." Hallock shifted his attention to Henrietta, his

eyes filling with hope. "I shall go speak with Mr. Steele and let him know the decision."

"And I shall come with you." Henrietta snapped her parasol closed and bustled past Wyatt. Hallock held out his arm, and she slipped her gloved hand into the crook.

As they disappeared into Steele's office, Wyatt took a step toward Greta.

She inched back. "Even if I don't marry Phineas, I still have to sign the annulment papers, Wyatt."

Greta's chest pounded with what she needed to do. During the walk from the hotel to Mr. Steele's and the time they'd been in his office, she sensed the same distraction and despondency from Phineas that she had since they started their conversation.

Now she understood why. He hadn't wanted to marry her because he cared about the other woman he'd met, but he likely would have gone through with the wedding because he felt responsible for her. And now that Wyatt had come after her, everything within her wanted to run to him, throw herself into his arms, and tell him she'd stay married to him.

But the other part of her—the rational part—demanded she finish getting the annulment and set Wyatt free from any further responsibility for Astrid and her. She wouldn't shackle either of the men.

Wyatt took off his hat and dug his fingers through his hair. His jaw flexed, and his dark eyes turned murky. "I want to make our marriage work."

"I have to go away, and I'm not certain I'll be able to come back."

"I know." His tone was resigned though turmoil still etched his face.

"That's not fair to you—"

"Do you love me?"

His question threw her off guard. Yes, she'd admitted to herself that she loved him. But she couldn't tell him that. Doing so would only complicate matters. She pressed her lips together.

He waited, his brows furrowed.

"I won't give you false hope," she whispered.

"I love you." His voice was earnest and pricked her heart, causing tears to well up. "If you can look me in the eyes and tell me you don't love me—even a hair—then I'll let you go and won't bother you no more about it."

She shut her eyes so he wouldn't see the truth.

His footsteps clomped nearer, and she could feel his presence directly in front of her. When his hands grazed her shoulders and brushed down her arms, she couldn't keep from turning into a puddle under his touch.

When he drew her to his chest and enveloped her, she rested her head against him. This was home, this was where she belonged, this was where she always wanted to be. Regardless, she forced out the words she knew she had to say. "You'll be better off without us, Wyatt."

He tightened his embrace. "Remember what you told Astrid earlier? You told her not to think that she'd be better off without you."

"That was different—"

"Nope. It ain't any different. We're here for each other. And because of that we make each other stronger. You make me a stronger and better man."

She pulled back so she could see into his eyes—his beautiful, dark eyes surrounded by his beautiful dark lashes. "Oh, Wyatt."

"Then you won't sign the annulment papers?"

"Are you sure you won't come to regret it?"

"Never."

"But you know I have to leave with Astrid."

He brushed his hand over her cheek and smoothed back her hair. "Yep."

"And you know you have to stay here and keep the ranch running?"

"Yep. As hard as it's gonna be for me tomorrow, I'm letting you go."

The sadness in his eyes and voice told her he'd resigned himself to whatever the future might bring, and that through it all, he would be there for her.

The words *I love you* pushed for release. But somehow they couldn't get past the tightness in her throat. Instead, she slipped her arms around him and hugged him, praying that somehow, someway, they could eventually be together.

CHAPTER 28

Wyatt ripped the last portion of the annulment and tossed the pieces onto Steele's desk.

"McQuaid, you should have told me you loved Greta back at the hotel." Steele tapped his cigar over an ashtray. "Then we could have avoided all of this unpleasantness with Mr. Hallock."

"I was aiming to until I got a look at Hallock standing there."

Hallock had already left with his new lady friend to track down Reverend Zieber to marry them as quickly as possible. Wyatt didn't blame his friend for being eager to see the deed done before anything else put a hitch in their plans.

He'd been biting at the bit too, ready to get out of town with Greta, away from anything else that might try to take her away from him. But while he'd been wrapping up things with Steele, she headed over to secure her spot on the stage-coach.

"I had the feeling the two of you would be good for each

other." Steele allowed himself a smile. "I'm just glad I was right and that everything worked out well in the end."

If everything had worked out so well, why did Wyatt feel as if he'd been plowed over by a dozen steers?

Steele's assistant was in the process of writing out the official agreement for their cattle deal, including Steele's percentage of the investment. "Sign right here, Mr. McQuaid." The assistant held the pen above a blank line at the bottom of the sheet.

Wyatt glanced over the paper, took the pen, then scrawled his name. As he straightened and glanced out the front window of Steele's house, his sights snagged upon the tall, lanky form of Roper Brawley crossing the street with his two cowhands on his heels.

He'd had to bank his anger toward Brawley while searching for Astrid, but now that the little girl was found, he allowed the embers to fan to life. "Ain't right that Brawley's getting away with killing my herd."

"We can't do much about it since he's claiming you took the cattle from him in the first place."

"You know that ain't true," Wyatt said, just as he had the last time he'd talked to Steele about it several days ago, right after the slaughter. "I bought those cattle fair and square from miners coming over the Front Range. And they had my brand on them."

Steele took a drag on his cigar, then puffed out a cloud of smoke that added to the spicy haze filling the room.

"What do you want me to do, son? Get the vigilance committee together and string him up?"

Wyatt rubbed at the tension building in the back of his neck. He sure as cow patty didn't want to resort to a lynching. But in this part of the territory, the lynch law and the vigilance committees were all they had to see justice done.

Made up of stable and prominent men, the vigilance committee usually sent a warning to the offender in the form of a letter with a drawing of a tree and a man hanging from it. The word *forewarned* was penned into a picture of a coffin at the bottom.

As angry as he was with Brawley, the man didn't deserve to die for killing his cattle. He needed to pay Wyatt back, maybe serve some jail time. But his offense wasn't the hanging kind.

"Don't know what to do," Wyatt said. "But we can't sit back and let him get away with this. If we do that, then he's gonna think he can harass me come summer when I drive my Shorthorns here."

"True enough."

Brawley sauntered across the street, kicking up dust. He approached the livery just as Greta exited. She nearly collided with the man but recoiled just in time.

When Brawley grabbed her arm, Wyatt released a low growl and bolted to the door. He'd told Brawley not to touch Greta again. And he meant it.

"Where are you going?" Steele pushed away from his desk.

"Brawley's out there," Wyatt called over his shoulder. "And he's got ahold of Greta."

Wyatt charged out of the house and onto the street, his revolver out of his holster and aimed at Brawley, who was still holding Greta by the arm.

"Let her go, Brawley." Wyatt cocked the hammer. "Or I'm shootin'."

In the process of trying to shrug free of Roper Brawley's grip, Greta halted. Wyatt stood in the street outside Steele's house, his revolver aimed at Brawley. His feet were spread, his arm outstretched, his jaw rigid. And his eyes . . . they were already shooting bullets.

"She ain't yours," Brawley shouted, his rancid breath assaulting her. "Everyone's sayin' you ain't been living as man and wife. That means she's free for the taking."

"She's mine." Wyatt's voice was low and hard. "And she will be 'til my dying breath."

Roper's free hand dropped to the ivory handle of his revolver, his weathered skin and dirty fingernails contrasting against the smooth cream color. Her mind flashed with the image of the stagecoach robber's hand when he'd pointed his revolver at them. Of course, any number of men could have the same brown fingers, crusty fingernails, and ivory-handled revolver.

Greta recalled Astrid's statement from a few days ago, that Brawley sounded like the robber who'd held up their stagecoach. Had she been too quick in dismissing the possibility because the robber hadn't been wearing an eye patch?

"Now step away from Greta real slow and easy."

Brawley dragged her around, forcing her to stand in front of him. "You're gonna have to fight me for her."

Wyatt's revolver wavered, and he flicked his gaze to her before he fixed it once again on Brawley.

Behind Wyatt, Mr. Steele stepped out of his front door, a revolver in his hand, and all around men were pouring out of the hotels and taverns and shops.

A chill swept under Greta's cloak, which had nothing to do with the breeze that had been getting colder as the day progressed. She had to do something to put an end to the conflict before it got out of hand and people were needlessly hurt. Especially Wyatt.

"Brawley, please unhand me. Wyatt and I agreed that we're planning to stay married."

"I think I'm aimin' to keep you for myself." Brawley drew her back into the crook of his arm. "That is, unless McQuaid wants to strike a deal."

Wyatt started across the street toward her, his revolver trained upon Brawley's head.

The cold steel tip of Brawley's revolver pressed into her neck, sending a shudder through her.

Wyatt froze, his attention riveted to the weapon. "Now hold on, Brawley. Put the gun down."

"Come on, Brawley," Mr. Steele called. "Don't do this."

Brawley laughed and pressed the barrel into her more firmly.

Wyatt's eyes rounded, and he held out a hand as though that would stop the man. "What kind of deal do you want?"

"This purty little thing for the land."

The land. Brawley wasn't going to stop tormenting them until he wrested the homestead away from Wyatt. That much was certain.

"Fine." Wyatt spat out the word. "You win. You can have it—"

"No!" Greta twisted and grabbed at Brawley's face. She wasn't about to let Wyatt lose his land. Not today, and not because of her.

"Greta, wait!" The fear in Wyatt's voice drove deep inside her.

But her fingers were already connecting with Brawley's eye

patch. She wrenched at it as he jerked his head back, panic flashing across his features.

She didn't release her hold, and as Brawley stumbled backward, the string holding the patch in place snapped, so she was left holding the felt cup.

Brawley fell to the ground, taking his revolver with him. "Give that back, woman!" He looked up at her long enough for her to see a lazy eye—the same lazy eye that had plagued the stagecoach robber.

Astrid had been right. Brawley was the leader of the Crooked-Eye Gang. And that would explain why he always had more than enough money to purchase oxen from miners when Wyatt struggled to come up with the necessary cash.

Before Brawley could right himself, the crack of a gun came from Wyatt's direction. An instant later, a bullet tore into Brawley's hand. He bellowed in pain and dropped his revolver.

All around men jumped into action. Several lunged for Brawley. Some grabbed his companions and disarmed them. Through the commotion and shouting, Wyatt stalked toward her, his worried eyes taking her in. "You alright?"

"I'm just fine." She held out the eye patch. "Astrid told me Brawley was the leader of the Crooked-Eye Gang and now we have proof."

Mr. Steele was right on Wyatt's heels. "Proof of what?"

"That Brawley has a crooked eye, which is evidence that he and his men have been the ones robbing the stagecoaches coming over Kenosha Pass."

Wyatt took the eye patch from her, examined it, and then handed it to Steele.

Brawley was clutching his injured hand, clearly in too

much pain to think about the fact that he was showing his lazy eye for every man in town to see and revealing the lie he'd perpetuated about losing his eye in an Indian attack.

Mr. Steele glanced from the patch to Brawley and then back to Wyatt. "Guess I need to pull the vigilance committee together today after all."

Wyatt's expression turned grave. "Didn't want things to come to this."

Mr. Steele holstered his gun. "Me either. But we can't let Brawley and his men rob and kill any more innocent people."

"Reckon so." Wyatt's voice was soft, and his eyes radiated resignation.

Greta pulled her cloak about her tighter so Wyatt wouldn't see her trembling hands. Now that the ordeal was over, she wanted to sink to the ground and give way to tears of relief that Wyatt was safe and Brawley could never again threaten him or the ranch.

The men pulled Brawley to his feet and began shoving him and his partners down the street. Wyatt watched for only a few moments before leveling a gaze at Steele. "I'm gonna take Greta on home if that's alright by you. She's already been through enough for one day."

At their somber exchange of glances, Greta guessed Wyatt didn't want to subject her to whatever the men planned to do to Brawley and his men. She could only shudder at the prospect.

When Wyatt reached for her hand, she didn't resist. She grabbed hold of him and allowed him to lead her to her horse.

Chapter 29

In the fading evening light, Greta kept looking at Wyatt and memorizing him, from the strong way he held himself in his saddle to the powerful build of his torso. The determined tilt of his hat. The scruffy dark layer of whiskers on his face. The tough set of his jaw.

She loved everything about him and wanted to carry every detail with her when she left tomorrow. As much as she wanted to delay a few more days or even a week, the stagecoach driver had warned her that this might be the last ride out. Already they'd had a hard time pushing through the highest passes with snow up to five feet in some places and the trail covered in ice in other spots.

Now that the plans were final, Greta's last hurdle was convincing Astrid of the need to leave. Wyatt had promised to help. "She'll go if she knows she can come back," he'd said.

Greta prayed he was right.

"Let's wait to tell her until the morning," Greta said as the cabin came into view.

"Then you're afraid she'll run away again?"

"I don't know what she'll do." The closer they drew to home, the more she dreaded facing the child with the news. Astrid would be devastated, maybe even feel betrayed, especially after how they'd bonded earlier in the day.

Wyatt reined in his horse, and Greta did the same.

Ahead, the cabin and barn sat against the backdrop of the mountains with the glow of the setting sun reflected on the golden aspens, dark evergreens, and gray rocky crags. The few remaining cattle grazed in the barnyard along with the chickens. It was a stunning view, one she wanted to capture and take with her so she could remember everything about this rugged place during the days to come.

"It's beautiful," she breathed. "And has so much potential."

"It is mighty beautiful." He swept his gaze over the landscape too. "But I can't deny that I'm scared to death of what the future holds."

She was scared too. Nothing was certain in life, not in this wild land where anything could happen—dangerous thieves, inclement weather, unpredictable Utes, wild animals, and crooked neighbors. The odds of being able to make it were stacked against them. Just like the odds were stacked against Astrid.

However, Greta refused to accept defeat with the ranch every bit as much as she refused to accept defeat with Astrid's consumption. She had to cling to the impossible. Could she do so with their marriage too?

As though sensing her question, Wyatt dismounted, came around to her horse, and reached out a gloved hand. His eyes beckoned her to take hold.

She placed her hand in his and allowed him to help her down. When she was standing next to him, he slid his arm behind her and drew her into the crook of his body so they stood side by side gazing at the ranch together.

A red-tailed hawk soared above the open grassland with its wingtips spread and separated like fingers, the sun glinting off its rusty tail feathers. In the distance, a herd of pronghorns grazed along the foothills, seemingly without a care in the world.

She breathed in deeply of the glorious view and prayed she'd be able to come back and stand by Wyatt's side in this exact spot for many years to come.

"This is ours, Greta. Yours. Mine. Ours."

She nodded.

"Don't you forget it."

"I won't."

"Promise?"

"I promise."

His arm tightened around her. "And you won't forget about me?"

"Of course I won't." Somehow this already felt like goodbye, and she didn't like it. She sensed tomorrow morning would be worse. Especially for Astrid.

Greta focused on the cabin. The wisp of smoke rising from the stovepipe and the light glowing from the window told her that Astrid and Judd were probably having supper, or at least that Judd was cooking something.

Was she really doing the right thing by taking Astrid to Denver? The little girl's impassioned plea came back to her: *"Please, Greta, let me die here where I'm happy."*

Greta couldn't deny that Astrid was happy here, happier

than she'd been in a long time, in a way she wouldn't be in Denver. Would it be better for Astrid to stay? Even if she never got well?

No, they couldn't give up now. Not after all they'd already been through.

"When you're in Denver, I want you to think of this picture." Wyatt nodded ahead to the grandeur. "And remember all you're missing."

She lifted her hand to his chest and spread her fingers, relishing the solidness. "I won't have any trouble remembering all that I'm missing."

"You sure?"

"The trouble will be thinking about anything else."

"Good. Here's one more thing to make sure you don't forget what you're leaving behind." With that, he shifted her, then touched his lips to hers. The pressure was sweet and light, and his mouth clung to hers for an extra heartbeat, as though he couldn't quite let go.

When he started to pull back from their kiss, a swell of need rose within her, and she chased after his lips, pressing into him, wanting more.

He paused for only an instant before he fused his mouth to hers again, the gentleness gone and in its place a desperation that told her so much more than his words had—that he needed her and didn't want to let her go.

Her skin was strangely alive and heat skipped along her nerve endings. His hands sliding over her back pressed her closer, the touch searing through her cloak. She didn't want this taste of closeness to end, a taste that made her hungrier.

As though experiencing the same hunger, Wyatt started to lift her off her feet. She had the picture of him carrying her someplace private and spending the rest of the night showing her exactly what she was going to miss by leaving him.

She couldn't let that happen.

With a force of will that had been born out of always doing hard things, she dropped her arms and broke from him. As she stepped away, he clung to her, his fingers gliding up her arms, to her neck, to her cheeks, beckoning her to be back against him where she belonged.

The truth was, she loved kissing him and loved the way she felt when he kissed her. But the other truth was, that if she let their passion take root tonight, she wouldn't be able to yank herself up and leave him tomorrow.

His breathing came out uneven just like hers. The intensity of his gaze, the longing etched into every handsome line of his face—it made her heart race with strange anticipation. And fear.

How could she leave him? How could she possibly ride away from him tomorrow?

He reached for her. "Greta." The one word contained all his desire.

"No, Wyatt." She held up her hands and took another step away. She couldn't kiss him again, or she'd never be able to let him go. With tears stinging her eyes, she spun and stalked back to her horse. She climbed up into the saddle, blinking back the pain of their parting.

With a safe distance between them, she finally drew her emotion under control. "I'm leaving tomorrow, and I don't want to complicate our good-byes."

"I understand." He stood motionless where she'd left him. Strong and proud and yet so humble.

"Good-bye, Wyatt. I love you." The words tumbled out.

Before he could respond or she could say or do anything else she might regret, she dug her heels into her horse and urged it homeward.

I love you. Her words lingered in the air long after she'd ridden away. He'd wanted to hear them, just not in the same breath as good-bye. Still, his heart thrilled in the knowledge that he hadn't been mistaken. She loved him too.

Blast it all. Although he'd managed to keep her from marrying Hallock, in the end he was losing her anyway.

He gazed at the distant Kenosha Peak. Was he a horrible sinner for hoping it would snow tonight so the pass would close and prevent her from going?

But even as he wanted the weather to trap Greta and Astrid, deep inside he didn't want to win them by default. If they stayed, he wanted Greta to make the choice, willingly. Which wasn't about to happen . . .

All he could hang on to was that they'd only be apart till spring.

He drew in a deep breath. Somehow they'd have to be okay. They loved each other, and that would see them through the difficult days ahead. That and a lot of hard work. He'd drive himself hard over the winter and keep himself too busy to think about her.

He had a heap of work to do to get ready for his herd of Shorthorns. And although part of him wanted to give up the new herd in order to be with Greta, another part of him thrummed with the anticipation of seeing the herd and driving them up onto his land.

If only she didn't have to go away . . .

With a whispered prayer for strength to release her and to keep persevering, he mounted his horse and started toward the barn. As he drew closer to the homestead, he saw her touch everywhere, from the clothesline to the cellar to the new chickens. He even saw her in the little details like the braided cornhusk rug outside the cabin, the curtain she'd fashioned for the window, and the new huckleberry patch she'd cut and transplanted from the foothills.

In the weeks since she'd arrived, she'd transformed the ranch into a home. And he didn't know how he could live there without her.

Pain pounded against his heart, and he forced himself to ride directly to the barn. He couldn't spend the evening with her or see her again. If he did, he'd beg her not to leave.

Chapter 30

Strange silence settled around Greta as she stretched to wakefulness. Silence. It was blissful. For a moment, she burrowed under the warm covers, unwilling to face the chill of the cabin before the stove pumped out its heat.

But the quiet was too abnormal, and it could mean only one thing. She flipped over and felt the spot next to her. It was empty.

Greta's eyes flew open to find the bedroom dark with only the first hints of dawn. Panic erupted. She scrambled up and pushed the covers away.

"Astrid?"

The stillness from the other room confirmed her worst fear. Astrid had run away again.

But why? When Greta had arrived home last night, she hadn't mentioned anything to the little girl. Since their belongings were still packed from earlier in the week, she'd decided to finish readying to leave in the morning so she wouldn't alert Astrid to the plans.

Perhaps she'd read the truth of their plans from Greta's mood. Although Greta had tried really hard to mask her sadness, Astrid had pressed a hand against her cheek at bedtime and told her not to worry, that everything would work out the way it was supposed to.

What had Astrid meant? That she planned to run away again so they wouldn't be able to leave?

Greta prayed the girl had only gone back to the hot spring and hadn't decided to hide elsewhere. Though Astrid had been safe, she wouldn't be so lucky twice. Surely Astrid understood that too.

"Astrid," she said again, knowing it was futile. The silence was too deep, too consuming.

As Greta's feet touched the cold floorboards, her wildly careening thoughts stumbled to a halt. Usually Astrid's coughing woke her up at least several times a night. But Greta couldn't remember waking last night—not even once.

Of course she'd been exhausted after the past few days of so little sleep and worrying about Astrid. Perhaps she'd slept through Astrid's coughing fits?

Greta shook her head, her long hair falling around her in disarray. The reason she hadn't heard the coughing was because Astrid had likely run away the moment Greta had fallen asleep. She wouldn't have been able to take a horse this time, not without waking Wyatt and Judd. No doubt Astrid realized that by foot she'd need a greater head start to find a new hiding place.

Her heart thudding with the urgency to find the girl, Greta donned her clothes, all the while plotting where to go. As she sat down on the edge of the bed to tug up her stockings, she halted.

If Astrid was so determined to stay, even to the point of putting her own life at risk again, then how could she force the child to leave?

Greta let her stocking fall to the floor. For the first time, Astrid was in a place where people loved and wanted her, where she was accepted for being sick, and where she wasn't shunned or made to feel like an invalid. Here she could be herself and find joy in the simple things of life like other children her age did.

How could she possibly drag Astrid to Denver against her will? The crying and resisting would make her weaker. And then once they got there, would Astrid try running away again?

Greta bowed her head, defeat crashing upon her and crushing her spirit. Was it time to admit she couldn't find a cure? That Astrid probably wouldn't fully recover, no matter where she went? That there were no guarantees in Denver any more than here on the ranch?

Maybe the physicians would prolong Astrid's life by a few months or a few years. But what good would that do if Astrid was miserable?

"But I don't want her to die. It's my job to make sure she lives." As soon as the hoarsely whispered words were out, Greta realized the impossibility of such a task.

She'd already done everything she could for Astrid, including being willing to marry a complete stranger in order to move to the West. Now the rest was truly in God's hands. He'd counted Astrid's days, and nothing Greta did or didn't do could take away from the number He'd already established.

Someplace inside, she knew all that. Now she just needed

to live it out. And let Astrid know she was done trying to control everything. Once she found Astrid, she'd tell her that if she really wanted to stay, they would. Greta wouldn't fight her anymore but would honor her plea to live out the rest of her life in this one place that had brought her joy.

With fingers now stiff from the cold, Greta finished putting on her stockings and shoes. She twisted her hair into a simple knot, grabbed her cloak, and then crossed to the barn. The door was ajar, and she peered into the dark interior. "Wyatt?"

"He's down by the river fishing," came Judd's sleepy response.

She needed to tell Judd that Astrid was gone again, but the words stuck in her throat. Instead, she backed away from the barn and started toward the river path. Judd would be devastated once more, but she'd wait to tell him, at least until she had the chance to inform Wyatt.

Her heart weighed heavier with each step she took. She was to blame for Astrid running away again. If only she'd listened to the little girl and paid heed to her real needs—especially for belonging and acceptance.

As she passed the chokecherry bush, a furry creature darted out, nearly tripping her. Startled, she halted. A yip was followed by wet paws jumping up on her skirt.

Squinting through the dark shadows of dawn, she made out the pointed snout and floppy ears of a puppy. "Chase?"

Hope spurted through her as she bent and picked up the squirming bundle, who proceeded to lick her face. "Where's Astrid?" Surely her sister wouldn't have gone far without the pup.

Did that mean Astrid hadn't run away after all?

With a racing heart, Greta hurried down the rest of the

path. Upon reaching the bank, she didn't see Wyatt anywhere and guessed he was in his favorite fishing spot upriver. She whispered a prayer that Astrid was with him. Then she set Chase down and let him lead the way.

The pup took off, and Greta stumbled to keep up. Within minutes, the bank opened up into the wide spot, its waters rushing against the large rocks.

At the sight of Wyatt's tall frame standing on the bank and Astrid's smaller one next to him, Greta nearly fell to her knees in relief. The tears she'd been holding at bay spilled over.

Wyatt was the first to glance in her direction. Astrid followed his gaze.

"Hi, Greta," the girl called cheerfully. "I'm helping Wyatt catch fish for breakfast. I've already got one. Want to see it?"

Greta swallowed the need to cry and brushed the tears from her cheeks. "Of course I do." Her voice was shaky, but she drew in a breath and crossed toward the two. Astrid explained how she'd caught the fish, reeled it in, and then helped to string it to the line in the shallow pool nearby with the fish Wyatt had caught.

"You're becoming quite the fisherwoman." Greta couldn't keep herself from smoothing the girl's flyaway hair, needing to touch her and reassure herself that Astrid was here, safe and happy.

"Someday I'm gonna be as good as Wyatt." Astrid cast her line again, biting her lip in concentration.

She glanced at Wyatt, but he avoided her gaze. The faint dawn light revealed the haggardness in his face and the dark circles under his eyes. He hadn't slept well. Certainly not as well as she had.

"I slept so soundly I didn't hear you leave." Greta once

again glided her fingers through Astrid's hair. "And I didn't hear you coughing last night either."

"That's because I didn't cough."

That was impossible, but Greta refrained from saying so.

"I'm better now," Astrid said, with a confidence that hurt Greta's heart. "The hot spring water is helping me get better."

The child certainly had looked better after her few days at the hot spring. Even last evening, Astrid had talked and played a game of checkers with Judd and helped with chores almost like a normal child. She'd tired easily and had gone to bed early. But she had much more energy than she'd had in a very long time.

"You really didn't cough last night?" Greta studied the child's face, noting fresh energy.

"Honest. I really didn't. I slept so good that I woke up early. When I couldn't fall back asleep, I saw Wyatt coming out of the barn and asked if I could go with him."

Greta stared at Astrid, a new sense of wonder pushing away the despair. Was it possible Astrid could find some relief after all? From the hot spring?

While she doubted the spring had the ability to truly cure an illness, what if the water somehow contained medicinal properties? If bathing there could diminish Astrid's symptoms, even just a little, then why not try it again? "I guess next time you start coughing, we'll have to ride down to the spring again. What do you say to that?"

"W-e-l-l yes!" She peered up with a wide smile.

Wyatt's fingers tugging expertly against his fishing line came to a halt, and he stood motionless.

When Greta chanced a look at him, he was watching her with rounded eyes full of questions. She lifted her hand to his cheek, relishing the rough scratchiness of his dark stubble. Her heart sang with a new, sweet melody. She and Wyatt didn't have to go through the painful process of living apart this winter. They could stay together.

He tipped up his hat as though trying to get a better read of her face.

Inwardly Greta smiled while she tried to remain outwardly composed. "What do you think?" She nudged Astrid. "Should Wyatt and I take a trip to the hot spring? Just the two of us together? Maybe today. Or perhaps tomorrow."

"Oh, I dunno." Astrid wiggled her line. "The Indian said the water is for the sick. You're not sick, are you?"

Greta could hardly pay attention to Astrid's answer as Wyatt made sense of her insinuation. His oh-so-handsome face registered first surprise and then hope.

"Are you sick, Greta?" Astrid's voice contained a note of worry that caused Chase, now lying at Astrid's feet, to lift his head off his paws and perk his ears.

"No, I couldn't be better. But I'm noticing Wyatt is looking tired and has such dark circles under his eyes."

"I have an ache right here." He pressed a hand to his heart. "But I'm guessing a day at the hot spring with Greta might make it better."

"Might?"

"I reckon I'm gonna need two days to completely heal and not just one."

She couldn't contain her smile any longer.

He lowered his pole and in the same motion pulled her against him.

She came to him eagerly, wrapping her arms around him and breathing him in.

"You don't have nowhere else to be today?" he whispered so Astrid couldn't hear.

She shook her head. "No. Nowhere but with you."

"You sure?"

"I'm sure."

As his arms tightened, she sensed he understood that she'd explain everything to him later.

"So when can we leave for the hot spring?" His voice rumbled by her ear with the hint of a promise.

"I'm ready whenever you are, Cowboy. As long as you're sure that'll cure your heartache."

"Ah, darlin'. There ain't nothin' that could cure it more." His lips connected with the pulse in her neck, and she nearly gasped out her pleasure. At Astrid's wide, curious eyes upon them, Greta swallowed her reaction but couldn't control the slow burn that spread to her limbs.

"I know something else you can do right now to cure my heartache," he whispered on the edge of a kiss by her ear.

"What?" She dug her fingers into his shirt to hang on, then shifted so he could have access to her mouth.

But instead of kissing her, he released her.

Without his touch, she felt strangely barren and started to grab a fistful of his shirt again to pull him back. But he was already digging in his coat pocket. A second later he tugged out a ring. Her wedding band. The precious one he'd purchased for her.

He held it up and reached for her hand. "Promise you won't ever take this off, so long as we both live?"

The beautiful gold-leaf design glimmered in the dawn light. "I promise."

Something in his eyes told her they'd only faced the first

of many trials to come. But something else there reassured her that they'd face those future hardships together, side by side, as man and wife, bearing each other's burdens.

"I'll always love you." He slipped the ring on, his eyes brimming with so pure a love it left her breathless.

"And I will always love you." She rose onto her toes and touched her lips to his, her promise in return, to love him all the days of her life. He was her cowboy for keeps.

Chapter 31

Flynn McQuaid
Southwestern Pennsylvania
Early November 1862

Flynn McQuaid spread his feet apart and crossed his arms, blocking the barn doorway. He wasn't about to let Brody leave. Not even if he had to tackle his brother to the ground, hog-tie him, toss him in the cellar and throw away the key.

"You ain't going," Flynn said again more firmly. "And that's all there is to it."

Brody fisted his hands, causing the muscles in his arms to bulge. His dark brown eyes glowered and his nostrils flared. He was like an angry bull about to charge, and Flynn braced for the impact.

"You ain't my pa." Brody's tone was low and menacing. "Stop acting like it."

Flynn wanted to roll his eyes. If he had a penny for every time he'd heard Brody and Dylan spout that line, he'd be a rich man. The almighty truth was, he was the closest thing the kids had to a pa, and they knew it. If only they'd listened to him.

"Whoa now, Brody." Flynn forced himself to remain calm. "You don't have to do this. You're still a boy."

"I ain't a boy!" he roared, causing one of the barn cats to jump and scurry away in fright. "I'm eighteen now and old enough to fight."

"Eighteen's plenty old." Dylan piped up from where he straddled one of the horse stalls, his trousers too short, revealing skinny legs and dirty bare feet. "Don't matter how old. Matters how well you can shoot, and you know I'm the best sharpshooter around."

"Stay out of this, Dylan." Flynn threw a scowl at the boy. At fifteen, Dylan was way too young to enlist. But with all the talk of war, the boy wouldn't hesitate to run off and join first chance he had, same as Brody.

A few weeks ago back in October, Pennsylvania had started the draft. They'd heard of riots in some places. Over in Berkley in Luzerne County the military had been called in. They fired on a mob of rioters, killing four or five of them—if the stories about it were true. For a lot of people, the draft only served to remind them the war wasn't going away as fast as everyone said it would.

Flynn reckoned the fighting would be over in another six months. No more than nine, which was the length of time for the conscription outlined in the bill President Lincoln had signed in July.

Six months was still long as far as Flynn was concerned, especially after reading reports about the Battle of Antietam and the horrific casualties, along with the stories about Bloody Lane with over five thousand injured or dead on

Sunken Road alone. There was no way on God's green earth Flynn was letting Brody join the Union Army, even if they'd supposedly won the battle.

"You ain't going. Not unless they march in here and make you. And so far they haven't."

Brody's dark brows came together in a ferocious scowl. More and more, the boy reminded him of Wyatt. Although Brody was bigger boned and brawnier than their oldest brother, he had the same swarthy dark hair and eyes and handsome features. They both took after their pa with their looks, whereas Flynn and Dylan had ended up with more of Ma's fair complexion—green-blue eyes and light brown hair.

The older Brody got, he was starting to resemble Wyatt in more ways than just looks. He was ending up as stubborn and strong willed. And lately Flynn was getting along with him about as well as an old goat.

"I ain't waiting to be drafted." Brody picked up the rake he'd been using to muck a stall. "I'm no coward, and I'm aiming to go fight because it's the right thing, not because someone's telling me to."

"Who says it's the right thing?" As Flynn tossed out the challenge, deep inside he knew if not for his lame hip, he'd have enlisted already. Many a day over the past year he'd cursed his hip and Rusty for breaking it.

But he wasn't cussing anymore. Nope. Instead, he was trying to focus on the good—as hard as that was. Like the fact that after the injury, Rusty hadn't hit any of them again, including Ma. Like the fact that if he'd been able to go off to war, he would've been worrying about the kids the whole time, wondering where they were living and how they were making ends meet.

At the creaking of the barn door, Flynn tensed and grew silent, as did Brody and Dylan, waiting for Rusty to saunter in and tell them all to get back to work, that the corn wouldn't harvest itself.

They all knew the reason Rusty was letting them stay on the farm was to help with the harvesting. Although he'd told them they had until spring, no doubt he was waiting to kick them out just as soon as the harvesting was done and he didn't need their free labor. Ma was hardly in the grave two months, and he was already courting Widow Flores, who had a couple of strapping boys.

Flynn figured he had a few more weeks left before he needed to have a job lined up along with a place for them to live. But the thought of leaving the land was intimidating. All he knew was farming.

Just thinking about losing everything to Rusty made his whole world tilt, almost as if he'd gone lame in both legs instead of one. Didn't matter that the McQuaid ancestors had owned and worked the land for generations. Rusty had the deed. It was legal. And there wasn't a blamed thing that could change it.

As the barn door squealed open farther, a lithe girl slipped inside, and Flynn released a breath.

"Come on now, Ivy." From his spot on the stall, Dylan paused in chewing a long piece of hay to scowl at her. "You're supposed to do the secret knock so we know who's a-comin'."

Ivy closed the door, her dark hair unbound and flowing in wild tangles. At eleven, she was old enough to brush and plait her own hair, but ever since Ma's passing, Ivy hadn't bothered with the upkeep. And no amount of Flynn's pestering had motivated the girl.

Even with her messy hair, Ivy was pretty. Trouble was, she'd much rather go hunting and climb trees than sew and cook like Ma had taught her. And in the weeks since Ma's death, Ivy had taken to imitating him and the boys more, not less. She was in sore need of a womanly touch.

His failure in raising his sister properly was just one of his shortcomings. The biggest failure facing him was with Brody. Flynn couldn't let him enlist. Brody was as sensitive as a man came and wouldn't be able to handle all the death and bloodshed. He couldn't stand seeing a lame horse, much less a man losing his legs, which was what he was gonna see and worse if he went to war.

"Got something for you, Flynn." Ivy hid the item behind her back as she bounded across the haymow, her bare feet sinking deep into the alfalfa. Her eyes glimmered with her usual mischief.

"What is it?" He knew better than to hold out his hand. The last time, she dumped a spiny lizard in his palm. Time before that had been a spider's nest with a whole passel of baby spiders crawling all over the place. Once, she'd even given him a rotten duck egg.

She stopped directly in front of him, providing him full view of her unwashed face and the dirt coating her skirt. Thunderation. He had to figure out a way to get her to take baths.

"Hold out your hand," she insisted.

"Not in a hundred years."

"Come on, you big 'fraidy cat." Her smile widened and seemed to bring with it all the sunshine of the early November day.

He reached out and tweaked her nose. He didn't have time

right now for her practical jokes, but he did want her to know he cared about her.

"I promise you'll like what I have this time."

"Heard that before."

"This time I mean it."

He mussed her hair and then turned back to Brody who, thankfully, was still standing in the same place.

Before he could resume their conversation, Ivy thrust something into his face. "It's a letter from Wyatt."

Flynn froze.

As Ivy waved the envelope, he caught sight of his brother's bold handwriting. Wyatt must have received his letter about Ma's death and decided to send his condolences.

But as usual, it was too little effort, too late.

Frustration burned inside Flynn, frustration that had been simmering since the day Wyatt had walked away from Rusty and the farm and left Flynn to be the responsible one and deal with all the problems. While Wyatt gallivanted all over God's green earth, Flynn had been left to protect his ma and help raise the kids. And he was left trying to figure out what to do now that they were practically homeless.

He stared at the letter, then spun and strode toward the door as fast as his limping gait would allow. "I don't care one whit what Wyatt has to say."

"He's got a ranch in Colorado and wants us to move there and live with him." The words slid out of Ivy's mouth faster than butter sliding off hot sweet corn.

"A ranch?" Dylan hopped off the stall and spit out the piece of hay, his face lighting with boyish enthusiasm. "Where we get to be cowboys?"

"The last thing we're doing is moving in with Wyatt." The

very core of Flynn's being protested the prospect of relying upon Wyatt. "He's never cared about us before, and there's no reason for him to start now."

Ivy's expression fell. "He said he's got a wife who has a little sister about my age living with them."

"It don't matter—"

"A ranch, Flynn!" Dylan's voice rose. "Just think about it. We'd get to ride horses and raise cattle and fight Indians."

"He says there's plenty of space and lots of work for every one of us," Ivy added. "And he really wants us to come, especially Brody."

Brody. Flynn's attention snapped back to his brother, who'd resumed his work cleaning the stalls. In his letter to Wyatt, Flynn had briefly mentioned Brody's intention of joining the war efforts when he turned eighteen along with Dylan's interest. Flynn wasn't sure why he'd said anything, other than maybe attempting to make Wyatt feel guilty for being gone. Or perhaps he'd wanted Wyatt to know the pressure he was under in raising the kids, pressure Wyatt had run away from.

Ivy took out the letter and scanned it. "He says he don't have a lot of extra money to help with the passage west, but that he'll do what he can."

Flynn's backbone stiffened. "I don't need Wyatt's money."

"Then that means we're going?" Dylan's eyes widened.

"Please, please, please." Ivy was standing next to Dylan, their two young faces turned up to him, eagerness and excitement radiating there.

"We don't have nothing left for us here," Dylan said. "Nothing holding us back."

Was Dylan right? Was there really nothing holding them

back? Flynn's mind flashed with the image of Helen's face and the tears she'd shed the day he ended their relationship and told her he didn't want to get married. It had been the day after Ma died from another awful childbirth, the day he vowed he wasn't ever gonna get married and put a woman through the torture of birthing.

In the months of nightmares since, his resolve had only strengthened. He'd decided the Lord Almighty had given him the responsibility in raising Ivy, Dylan, and Brody. That was enough for him. But it still didn't make the parting with Helen any easier, especially whenever he saw her at church and she watched him with hopeful eyes, as if he'd eventually change his mind and marry her after all.

"Rusty wants us gone." Ivy glanced nervously toward the barn door.

"I think I know that well enough." Since the day of his broken hip, Flynn had stopped being afraid of Rusty. But he'd never stopped hating the man for the way he'd ruined their family. And now stealing the farm from them.

"I'm sure Colorado and those mountains will be mighty fine." Dylan slicked back his hair. "And besides, out there we'd be real far away from the war. That's what you want, ain't it? For me and Brody to be far away so we can't enlist?"

Brody's too-small shirt stretched against his muscles. He worked silently, clearly pouting over Flynn's decision not to let him join the fighting. Maybe it would be best to go west where the lure of adventure and the prospect of a new life could help Brody forget all about the war.

Watching Flynn's face and reading his decision, Dylan grinned, well aware of his charm and the fact that he could sweet talk a mule into doing a song and dance.

Flynn held out a hand to Ivy.

Ivy gave him the letter and then hopped up and down. "Does that mean we can go?"

"It means I'll read the letter."

Dylan and Ivy exchanged grins. They knew him too well, especially that he cared about his family more than anything else. If going west would save Brody, he'd do it. In fact, nothing—not even his estrangement with Wyatt—would stop him from doing the right thing.

Jody Hedlund is the bestselling author of over thirty historical novels for both adults and teens and is the winner of numerous awards, including the Christy, Carol, and Christian Book Awards. Jody lives in Michigan with her husband, busy family, and five spoiled cats. Visit her online at jodyhedlund.com.

Sign Up for Jody's Newsletter

Keep up to date with Jody's news on book releases and events by signing up for her email list at jodyhedlund.com.

More from Jody Hedlund

Upon discovering an abandoned baby, Pastor Abe Merivale joins efforts with Zoe Hart, one of the newly arrived bride-ship women, to care for the infant. With mounting pressure to find the baby a home, Abe offers his hand as Zoe's groom. But after a hasty wedding, they soon realize their marriage of convenience is not so convenient after all.

A Bride of Convenience
The Bride Ships #3

BETHANYHOUSE

Stay up to date on your favorite books and authors with our free e-newsletters. Sign up today at bethanyhouse.com.

facebook.com/bethanyhousepublishers

@bethanyhousefiction

Free exclusive resources for your book group at bethanyhouseopenbook.com

You May Also Like . . .

Marianne Neumann became a placing agent with the Children's Aid Society with one goal: to find her lost sister. Her fellow agent, Andrew Brady, is a former schoolteacher who has a way with children and a hidden past. As they team up placing orphans in homes in Illinois, they grow ever closer . . . until a shocking tragedy changes one of their lives forever.

Together Forever by Jody Hedlund
ORPHAN TRAIN #2
jodyhedlund.com

When Madysen Powell's supposedly dead father shows up, her gift for forgiveness is tested and she's left searching for answers. Daniel Beaufort arrives in Nome, longing to start fresh after the gold rush leaves him with only empty pockets, and finds employment at the Powell dairy. Will deceptions from the past tear apart their hopes for a better future?

Endless Mercy by Tracie Peterson and Kimberley Woodhouse
THE TREASURES OF NOME #2
traciepeterson.com; kimberleywoodhouse.com

Nate Long has always watched over his twin, even if it's led him to be an outlaw. When his brother is wounded in a shootout, it's their former prisoner, Laura, who ends up nursing his wounds at Settler's Fort. She knows Nate wants a fresh start, but struggles with how his devotion blinds him. Do the futures they seek include love, or is too much in the way?

Faith's Mountain Home by Misty M. Beller
HEARTS OF MONTANA #3
mistymbeller.com

BETHANYHOUSE

More from Bethany House

Assigned to find the kidnapped daughter of a mob boss, Pinkerton operative Calista York is sent to a rowdy mining town in Missouri. But she faces the obstacle of missionary Matthew Cook. He's as determined to stop a local baby raffle as he is the reckless Miss York whose bad judgement consistently seems to be putting her in harm's way.

Courting Misfortune by Regina Jennings
The Joplin Chronicles #1
reginajennings.com

After receiving word that her sweetheart has been lost during a raid on a Yankee vessel, Cordelia Owens clings to hope. But Phineas Dunn finds nothing redemptive in the horrors of war, and when he returns, sure that he is not the hero Cordelia sees, they both must decide where the dreams of a new America will take them, and if they will go there together.

Dreams of Savannah by Roseanna M. White
roseannamwhite.com

Troubled by painful memories, Olivia Rosetti is singularly focused on running her maternity home for troubled women. Darius Reed is determined to protect his daughter from the prejudice that killed his wife by marrying a society darling. But when he's suddenly drawn to Olivia, they will learn if love can prove stronger than the secrets and hurts of the past.

A Haven for Her Heart by Susan Anne Mason
Redemption's Light #1
susanannemason.net

BethanyHouse